Out Backward

Out Backward

ROSS RAISIN

HARPER  PERENNIAL

NEW YORK • LONDON • TORONTO • SYDNEY • NEW DELHI • AUCKLAND

HARPER ● PERENNIAL

First published in Great Britain as *God's Own Country* in 2008 by Viking, an imprint of Penguin Books.

P.S.™ is a trademark of HarperCollins Publishers.

HarperCollins books may be purchased for educational, business, or sales promotional use. For information please write: Special Markets Department, HarperCollins Publishers, 10 East 53rd Street, New York, NY 10022.

FIRST U.S. EDITION

Library of Congress Cataloging-in-Publication Data is available upon request.

ISBN 978-0-06-144875-1

08 09 10 11 12   OFF/RRD   10 9 8 7 6 5 4 3 2 1

To Margaret
1948–2005

Out Backward

I

Ramblers. Daft sods in pink and green hats. It wasn't even cold. They moved down the field swing-swaying like a line of drunks, addled with the air and the land, and the smell of manure. I watched them from up top, their bright heads peeping through the fog.

Sat on my rock there I let the world busy itself below, all manner of creatures going about their backwards-forwards same as always, never mind the fog had them half-sighted. But I could see above the fog. It bided under my feet, settled in the valley like a sump-pool spreading three miles over to the hills at Felton.

The ramblers hadn't marked me. They'd walked past the farm without taking notice, of me or of Father rounding up the flock from the moor. Oi there ramblers, I'd a mind for shouting, what the bugger are you doing, talking to that sheep? Do you think she fancies a natter, eh? And they'd have bowed down royal for me then, no doubt. So sorry, Mr Farmer, we won't do it again, I hope we haven't upset her. For that was the way with these – so respect-minded they wouldn't dare even look on myself for fear of crapping up Nature's balance. The laws of the countryside. And me, I was real, living, farting Nature to their brain of things, part of the scenery same as a tree or a tractor. I watched as the last one over the stile fiddled with a rock on top the wall, for he thought he'd knocked it out of place weighting himself over. Daft sods these ramblers. I went toward them.

Halfway down the field the fog got hold of me, feeling round my face so as I had to stop a minute and tune my eyes, though I still had sight of the hats, no bother. They were only a short way into the next field, moving on like a line of chickens, their heads twitching side to side. What a lovely molehill. Look, Bob, a cuckoo behind the drystone wall. Only it wasn't a cuckoo, I knew, it was a bloody pigeon.

I hadn't the hearing of them just yet, mind, but I knew their talk.

I followed on, quick down to the field bottom and straight over the wall. Tumbled a couple of headstones to the ground as I heaved myself up, but no matter. Part of Nature me, I'd a licence for that. They couldn't hear me anyhow, their ears were full of fog. I was in the field aside theirs and I slunk along the wall between, until they were near enough I could see them through the stone-cracks, bobbing along. I listened to them breathing, heavy, like towns always breathe when they're on farmland. Weekend exercise for them, this was, like sex. Course they were going to buy a pink hat to mark the occasion.

A middle of the way down the field and they stopped. They parked down in a circle like they fancied a campfire but instead they whipped out foil parcels and a Thermos and started blathering.

I've got ham. Who wants ham?

I'll have ham.

Oh, wait a moment. Pink Hat inspected the sarnies. We have a choice – ham and tomato, or ham and Red Leicester?

He gave them each a parcel, then stood the Thermos in the middle of the circle.

Nasty old day still, he said. Wish it would perk up a little.

Doesn't look too promising, though, said one of the females.

I teased a small stone out the wall and plastered it in sheep shit.

That is such nice ham.

Isn't it? Tesco, you know.

Crack. I hit the Thermos bang centre, tea and shit splashing up the fog.

They hadn't a clue. It was a job to keep from laughing as they skittled about and scanned the sky as if they were being bombed. Or maybe they feared they'd pissed the cuckoo off – upset Nature's balance, sitting in a field. Didn't think to look over at me crouching behind the wall. So down I went for the shit pile and I threw another stone, but it missed and hit a female on her foot. I might've flung a headstone at her and she'd not have felt it through them walking boots but that wasn't going to stop her screaming her lungs out her windpipe. Behind the wall, there's someone behind the wall, quickly let's go. Quickly! They were all on their feet soon enough, grabbing up the phone and escaping down the field. Run for your lives, towns, run for your lives. When they were out of range, Pink Hat turned and blabbed something about a peaceful day out, they meant no harm please leave them alone.

But I couldn't be fussed with them any more. I waited for them to scarper then I started back to the farm. The pups would be needing a feed, and I was rumbling for a bite myself.

Near the top the field I looked round to see how far they'd got, likely they were halfway to Felton by now, they were that upshelled. So I was fair capped when I saw they'd come back. I couldn't rightly make out what they were up to at first, all I could see was their heads huddled behind a wall and Pink Hat galloping up the hillside. He snatched something up off the ground and it glinted an instant before he put it in his rucksack. They'd left the tin foil behind.

In the old stable the pups were asleep, the four of them piled up snuffling against Jess's side. She had an eye awake, looking on while I took a plate of chopped liver off the shelf and lay it by for when they were ready. Then I went in the kitchen, and there was a smell drifting about that got in my nostrils and reached down my gullet. Biscuits. I opened the oven, but it was empty. Door was warmish, mind, like a cow's underbelly, and I pressed my hand against it a time, letting the heat slug up my arm before I stood up and went for the cupboards. No biscuits in any of them, so I sat down by the fire.

Mum was in the other room, and she was all I could hear but for the fire and the honeysuckle flapping against the window. She was on the phone to Janet. That, or she was talking to the budgerigars. Fat little fuckers, up to nothing all day but rubbing their heads together and gawping in the mirror. I got up and pushed the door to the other room, just a nudge, to poke my eye in. She was on the phone, and she had the biscuits. She was gobbing them whole while she yammered on to Janet.

Happy as a pig in trough he were, Janet, happy as a pig in trough . . .

3

I went for a gleg in the freezer to see if she'd done another batch, but it was just bags of sprouts and vaccination packs like always, so I gave up the biscuits and stood by the window, where just a chunter of talk came through the door-crack with the scratch of fingernails on the tin. The fog had cleared some and I could see the lump of Felton Top other side the valley. I knew them ramblers were headed for the Top, filing downriver till the path jutted left up the hillside. Blimey, it's a fair old climb, but not to worry, there's a pint waiting for us on the other side.

I settled into the chair by the fire and let my body go to rest. The pub round the Top would be thronged today, full of ramblers. I didn't think on it much longer, mind, for I dropped off soon enough, I was that snug, only the tap of honeysuckle on the window to listen to. Mum had quieted – Janet was on one – so I drowsied on, my head bare of thought until the wind got up and the tapping hardened. Is there no peace round here? I said, the one eye open. The honeysuckle wasn't moving, though, and I knew right away that sound, it was Father's boots on the path, and I straightened up.

He came in, didn't speak. In his left hand he had a dead rabbit. I could see by his face something was nettling him. He strew about the letters and papers on the tabletop, turning them over and knocking the salt so as it sprayed on the cloth. Then he was in the cupboards, leaving them all open before he turned back and the rabbit's head banged on a chair. He had it by the legs and there were spots of red on the floor where he'd walked through the kitchen. He took the cushion out the armchair aside me and jammed his hand down the back of it. He wasn't after the biscuits, then. I kept lipped up while he frisked the inside of the chair, dangling the rabbit by my feet, and Mum came in, the tin in her hands.

Guy. Have a biscuit. She offered him the tin, but he ignored it. What you looking for? she asked.

Whistle.

Here. She picked his whistle out the egg bowl then righted the salt up. Near went through t' washer, it did. You left it in your other trousers.

He put the whistle in his pocket and slumped into his chair.

Bending toward the fire, he set the rabbit on the hearth, laid out on its side so as it seemed to be stretching in the warmth with its eye fixed on me. Mighty fine spot for a snooze, this, it said. Father gave a stab to the fire and the room swelled with heat.

He looked at me. Them who've bought Turnbull's farm move in day after tomorrow, d' you know that, lad?

No. Who are they?

Towns. And you'll let them alone, an' all. He took himself a biscuit from the tin. They've a daughter.

I sat up top the field and watched them all the afternoon while the pups scuffled about me and my arse proper boned into the rock. I'd been in the yard messing about by the sheep-dip when I heard the cattle-grid rattling other side of our hill and I thought, hello, they're here, for I could tell between rattles and that wasn't one I had the knowing of. I was in my place before they even showed on the skyline. A mighty blue van coming along the track. I watched as it took the fork toward Turnbull's old place, slowing for each cattle-grid, until it disappeared a moment in the thick of trees in front the farmstead before pulling into the gateway. I fetched the whelps and sat them two each side of me, fooling myself they'd be mooded for staying put, and I settled in to view the doings half a mile down the hillside.

And look who was first out the van. The girl. Young. Fifteen maybe. The others got out – mum, dad, kid brother, two furniture lugs – and they went at clearing the van, mum and dad pointing commands, the fridge, yes, that goes indoors, as if they feared the lugger-buggers might set it in the vegetable plot, and the boy skittering about, unsure, like a louse on the flat of your hand. The girl got stuck in, mind, bounding back to the van after each round, her ponytail flop, flop on her shoulders.

I watched on, the whelps racing and tussling round me on top the rock, never losing sight of me or jumping down. Mighty jump for them that, small souls that they were. They were seven weeks. Not a bad lap of life, when fighting is just play and most the times you're not asleep you're chasing Twat the cat around the yard, and seven weeks was old enough they'd live on. The first month is the parlous one, while they're still soft to the cold and the cat, and to each other, so that each morning you have to ready yourself for a warmish lump or two trod into the straw by the other little guzzlers. We lost three the first few weeks. You had to be fair solid, being a sheepdog. Or a farmer. Or a furniture-lugger, come to it, carrying fridges about the place all day.

The lugs were taking a break, one of them sat in the van and the other searching about for something. He was looking all round a big cabinet on the path, well blow me, I know I left it someplace here I wonder where, until the girl came over and set him straight, pointing at something on top the cabinet. A mug of tea, seemed like. It must've gone cold for he slurped it straight down, both hands, the knobbly-arsed monkey.

Sal was biting on my finger. I let her, because it didn't smart that much and she needed to train up her teeth. She was the boldest of the whelps, spite of being a female. The others were happy getting a mother-smothering from Jess, but Sal had started to break from that, partial now to following me round instead. Mostly the tickle on my trouser leg would tell me she was there, but sometimes I'd not mark her until I'd kicked her five yards forward and she'd yap on back to me, what you do that for, you big old bastard? She was the biggest of the litter too. The size of my head, fair exact, for when I played with her and put my cheek to the ground, she fit snug against my face, a damp spot of nose on my forehead. And I had a big head. Long thin head, long thin body. Lankenstein, they'd called me, in them days I still went to school, until three years ago when they sided me off. Cheerio, Lankenstein, we'll not be seeing you again, I hope. Too fucking right you won't.

The inside the van had been gutted and their belongings were lined up on the path to the front door. The pups had quit scuffling, their heads up having a watch, same as I was. Five of us in a row, picture-house style, curious over these towns. A person might've looked on us and guessed we were all thinking similar, though they'd be wrong, likely, for I was eyeing the furniture and figuring how much it'd sell on for. A fair pocketful, certain.

The girl let her hair out. A blondie, looked like. The family were all indoors and she was leant up against the side the van talking to a lugger-bugger. A nice chat they were having. He had his arms folded all attentive but I couldn't get a proper sight on him as he had his back-end to me, so all I could see was the great stump of his back. Probably looked much the same both ways round, mind. She touched him on the arm. Then the wind gave a gust and our ten ears pricked up as laughter drifted up the hillside toward us, her laughter. A pearl of a noise, that danced about our heads a moment then spun off over the Moors behind. She must've laughed first, then touched him, and we'd got them wrongways – Sound is Light's clog-footed brother, always lagging behind. What had a lug such as him said that was so funny? I'd never forced a laugh like that from a person, not a girl, certain. Myself, I'd more likely rile folk up, cause them to shout or bluther, than honey-talk them. That was my talent. Maybe that was what he'd been telling her, maybe they could see me up here with the whelps and he was having nine yards of fun out of me. There's a lad lives up there, do you see him? Sam Marsdyke. He's mighty popular round these parts – you won't find a sheep that has a bad word to say on him. Ha, ha, that's a good one, you are funny, Mr Lugger-Bugger. Oh, I don't know about that. Not half so funny as Marsdyke's face, I'm telling you!

She was at it again. Laughing away, what a man you are, let me just steady myself against the van here.

She'd know me before too long. Not me, course, but my history, painted up in all the muckiest colours by some tosspot, gagging to set her against me. A piece of gossip travels fast through a valley. The hills keep it in. It goes from jaw to jaw all the way along till it's common news, true or not. Specially when the valley's full of tosspots, such as this one.

Delton was the worst. That crick of the kitchen curtain each time I passed by their farm at the bottom of the track, on my way to town. She was spying out, brewing her gossip. Never mind we were in as bad shape as them with money, and we should've stuck together, she'd never be warm on us. Specially me. So I knew she was out for me now, the blatherskite, brooding round the hillside with her cats whipping round her ankles. Just ripe for an introduction to these towns. And the second she spies her chance – that Sam Marsdyke, let me tell you what he does to young girls like you.

Sod that. I'd let them know I wasn't so foul-smelling as Delton had me for. I'd meet them in flesh first, before they met my shadow.

2

I was up early. The sun had just started to show himself when I stepped into the yard, a ball of orange half-hid behind the Moors. That was the best time, when the Moors were coming alive with creatures waking in the heather, and the dark was shifting to reveal a mighty heap of purple spreading fifty miles to the sea. This new family weren't fussed about that, mind. Their sort were loopy for farmhouses – oh we must move there, the North York Moors is God's own country – but they couldn't give a stuff for the Moors, all they wanted was a postcard view out the bedroom window. They knew nothing what I knew of it. Spaunton, Rosedale, Egton, thirty moors each bigger than your eye could frame, fastened together by valleys cutting into the earth between, lush with forest, flowers and meadow grass, where there weren't towns and villages drying it all up. I turned round from the Moors to look down the sloping green farmland that shaped the side of our valley. It must've been full of trees once, but now the whole valley was scarred with grey roads and homesteads, and the town.

I fetched a basket, cloth and some other trunklements, then I set off down the hillside. It didn't take much searching before a small circle of mushrooms came into view, four perfect ones down the bottom the first field. I plucked them out the ground, laying them in the basket before I made for my next sighting.

It was the calendar for picking, arse-end of summer, and there were plenty of sproutings. They were most fertile around the borders of the fields, as the grass grew clumpy by the walls where the sheep hadn't mown it up. There, and through dung piles. That was where I found the biggest mushrooms, groups of them sharing the shit, slurping up the goodness through their lime-white stalks. The stalk-ends were clung with muck after I picked them, so I rubbed them down with the cloth. I knew towns. I knew how they were mooded toward muck. I carried on down the fields and my sight of the valley floor sharpened to take in the groups of houses patching the land, bunched in villages along the river's side. The biggest patch was the town, stretching out to the base of the hills either side. It was early yet but vehicles were moving through it, so folk were up and about already, going about their business.

These who'd moved into Turnbull's were a different sort to the folk from town. They had brass, and folk with brass always wanted to keep themselves separate, not have their snouts in other people's doings the whole time like them lot down there. But they were still towns, mind. They knew sod-all about mushrooms, or much else besides. The country was a Sunday garden to them, wellingtons and four-by-fours and glishy magazines of horse arses jumping over a fence.

And here was me fetching their breakfast. A girl shows up and I'd turned into a half-brain.

My basket was filling nicely, but I kept on, starting a second layer. Mushroom breakfast for a week, and each time they sat down to eat they'd remember who gave it them and Delton could say what she pleased, she'd have to scratch the polish off my arse.

I walked round the fields until the basket was brimful, but I wasn't sure they'd be up and I didn't want to wake them, so I sat up against a tree to wait a while. It was a champion collection, all different sizes of plump, dew-damp mushrooms. I took one out the basket and held it in the nubs of my fingers. A babby little feller, perfect round and white, no older than an hour or two. He'd poked his head out the ground same time I was getting from my bed. I turned him stump-up and felt along the pink fronds, fine and delicate like the gills of a fish. It was a gradely welcome. Delton wasn't going to match this.

I got up and trod for Turnbull's farmstead. The towns' farmstead, as was fitting to name it now, daft as that was, when the only livestock they'd be keeping was cats and dogs and Fluffykins the rabbit. The kitchen light was on. I stood by the gate a moment then unsnecked the chain, but soon as it clinked off some great barking article came lolloping out the garage and near caused me to flip the basket over. Hello boy, shush up now. Woof, Marsdyke's here! A Labrador. He jumped up to the gate and jowled the top of it with drool.

Lionel, come here! The dad was at the back door in his pyjamas, stumbling into a pair of wellingtons.

Lionel!

Lionel kept slopping up the gate.

He came toward me. Proper smart pyjamas, probably went to work in them.

I do apologise for him, he's dreadful with strangers. He bent down to quieten the dog and I saw the top of his head shining under scrags of hair. Especially with the move . . . he shot his eyes up at me. He hasn't been bothering your animals, has he? I mean, your cattle, with his barking?

No. They're grand.

Oh, good. I'm Graham Reeves. We've just moved in. They were southern, clear enough, from the sound of him. He held a wobbling hand out to me.

I know, I said. Sam Marsdyke. Guy's son.

He spotted the basket.

They're for you, I said, you and your family.

Gosh, thank you, wild mushrooms. There's so many, blimey, thank you. He stood up straight to take the basket, the dog butting at his legs. There was a dark blotch of wet damped in the groin of his pyjamas. I must've got him off the bog.

Well then. I stepped back from the gate. We're up the hill, if you need something doing. I turned to leave, a quick gleg past him at the back door, but he'd not done talking yet.

Are you the local farmers, you and your dad?

Us and Deltons. And Norman other side.

I see. He looked up toward our farm. Lionel was eyeing the mushrooms.

I'll be going, I said.

Right, okay, thank you again. Hope to see you around.

I made off and started back up the track, but after a few steps I stopped, and watched through the trees. He was taking his

II

wellingtons off, fending the dog from the mushrooms. Then the both of them went in. Don't worry, darling, it was just our new neighbours, the Marsdykes. Look what they gave us. She'd bust her eyelids, the mum, when he showed her the basket, she's never seen so many mushrooms. Oh, my word, mushrooms on toast, don't you just fancy that? He kisses her on the cheek as he hands over the basket. Don't you see, he tells her, I told you it would be wonderful, it's God's own country here. They go into the kitchen together, and it's quiet a moment until, hello, who's this padding down the stairs? It's the girl. What's going on? she says. She rubs sleep-dust from her eyes and two small swellings push against the cotton of her pyjamas. Mushrooms, they cry together, from Sam Marsdyke!

I pressed up against the back the house, checking I'd not been seen, and snuck round, nice and quiet.

Cluck, went a chicken that was scrabbling away outside the coop in the backyard. They'd taken a fancy to Turnbull's poultry, then – ducks, geese and all judging from the sounds inside the coop. The chicken came toward me, she thought I had a feed for her. Sorry, old lass, I gave it all to them in there, and I'd get back in that coop if I were you, there's a fox about this past couple of weeks who'd love to get his chops round you. I knew when I was outdoors of the kitchen because it was the only room that side the house. I'd been in it, plenty enough. Turnbull and Father had been a right pair, always helping the other and getting leathered down the Grouse together. Father had been a miserable old bastard since Turnbull died, owing as he had no one to go down the Grouse with to get leathered.

I hunched down and shuffle-stepped till I was underside of the kitchen window. It was open a little way, but there wasn't a sound. I eased upward to slip an eye over the sill, but there was a wall of books blocking. They were stood paper-end to me, though two of the flat ones sat on top had their spines showing. *The Good Barbecue Chef* and *Indian Adventure: All Things Spice*. Some prize reading there. They'd have an adventure if they went to the Indian down the valley, certain, but I didn't likely think they'd be doing much of their eating down there, not with all these cookbooks. That was their sort for you – the sun hadn't done a lap round their house yet, but the cookbooks were settled up. I was about to creep higher, till I saw a thin snicket between two books cocked against each other. I looked through. The mushrooms were on the table, and I could see most the middle part the kitchen. There were cardboard boxes piled up on the floor, and a big gap in the sideboard where the washer had been took out, but not a body in view.

I sided my head to the glass to get a listen. Nothing, so I pressed my ear harder, with my eyes straining sideways to get a squint on them if they came in. My eyeballs were tether-end of their range and all I had proper in my focus was the front of the cocked book, some grinning prat in a stripy apron holding up an onion. Just wait and see what I can do with this onion, he was smiling, but I couldn't give a toss what he could do with onions, I just didn't want to get spotted and everything to bugger up.

Likely they were in their beds. All I heard for five minutes was the echo of blood pumping in my ear, so I turned and looked again through the snicket. My lugs needed a clean, it seemed, for I'd not heard the dog come in. He was stood with his paws on the table, snouting at the mushrooms. Sniff, sniff, what's this? Drool all over them. Lionel! came a voice dim through the window. Naughty Lionel! The kid brother ran in. He flung himself on to the dog and lolled over its back while Lionel lurched up the shreds of a mushroom he'd knocked on the floor. Then the kid flopped off and ran for the table to dump his hand in the basket, and a load of mushrooms spilt out. He tossed one in the air for the dog to catch. Gulp, down the gullet before his paws hit the floor. Again! he squealed. But the next mushroom bust apart in the air, befuddling Lionel, who pushed a splinter of it behind a box, scratch scratch, where's it gone? I was near ready to bang on the window, distract them, but I stopped myself straight off when the girl walked in.

She clapped the dog away. Her hair was dark with wet, but I could still mark that I'd been right, up on the hill, she was a blondie. She turned to the kid. What are you doing, Oliver, you little shit? Uh-oh, I'm telling Mum, you said shit. Shut up. Little shit. She came to the table and looked at the basket. Her face was near enough I could see the little brown ferntickles speckling her nose and the tops of her cheeks. I had to move aside, in case she saw me over the top the books. Where did these come from? Me, I almost spoke out, but I kept it in my pipes. The dad stepped in the frame, dressed now. Ah, now that I can't tell you, he said, tapping twice on his nose, like he was trying to wake it up. It's secret information. The kid clomped and squawked, Dad, Dad, where they from? But the dad just smiled and touched his nose again.

She sat down, opened a magazine. She'd lost interest who gave the mushrooms. A sliver of skin was showing under her shirt-tail, the flesh furrowed at the base of her spine, delving into her jeans.

The kid squawked again, where they from, Dad, where they from? He looked down at the kid. The Bogeyman gave them to me. The mum came into the room then. Graham, she said, don't tease them, and she stooped for a box by the table, pulling out a frying pan. Her hair didn't move a twitch as she bent, it was set in a sleeky-soft ginger mould, as if her head was jammed inside a chicken. The mushrooms are a present, she said, but I missed the next piece because she walked off toward the sideboard . . . one of the local farmers.

One of the local farmers? Might as well have been Norman collected them, for all the girl knew. Chickenhead thought we'd had a get-together, planned the bleeding thing.

The girl slipped her forefinger over her tongue, and flicked the page of her magazine. See, Mum, her eyes still on the magazine, told you they'd be friendly, didn't I?

Yes, oh, I'm sure they are, I just think we should be careful not to antagonise them, that's all, make sure Lionel doesn't run amok with the sheep, that sort of thing. Lionel was slumped against the table leg, licking his knackers. They're not exactly known for their patience, are they? And they carry guns, she said, turning on the tap. The dad piped up – do give the mushrooms a good wash, there's droppings on some of them. What's droppings? the kid said from underside the table, where I couldn't get a fix on him. The girl ducked her head toward him. Shit, she said, too soft for me to hear, but I traced the lines of her lips. It's plops, Oliver, said the

dad, sheep plops. Yuck. I'm not having any. Chickenhead clobbered
a clove of garlic with the stump of a knife.

Who was the farmer, Dad? She looked up from her magazine,
stroking a tress of hair behind her ear to expose her throat, smooth
and white. Sam Marsdyke, he said. You said it was the Bogeyman,
squawked under the table. Well, Oliver, perhaps he is the Bogeyman, said the dad. Who is he, Dad? she asked. A page of her
magazine flipped over, but she didn't notice. A young chap, bit
older than you, the dad said. Mind you, it is hard to tell sometimes
with these farmers, they are rather grizzly-looking. Bogeyman!
Bogeyman! under the table. The dad laughed, yes, he's no oil
painting. All arms and legs, and a nose like – her lips puckered,
waiting – an old tree stump! She smiled. A knurl of butter slid in
the pan. This won't be long, said Chickenhead, and the dad fumbled
in the boxes until he pulled out a fist of cutlery. The girl flicked
through her magazine, each while a little smile.

They were sat so near I had to squinny through the crook of the
dad's pit to get a look at her, other side the table. Behind them,
the pan steamed curls into the air from the juice sweated out
of the mushrooms. Well, said the dad, you've got to hand it to
the Bogeyman. I thought we might saunter up to their farm after
breakfast, drop off the basket, then we can kick on with the lounge.

I was rubbing my brain trying to think was it today Mum was
going into town for her hair, when the kid's plate smashed on the
floor. Lionel was whipped up, woof, woof, what's this, why's the
boy screaming like a throat-slit pig? Oliver, what on earth? He was
on the flagstones wriggling and retching up his breakfast, Oliver!
Shut up, Lionel! He retched again and they fussed around him,
what's wrong with him, what's wrong, Oliver? The dog was nosing
in the slop the kid gipped up. Chickenhead flashed a look at the
dad, I told you he hated mushrooms, she said. The girl knelt down.
It's all right, Oliver, it's all right. Her shirt rode up her back far
enough to see the ridge of her backbone. Ugh, fuck, she sprang up
slipping on a patch of slop. Maggots! she hollered, there's maggots
in the mushrooms!

I felt my guts wither up. I'd forgot about that.

He's given us maggoty ones, Chickenhead shouted, and the girl ran for the sink to gush the tap on and swill her mouth out, water running down her neck. I'd have told him if it wasn't for that sodding dog. Check for maggots, some of them'll likely be mawky. Cut through the stem and look for riddle-holes – those are maggots, chuck them ones out. But I'd forgot, and now they were turn-taking waterfalls in the sink, all owing to me, the Bogeyman, local farmer.

Course, they thought the whole lot was rotted, that I'd picked them specially. The maggots were dead before they ate them anyhow, but they weren't thinking about that, they all had sodding foot and mouth now.

She sat down and the kid parked himself, quiet, in front her chair. She stroked his hair and I tried to see what her face was showing, but I couldn't tell. Her collar was wet with water. It glimmered on her neck.

I slunk off. My eye glanced past the cookbooks and a smear-stain on the glass I must've made with my hair. You've buggered it now, the onion man grinned at me in his stripy apron. Oh yes, you've buggered it now.

3

She'd find out soon enough. If I'd not been such a gawby forgetting about maggots she might not've believed them, but she'd believe them now, certain. And it'd be Delton that told her. Katie Carmichael. How I had to quit my schooling when I was sixteen on account of trying to rape her in Wetherill's formroom.

She never pressed charges. A court case would've messed up her exams, poor girl, though bugger knows why her exams were so important, she was only third year, and I didn't know why there should've been a court case anyhow because I didn't rape her, as it happened, and even if Wetherill hadn't come back for his fags I wouldn't have done, neither. We won't press charges so long as that monster is taken out of school, was the trade. And they said I was lucky, because I'd forced her against her will, but I didn't know what was lucky about missing my GCSEs and having to work the farm with Father. I'd have bobby-dazzled them and all – I got the best marks in class for the mock exams, not far off. There were some proper nimrods in my class, mind.

You're Sam Marsdyke, aren't you? she said to me. That set it off, her speaking to me, for I'd have sloped past otherwise, just a quick gleg at her, sat on the window sill in her skirt. I am, aye. I scanned up the corridor to see if there was a bunch of them round the corner, all giggles. I've been sent out of class, she says. That right? I say, fumbling in my pockets, what's she doing talking to me, is she pulling my string? Do I stand here like a doylem or do I get on? But I stay put because she chelps away, all she did was she drew a picture of a cat in her textbook, it wasn't even in pen, that's hardly a crime is it? I don't know why she's telling me this. Probably thinks I'm right impressed at her getting sent out. I don't mind, though, for next thing I'm sitting down with her on the sill close enough I can feel her leg touching against my own.

She talks on at me, this, that, the other, it's not the first time I've been sent out of class. Isn't it? I say, and then I tell her about how the first time I was sent out was for throwing four pencil cases out the music-room window and she thinks that's proper funny, she does, and I knew that we were going to kiss because we'd moved closer and my leg was getting warm where it was pushed up. We talk some more or she talks, anyhow, as I'm not sure what to say, but it doesn't matter for next thing I'm pressing up on her and her neck smells of soap and I'm kissing her and our teeth clank together because I'm not in the knowledge of how to kiss a girl proper. Wait on, I tell her, Wetherill's out his room, let's go there. No, she says. Don't worry, it's all right, and I'm holding her by the forearm, it's only the next corridor. We go in the room shut the door it's cold inside someone's left a window open, but we're not bothered about that. I kiss her on the neck, soap gusting up my nostrils, a proper stalk I've got on now kissing her like that and her spread on the table. But then Wetherill comes in, he's left his fags in the desk. What's this? Marsdyke! and he's reaching for the blackboard eraser so I step back and he puts it down.

If Wetherill hadn't bust in when he did everything would have gone different, it wouldn't have looked so bad as it did, they wouldn't have said I planned raping her. You forced her against her will. Sod off, against her will. Yes you did, they said, and you're lucky she's not pressing charges because there are bruises all up her arm, what more proof do we need?

4

Any as had half a brain could've told Chickenhead was angry. She didn't say anything at first, just stood quiet on the doorstep while the dad gibbered on, we've brought your basket back, delicious mushrooms, and the like. They'd waited a day to frame themselves up before coming, but that hadn't bated her anger none, it bred in the quiet, and when finally she did speak I could hear it grating at the underside of her words. And so could Father. He was sat in his chair, the telly burbling away, but I knew he had an ear on the doorway.

Actually, she said, they were riddled with maggots.

I played with the whelps under the table, where she couldn't see me.

Well, that couldn't be helped could it, Helen? said the dad. Fact of Nature.

Oh, Nature, of course. It's Nature's fault my little boy hasn't eaten a jot in twenty-four hours, is it?

Mum was stood at the door with them. Our Sam didn't tell you to check for mawk-holes?

No. He didn't.

Play with the whelps. That was what filled my head. Just keep on playing with the whelps. Father was looking at me. I gripped Sal into my belly and thumbed her big ears over her eyes until she squirmed to get out, and I let her go, sniffling and shaking her head.

Well, said Mum, you'll know for next time, then.

All I heard after was the dad chuntering his goodbyes and the door closing shut.

Father sat stewing in his chair, silent. Mum went out to put the basket in the storehouse. And this is Laura, said the telly, doesn't she look stunning in this twelve-pound top from New Look? She looked half-decent, fair enough. My legs ached from being sat under the table so long. I could see the top of Mum's head out the window, she was fussing about in the yard because she didn't want to come back indoors. What can I do now? Ah, I know, I'll take this washing down off the line, it's a bit damp but no matter. He stood up then and came toward me. I didn't flinch, it was daft flinching, I just waited for it. He took his time, sod knows what he was waiting for, he was probably listening to the telly or something, then – clout – the back of his hand against my cheek. The whelps were scarpering, I fell to the floor and scrabbled up against the table leg.

What'd I told you, Nimrod? The tip of his boot was next my face. It was caked with shit. I could smell it. Eh, Nimrod, what'd I told you? I didn't answer him. I stayed there with my cheek flat on the carpet where I had an upskittled frame of the whelps cowering under Father's chair, chins hid between their paws. So it needn't cost you the earth to look a million dollars, but it wasn't Father said that, it was the telly. Father said, I'll smash your top, you goat with them again. Then he buggered off out the room.

I lay there a time looking at the whelps, a humdinger of a throbbing in my ear. There were small feathers and bits of hair matted into the carpet, too worn in for the vacuum to suck up.

She'd not come up with them – there was that, at least.

I was penning sheep in the top field when I heard the cattle-grid rattling. They were going out. Father was off in the tractor so I left the sheep half-penned and hoofed it round the hill to track where they went. Their vehicle was parked out front of Deltons'. I squinted to get a look inside the car but it was empty, far as I could tell, though it jipped to focus proper owing to the beltenger Father had gave me earlier. They were in the kitchen, listening to Delton. Devilry, that's what it was, nobbut devilry, but I can tell you worse. That's not the worst of it with him. Is it, Arnold? and she'd turn round to old Arnie Delton like he might say a piece himself, but he was taking no notice, sat farting in his chair with his eyes goggled on *Countdown*. Devilry. You poor dears.

They'd been parked up ten minutes. The engine still chugging away. A nip in, hello, we're the towns, is all they'd reckoned on but Delton had them hooked with her cats and grim mumblings. Mushrooms! Ee, you should've seen what he did to my poor little car, that'd mark you the nature of the boy. Daft old trull – I'd done nothing to her car, it was her own fault driving so slow. She'd been crunching along the track going who knows where, probably off to buy cat food, so course when I came round the corner I fucked into her back-end. Only a small dint in the tractor, mind, and Father never noticed. She had a whole load of stories like that she could tell them. Like the time she said I'd shot her cat, left it dead in a field someplace – only it turned up again the week after, she'd not had it neutered and it'd been copping off with every bitch between there and Whitby.

Chickenhead came out, then the girl, only the two of them. When they got to the car, the girl looked back and gave a little wave. The side of the house blocked my view of Delton waving back on the step, that gnarly smile on her, now just you remember what I told you, and don't think he wouldn't do it again in a flash.

I lay down with my hands behind my head and stared into the sky. I stayed like that till it was nearing dark, and the sky was bare save for Mr Moon and every while a bird flying home for bed. I shut my lids and fell asleep.

When I woke up and angled my watch in the moonglow it was fast on half-midnight. The hillside was settled with peace, not a sight or sound anyplace but for a breeze chirring through the tree next me, and the lines of orange dots running stitches along the valley below. I stood up and my knees cracked. There was Deltons' – a shadowy square in the dark – Delton asleep inside, the jowl wobbling, that gnarly smile on her. The girl waving, well done Mrs Delton, that was a good one today, he's real vermin, isn't he?

Ain't that right, Mr Fox, I said, for there was a scurvy old feller skulking over by the tree. He spun his head round to see who it was had said it. Real vermin, you and me, skulking round in the dark, eh? Speak for yourself, he said, and off he went. Folk had their chickens shut up tight these past few weeks, owing to him – same as they had their doors bolted to keep me off their daughters.

Fuck you, I shouted. The words jimmied off the hill back to me, and faded into the valley. Fuck you, but no one to hear it, not even Mr Fox, heh, heh, let's just see if I can't get in these chicken coops. I don't know who I was shouting at, mind. Delton, probably, because that was where I started walking when I'd said it.

There was a wall all round Deltons' for keeping out the vermin. Not a drystone wall, that wouldn't do it, but a high, solid affair with slugs of yellowy cement in the cracks. No bother for me and Mr Fox, though. I dumped down on the other side, into a bunch of nettles. They reached up to my pits, they were that overgrown. Not much of a weeder, are you, Delton? I lifted my arms like a scarecrow and trod through. It made me laugh, that did – me playing scarecrows middle of the night at the back of Deltons', but then a nettle snuck up my trouser leg and stung me to buggery. Delton smiled at that one. I wasn't bothered, though. She could smile all she liked now, the whiskery old trull. I slipped out the nettle-bush and smuggled round the house.

Each few steps I gave a rub on my calf to quiet the sting. It was a day for soreness, first my head, now the leg, pain see-sawing up, down my body, but I hadn't time to think on that now, I could tend to that later when I was back with the pups and Delton's smile had slid off her face in a slump on the floor. I tilted the latch off the chicken coop and creaked it open.

A dim bulb was dangling on the wall, sending a fuzz of yellow into the dark beyond the door-gap. In I went. My feet brushed fresh straw, a dull golden covering across the floor, and all these tufts sticking out from boxes and roof-beams, making the whole place snug. Not a hard life for these chickens. I wouldn't have minded a try of that – not an itch of worry, apart from where'd that worm go? And course the fox creeping in to snatch their heads off. I thought I'd just take a look so I stepped further in, stooping under the beams, peeking in the boxes where puffed-up chickens brooded nice and peaceful. We didn't keep chickens at our place. They make more shite than money, was Father's opinion. No shite on view

22

in Delton's coop, mind. She probably had them trained to crap in trays

Scratch, scratch, I could hear, so I followed on past a tower of sideways boxes, stacked up into a block of flats for chickens, and there was a mouse rubbing his hands behind a pile of long sticks. He fucked off when he saw me. As I walked back to the door, a chicken popped her head over the top of a box. Hello there. She sided her head so the eye was full on me. Cluck, cluck, Marsdyke's here. More heads popped up. Shut it, chickens, I said, you'll wake her up. Then the cockerel started up. Cock-a-doodle-doo, eh? You barmpot, it's the middle of the bleeding night, some alarm clock you are. But there was no talking to him, perched up on the beam there like a pineapple. Cock-a-doodle-doo, he called again, how many girlfriends do you have, Marsdyke? I've got twenty.

I got out the door sharpish and pulled it shut. Then I stood in the darkness behind the coop and waited for the gabble inside to quiet down as they went back to roost. When I was sure they were all settled and Delton wasn't coming inspecting I opened the door again, just a sliver.

I near took off then, near went home for bed and left Mr Fox to his midnight feast, but I didn't, because there was a chicken by the side the coop that had got out without me seeing. She was fair relaxed, for a runaway, poking in the ground for worms. God had certain wired chickens up nice and simple – switch them on and they look for food, never mind if it's the middle of the night and the fox is on his way. I watched her a moment. If there was one out, the rest would follow soon enough. I was two steps off but she didn't notice me. Some daft bloody chickens you've got here, Delton, and the gnarly smile comes out, you've done it now, Marsdyke, she'll never be warm on you after I tell her about this.

Poke, poke, poke, has anyone seen that worm? I'm sure it was round here someplace, oh, is that you Marsdyke? The head pricked on one side, then the other. Have you seen the worm? The fuck I have, I said, get back in the coop. I got behind her and shunted her with my boot. She clucked and fluttered some, and scooted in the door.

I followed her in. The place was at peace now, all snug and yellowish, and she looked up at me. You again, Marsdyke? You've done it now, that's for sure. The rubbery red jowl under her chin was wobbling. I moved toward her and she clocked me with her marble eye. Vermin, you are, nobbut vermin. I was near enough I could see the red rim of her nosehole. First the mushrooms, now this, dear me, poke, poke. Fuck you, I said, and I kicked her. She flailed through the air like a torn football. Heads popped up over the boxes but I ignored them and went in for her again. I belted her high this time and she thumped down in the corner where the mouse had been. Straw and feathers floated by my face. She was clucking something desperate now but she couldn't move apart from a shuffle as her wing was broke, hanging limp aside her. A hundred heads looked on, a hubbleshoo of noise starting to get up. I picked up one of the sticks from the pile. She scraffled through the straw away from me, but I stepped right up to her till she turned at me and clucked, the jowl wobbling, get off, cluck, cluck, she'll never warm on you now, not after I tell her about this. Fuck you, I said, and took a swing.

There was a crunch as the stick clobbered her head. She lipped up then, but her body jerked about in the straw, so I gave her another hit and this time her head flapped on the side, and I gave her another and it snapped clean off – like knocking the top off a thistle.

I stood a time, and my brain went quiet. I knew there was a noise all about the place for they were out the boxes and the cockerel was back on his beam, but indoors of my head was still. I leant the stick with the others, the damp end bedded into the straw, and I fetched up the body. It was heavy and warm. I tucked it under my arm, trying not to gleg the neck, all stringy red wires like the insides of a cable. It made me want to gip. I'd done it now. Done it, champion. I rooted about in the straw for the head.

The eye glinted up through cusps of golden straw flecked with blood. I picked it up by the beak, then I inspected quickly round the coop to make sure Mr Fox hadn't snuck in. I latched the door up, and bid my riddance. I wasn't mooded for letting him in any more.

I couldn't climb the wall with the body under my arm, so I threw it over first and listened for the thud other side, the head stored in my pocket, for I didn't want to toss it up and lose it in the dark.

I went down by the beck. All burbling water and a wriggly picture of the moon. It would've been postcard down there, a scene like that on a fine, clear night, if there wasn't a head sodding up the insides of my pocket. I buried the body and head together in the soft mud by the water, and I legged it for home.

5

I kept to the Moors after that. Each afternoon, when I'd filled the troughs or whatever else Father had said, I'd fetch the whelps and go up. I felt peaceable there, once I reached the brow where the Moors lashed out, a million miles of heather and gorse and rock but not a person in sight. The whelps were small enough still I could take them up in the wheelbarrow, though I let Sal ride on my shoulder. She lay there, serious as a soldier, scanning over the land, until I set her down with the others and spriggets of heather towered over them like giant bloody oaks where they gadabouted round.

I could stay up there a stack of hours, lost with myself, nothing to bother me but the slap of wind on my chops – time slowly emptying all thought out my body till I was light as lambs' wool. Except for her. Niggling at my senses. I kept playing the time outside the window when she'd said – who was the farmer, Dad? – only each time I heard her say it I got her voice mixed with a lass off some television programme about a school, even though her voice was nothing similar, far as I could remember. It was daft stewing on a girl like that. I tried to shove her to the back of my skull.

One of them moor days we wandered further out than normal, as far as the bridleway. There was a car parked up aside it. It was tottering in the wind. Likely it'd been junked – town lads sometimes goated about with thieved vehicles up here, because of the vast, and because they were bored off their backsides with canning lager and smashing up phone boxes. I left the whelps digging at the turf and nosed up to the car with my blood racing as I halfways expected a dead body inside. But when I glegged in, it was nothing dead, it was a pale, bare arse bobbing away. A pair of kids humping. I spied in, watching as he bred her, the car rocking with each shunt.

Fucking romantic, that, humping on a car seat in the middle of a moor. Hadn't they beds enough down there, they had to come up here in secret? Probably his sister.

I hadn't much of a view with him lying on top – all she had showing was a slop of hair and a shiny pair of knees – so I left them at it. I hadn't much of a care for watching his pimply backside.

You're keeping to the tops a lot, these days, Mum said to me one night.

I am. I'm walking the pups.

You shouldn't be getting too warm on them. They get plenty enough of that in the yard, and you know some'll be for t' bucket.

I didn't quit my wanderings, though. The whelps ran themselves empty each of them afternoons until I brought them back, pow-fagged, to Jess. Bleeding heck, she'd look up at me, you've fair knackered them out, and she licked them all over with her big scratchy tongue. Don't worry, old girl, I told her, I'm just training them up.

Mum hadn't nothing to worry herself about, neither. There was no trouble for me to start on the Moors. As long as I was up there, I couldn't be prowling about town or bothering the new family, so I didn't know what she was riled for. When I was a bairn I'd kept on the Moors all the time. She'd never been fussed then. I was always up there, them days, messing about with dogs, and some-times my friend from the school, making fires, rabbit-hunting. Them were good days. Even if I was pot-of-one, it didn't matter – when you're a bairn you can please yourself just digging a big hole in the turf until the water shows through the bottom – hello there, is that a worm? One for the collection – and you don't have to worry about dead chickens, or girls niggling at your senses.

Father told me he needed a stretch of fencing from the hardware store, so I had to forget the Moors one afternoon and take the tractor into town. It was looking like I'd be there a fair while and all, as I queued up behind old calf-head Jackie, listening to him moan on at Dennis Bennett other side the counter.

I'll tell you one thing, and I'd tell t' same to any as'd care to listen.

Go on, Jack, go on.

Well, I will. I'm telling you, I've supped my last in that establishment, for all I might be thirsty.

You do right, Jack, me an' all.

I rested my roll of fencing on the floor. A grand gesture, that was, Dennis Bennett refusing to sup in the Betty, seeing as he never went there anyhow, he drank in the Maypole.

Thirty-three year I've been drinking in that establishment, eh, said Jack. He paused, picturing up all the interesting things had happened during that time. And I wrote t' same on that there petition.

I thought it were just a list of names, the petition?

It was, aye, but I took meself two lines.

Bloody hell.

These were dark days for the old boys in town, certain. The shadows of the cities were sneaking in both sides of the valley, and there was nothing any of them could do about it but for mawnging, specially now the shadows had met in the centre of town – the Fat Betty. It'd sold for a fair pocket, Father said, and old Jackie could moan and keep me waiting all he liked, he wasn't going to stop them branding the Betty for a chain pub. The brewery already had a string of them down the valley – in Addleston, Lockby and Thorpe Head – the lot of them the same but with a *distinguishing feature*, like a family of inbreds.

Your father ne'er signed petition, eh, Marsdyke? Jack had bought his items and fixed his flappy old face on me.

He doesn't drink in town, I said.

Well, 'e should've signed, all t' same.

He picked up his items – a bag of screws and a saucepan – and buggered out the door, griping quietly into his beard. Daft old sod. He was half asleep most times he was in the Betty. What difference was it to him if they changed the decorations? Likely he was worried the brewery might bring in some other old calf-head with the new carpets and the wine glasses, who'd take over his buffit in the corner, mumble into his pint in Jack's place.

Doing some fencing, are you? Dennis Bennett eyed me down his nose. No, I'm making a bleeding cage, for to keep my victims in, what the hell did he think it was for?

I slung the fencing in the back the tractor and, as I didn't much fancy getting home yet, I took a walk through town. There were plenty of folk about. I didn't recognise many of them, though, as I went down the street, which was fine by me, until it hit me the family might be there and I stopped, looking around, only steadying up when I was sure they weren't near. There were other new families, mind. They all trotted round similar, gawping at the pubs and the hills as if they'd never seen the like. Because they hadn't, probably. Their places were different than this, places with jobs and wealth and land so flat you couldn't hide a gatepost sideways.

Wait on, lad! Wait on!

It was Norman, blustering up behind me, a waxy new Barbour on.

I'm fain glad to see you, I am. I want to ask on yer father. How's he keeping?

He's middlin'.

Grand. Grand. He put a hand on my shoulder. Turnbull and yer father were tight as nuts, weren't they?

They drank together, I said, inching back from the hand. He reeked of Saturday spray, tangling with his more natural reek of cattle-muck.

Get on! They were tighter than ale-partners, them pair. A pair of old rogues together, they were. His cheek bulged a slow wink over his eye. He wasn't a bad type, old Norman. Send my greetings to him, will you, lad? And yer mother too.

I nodded, and watched him cross the street to get in a new motor. A proper fancy one. Why the bugger Norman was sat in it, I didn't know. He was spending some fair brass, somehow, new coat, new car, Father wouldn't be happy.

I was hungry, so I went up the butcher's, my mouth juicing for a steak bake, but I'd forgot it'd been closed down a month since, and when I got there it wasn't the butcher's any more, it was The Green Pepper Deli. I took a look in the window. Last time I'd been here, there were rabbits strung up and bloody hunks of beef dripping on to the counter, but now it was all shiny jars on shelves and a tray of olives pricked with little sticks. Go on – try one. No, thanks, I'd rather get my jaw round a hot steak bake, do you have any of them in your jars? Do you bollocks.

I walked on. That capped it, the butcher's going. There were new shops going up all over, feckless articles no person could use. There was one now just for gift cards, and another that sold bunches of flowers – tall, daft, dangling affairs brought in from York and foreign places, no matter summer was seeping into back-end and the Moors were busting with meadowsweet and red campion.

I could see there was a crowd in the Fat Betty up ahead, because there were drinkers on the pavement and cars parked up both sides the road. Two-faced tykes. Normaltimes, the Betty was empty for weeks at a stretch, save for Jack chuntering in his corner, but now it was threatened the whole town had crawled out to show their support. They were wasting their time. The Betty was on its way, any with half a brain could tell that. There was a different breed to cater for now – this gawping lot from the cities with their fancy jars. The rambling class. Young folk hadn't brass enough to buy houses here any more, so they were sloping off, and all that left was the old-timers. Them that weren't for selling up sandbagged themselves in their homesteads for the remains of their time, and died with their chops in a sulk. This house hasn't left our family for near four generations, you know. As if the city folk gave a stuff for any of that. They were rubbing their hands waiting for the old-timers to clog it. Probably had themselves a phone hotline set up – how's old Elsie Metcalf's Parkinson's at the moment, not so good, you say, she's on her way before the year end? Marvellous news.

I stepped on, head down, through the pavement drinkers. I wasn't fussed about the Fat Betty. I didn't drink there. I was on my way to the Tup, for I could sup in peace there, it being a manky shit-pit no person went in.

The Betty and the Maypole weren't partial for serving me, anyhow. You're too young, Marsdyke, no matter I was turned nineteen, they just didn't want me on their property. They'd serve drunks and schoolkids, and they'd serve city folk who'd come to buy up the town and put everything in jars, but they'd not serve me. That was town for you.

The Tup was empty save for a barman reading a newspaper on the counter. He was glaring at a mighty pair of breasts. I ordered myself a bag of crisps with my pint, because I was hungry still, and as he poured the drink he kept slipping a look through the taps for his paper, like he was worried the breasts might bounce off down the bar counter. I took my pint and left him at it. There was a table on the pavement and I made for that – it was fresher than the musty, dank parlour that smelt of a hundred damp dogs. I was near the door when I saw a body on the other side the parlour. Seymour Swinbank. I hadn't spotted him when I came in, but Seymour wasn't a feller to make a show of himself. He came in because folk wouldn't ruffle him up here, and he'd not much of a welcome many place else. We had something of a likeness there, me and Seymour, only he was grandfathering age, and I hadn't crambazzled myself half to death with drink as yet. I went outdoors.

I sat down and took a slow gulp of my pint, looking out as the sun disappeared behind the hillside. I could just make out the farm from there, a tidgy speck right under the brown-edged horizon, and next to it, their house. Looking from this distance, it seemed like it was right up close to ours. They were probably in, cooking tea, inspecting for bugs, and her upstairs in her bedroom, flicking through the magazines. Inside the parlour I could mark Seymour moving toward the bar for another drink. He'd have one last, until the shops shut up and a few drinkers started coming in, then he'd be gone, slunk off to wherever it was he went. He was a fine article, once, was Seymour, it was difficult to believe that looking on him now. He was a fair show of how a person can mould and rot to naught. I glegged in at him, shuffling back to his seat, a generation of sorrow and drink worn into his face. In the good days he was a fisherman – him and his brother, Sidney. That was near thirty years back, it was said, when the two brothers spent their summers in Whitby, netting cod off the North Sea all day long, and not sailing shoreward till their boat was a giddy mountain of fish. Some said that was what did it for Seymour, the spray of salt and the stench of cod for days strung out, getting up his nose and addling his brain. They made some champion hauls them summers, so it went, and they returned to town for back-end and winter with brass stuffed in every pocket. Who's for a drink, then, fellers? they'd shout, lording it down the pubs each night.

It was a female, came between them. Like gulls after the boat, lasses started following on. Ahoy there, ladies, they'd say, don't we look dapper in our shiny oilskins? Well, you reek of cod, but s'pose you'll do, said the ladies. And then, course, the brothers fetched their net for the same lass. They scrapped over her all summer. Then one morning there's a beltenger of a storm on the ocean, but Seymour and Sidney take the boat out, no matter, and come evening Seymour docks up and there isn't sight or sound of his brother, only a steaming pile of fish. Where is he? they cry. He's gone! He's gone – I turned round and he'd fell overboard, says Seymour, all red eyes.

Poor Seymour, they said, losing his brother like that, though, course, there was always gossip. At least you have this bonny lass to console you, that's something – and so it was, for she consoled him right back to town and into his bed. And then it turned out there was insurance brass on Sidney's life, a tidy portion, all for Seymour. He consoled himself for six months with scarce anyone bothering their tongues on the dead brother, until he rolled up to town one day, not a scratch on him.

But you're dead, they told him. No, I'm alive as any of you, more alive than some by the looks on your fizzogs. But where've you been this six months? Well, on my way back here, of course. Took the scenic path. Now, where's that brother of mine? And they all lipped up then, for Seymour was down the street, the lass they'd scrapped over warming his bed. When the town woke up next morning Sidney was steaming. That raggald – he pushed me over the side! How could you do it, Seymour, they said, your own brother? And the lass was at it too, how could you do it, Seymour? No bugger asked why Sidney had took six months to tell what had happened. They were too busy with – you'll go to gaol, Seymour, you'll go to hell. He didn't, though – there wasn't evidence enough to send him down either of them two. He ended up in the Tup, instead, his money took off him, his lass won over by the brother, and folk steering out his path every place he went.

That was town for you. They picked the story that best suited their ears, but I never cared much for that account – I went for the other rumour. The brothers framed it up. They planned to bide out six months till the law couldn't take the death-money off them, then Sidney was to return, all smiles, and the brothers would split the brass. Only article in the deal had been Seymour would leave the lass in Whitby, and keep his paws off her. When Sidney found out what had happened, he made a new deal – that he'd shape his brother up for a murderer and honey-talk the girl away from him.

Oi, Marsdyke!

My dreamings flicked off as a car pulled up by the curb. A lad's face hung out the window.

On the lash wi' yer pals, are you?

He laughed. Another lad stuck his head out the back window.

Yer mates gone to the bog, yeah?

He laughed too. There were three of them in the car. Gommerils, the lot. I'd been at the school with them.

Bet you thought you were right smart, giving out them rotten eggs, did you? Nice house-warming that was.

Fucking town. How many jaws had the story passed through that the mushrooms had turned to eggs?

Yeah, right nice. Lay 'em yerself, did you?

They liked that one. They jerked with laughter, so as the car shook. Slap – the one in the back swung his body out the window and smacked the roof.

Fuck off back t' Moors, you inbred.

My skin tightened. I watched them, silent, while they laughed at me. I clammed my fingers round the arse of my glass.

Rapist.

My blood bolted and I stood up stumbling off the bench, he had a mighty grin on him, it was the funniest thing he ever said. But whatever I was going to do to him I never got the chance, for they sped off then, Ta, ta, Lankenstein, splining in the air. I just stood there, blood racing jenny-wheels around my bones as the noise of the car faded away. I was still stood, watching a slant of light shrink on the road as the sun dipped behind the Moors, when I heard her voice behind me.

You're Sam, aren't you?

I turned round, she was on the pavement two yards off, looking at me stood like a proper plank.

I am, I said, thinking that she must've seen the lads in the car.

I thought it was, she said. I've seen you about. I live in the farmhouse close to yours.

Oh, hello.

She shuffled some, not saying anything, and course I didn't speak, I was still trying to understand if she was real or not. I thought she'd take off, but she didn't, she stayed put and said, sorry about the mushrooms. I just stood there, still red from before with the gommerils. She must've thought it was from talking to her. Gawky fool, she was thinking.

She said, Mum can be a real sour-faced cow sometimes. I know you didn't do it on purpose – unless you've got X-ray eyes, or something. And she smiled, so I smiled back, my lumpy old smile. She stared down at her feet. I only marked then, she'd been at school, for she was wearing the uniform from the private down the valley.

I have to go, she said. My dad's picking me up. See you later.

I watched her walk off down the street, as the sun closed shop and the valley fell to shadow. Crease, crease, went her buttocks under the skirt.

Fuck you, town. Fuck you and your rotten eggs.

6

I glugged up my tea and followed Father out the kitchen. He went in the storehouse, fetching his toolbox and the battering hammer, and made for the fields. He didn't wait on me, so I tailed after, picking up the roll of fencing on my way. The fields were sogged, for it had rained in the night, and by the time I reached the bottom fence my boots were black-bright with mud.

It's fair buggered, he said when I came aside him.

The middle portion the fence was sagging to the ground, and the wire was all mangled and torn with a great hole gaping wide enough a Barnsley midget might've stepped through and not brushed a hair on his head. Father took hold the wire and wrenched it up. A shimmer of raindrops sprung out, arching a rainbow an instant, till they fell to the sod and he began pulling the wire off the posts with his hands. I joined him at it, starting other end the fence. The wire came off easy, for it was rotted with rust and snapped apart most the time, so we worked quickly and it wasn't long before Father had done his half. He took up the battering hammer and went at loosening the posts that were skewed all angles, clouting their sides until they were slack enough he could uproot them and dump them on the ground. I upped my pace, pulling off the last the old wire.

A group of sheep had crept down the field, noseying on at us like a bunch of schoolgirls, tell him, go on, tell him, until one of them pushed forward and stood looking at me. Excuse me, but what is all this racket about? We were eating in peace up there until you came. I ignored her and loosened the fenceposts aside Father. As I was doing it, a smile wriggled out the back my mind and on to my lips. I lowered my face so as Father wouldn't see it. Unless you've got X-ray eyes, or something. I had the voice fixed now, it wasn't muddled with any girl else. I could play it over, often as I liked.

Come here and hold this post, he said. I haunched down and gripped it steady while Father, taking a wide swing with the hammer, clobbered on top the post so it sank into the ground with a sludge. My hands jarped off from the vibration.

That too hard? he said.

Fine, I told him, never mind a wagonload of pain was juddering up my arm.

We carried on like that – me bent down holding the posts as he battered them in – and no matter he was right up close, near enough his smell clung on me, there was nothing I could do to stop that smile coming out again. I tried to think of something else, because if he saw me smiling like that he'd likely hammer me in the ground instead. I thought about the chicken. I pictured it in the mud, rotting, a gleam of bone showing through the damp leg feathers and maggots crawling out its beak. That pulled the smile off.

He had a sweat on, Father. His forehead was gleaming, but he'd not take his jacket off, or his cap. The cap never came off, not until the day was out and he came in the kitchen, set it on the back the door, and parked himself in front the fire with a circle on top his head like a patch of flattened grass.

He didn't let up until the last post was beaten in. I fetched the roll of fencing and unwound it a few curls, then held it against the first post while he hammered in the hook-nails. He seemed pleased, but it was hard to tell with him. You needed them X-ray eyes to know what was going on in his head, half the time, unless he was stewing over the subsidy cheques drying out, or – what'd I told you, Nimrod, what'd I told you? We had something in common there, me and her. A right pair they made, Father and Chickenhead. Mum can be a real sour-faced cow sometimes, she'd said, and I wasn't going to argue her on that. I looked over at their house, poking through the trees.

I saw Norman in town yesterday, I said.

Father went on with his hammering.

Saw him on the high street after I'd got the fencing.

We finished the post. I'd pushed him far enough with my talk, so I lipped up as we moved to the next, but when he started hammering again he spoke, his eyes fixed on the nail. D'you speak?

We did. He sends his best.

Does he? He said it quiet, out the side his mouth, like he was gobbing out a piece of gristle.

That was it for the time, and I thought on telling him about the butcher's, or the crowd outdoors the Betty, seeing as he was in a fair mood, but I thought better of it and we went silent again.

D'you see his motor? he said after a while.

I did. Must've cost him, eh?

Father banged at a nail. He'd never been as friendly with Norman as he had with Turnbull, but that was owing to distance, much as anything else, Norman's being three mile off round the hillside, Deltons' wedged between. They spoke to each other, though. They'd pass on the road to town, and shout conversations from their tractor seats. Blashy fuckin' weather, eh! Hast-ta the footrot yet? They passed the time like that, and it wasn't all gritted teeth. It'd been a while, mind, since I'd seen Norman in his tractor, and them high-up conversations aren't so easy if one of you's in a car.

We stood and looked at the fence. It was a champion job. The sheep trundled off up the field, happy we'd finished our banging and they could chew in peace again. I collected up the tools and we trod for home.

He had me on all manner of jobs after that – go see i' they want more feed mixin' . . . go fetch that old rannock 'as got herself split off . . . them stalls need muckin' out. Me and Sal were so busy going round seeing to the sheep we hadn't time for the Moors, or the town, the next few days. I tried to learn her about rounding the flock, but she wasn't much use, she was too young yet, she got panicked and buried herself in the grass yapping at them with her hind in the air.

We went down one afternoon to have a check on the fence, and it seemed the sheep had the same idea for when we got there they were lined up in front of it, taking an inspection. Hello there, ladies. One of them twisted her neck to look at me along the top of her back. It's quite a fence you've made – there's no getting through now, she said. That's right, ladies, there isn't, it's the end of your adventures, I'm afraid, you'll just have to keep yourselves busy munching your cud and practice-humping each other. I looked down at her house. They'd learnt how to get the fire going, then. Churls of smoke were floating out the chimney, and I didn't need my X-ray eyes to see them in their sitting room, the warmth slurping round them sat snug and fuddly in their seats. Chickenhead fluffed out, roosting. The dad smiling at a bookshelf, and the kid itching about on the rug. The girl was set off from the rest of them, upstairs. What did she want with sitting next to Chickenhead, the sour-faced cow? Likely she was at the magazines again, lying on her front on the bed, her feet rubbing in the air like a pair of swans twining necks. The room all neatly sorted – small, buckled boxes shelved up, full with a hundred types of trinkets, books and magazines about the place, and her school skirt and tights on the floor, folded, where she'd undressed.

I turned away from the house. Sal was off on a wander. The sheep were still by the fence, stooping for a bite of grass. One of them was set off from the rest, and I stepped toward her and stood in front until she marked me, lifted her head, the bottom half her mouth grinding slowly side to side.

Afternoon, I said. Then I walked back to the fence. I waited a moment, before stepping up to the sheep again. Hello. How you doing? She chewed on, looking blankly at me. Must've known you were coming past, somehow, I said. That'll be the X-ray eyes, that will. I smiled, just a showing, then wider, so my lips parted. I paused. Must've known you were coming past, somehow. Probably think I've eyes in the back my head and all, do you?

The sheep bent down and ate.

If you want, I'll show you what there is round here. I practised the smile again. There's more to do than just picking mushrooms, you know.

A few of the other sheep glegged up. What the hell's he braying on about? Hasn't he a feed for us? Then they put their heads down again to tear at the grass.

I left the tractor parked up and walked down the high street to the garage. I stood myself on the forecourt, outdoors of the shop, gawping at the newspapers. Well now, which one should I buy, I'll just stand here and think on it a moment. I looked them over, each while a squint down the street toward the bus stop. I waited ten minutes, then I buggered off back to the tractor. I couldn't likely spend all afternoon choosing a newspaper.

Next day, I came back, and I waited longer, but nothing happened still. Only folk I saw at all was the barman from the Tup, sneaking across the road for his paper. He didn't take much of a ponder, he picked one straight off the display, paid, and went back in the Tup to look at the breasts.

Inside the shop, Mrs Applegarth watched me from behind the counter. She came out twice and fussed about on the forecourt, picking up leaves or checking the paper towels by the pumps.

I took to buying a paper, and that kept her indoors.

A fair pile started building up on my bedroom floor. I put my boots on top of them at first, so as it looked I was keeping the carpet from getting mucky, but when the pile got big enough Mum would mark something queer about it, I threw them out. I began thinking I'd got the hour muddled, so I came down different times, but there wasn't sign of her still, and I knew I hadn't much longer before Father smelt something suspect, me taking the tractor out each afternoon. I kept at practising my conversation, anyhow, so as I couldn't be caught by surprise and forget it. Mrs Applegarth likely thought I'd flooded my banks, stood there each afternoon chuntering at the newpapers.

I got to know the world's turnings, mind, reading *The Valley News* each day, never mind none of it mattered anything to me. *The Blatherskites' News* is what they should've called it, for it was nobbut gossip-talk. Gossip-talk and, at the arse-end the paper – HATCH, MATCH, DISPATCH – a list of bairns, couplings and dead. For all Mrs Applegarth thought I was half-baked, I wasn't near so half-baked as the folk who bought this. Roadwork dispute deepens. Local dog wins prize. And, course, the fuss over the Fat Betty. Three hundred and ninety people signed the petition, *The News* said, and the matter was under consideration by the local council. It was front page one day – BRAND THE BETTY? FAT CHANCE – and all sorts of folk had spoke their tuppence, saying what a scandal it was, the pub was the heart and soul of town and how could a place survive without a heart? But I marked toward the other end the paper, near the clog-poppers, there was an advert for a new bar in the town. *Coming soon – comfort and class in the perfect countryside setting, with traditional ales and a comprehensive wine list.* It didn't have a name yet, but the address was certain familiar.

It was no use waiting in the garage the whole time if she wasn't coming past, so I went to the Tup and framed up a new plan. I nodded at Seymour as I walked through, but he didn't notice me, then I sat outdoors and turned it over, looking down the road toward the edge of town.

Just out of sight, round the corner, the private school bus would be dropping off soon, the rambler kids streaming out into a sudden hive of four-by-fours swarming round.

I crouched behind the hedge, spying through the mesh of thorns at the hubbleshoo of small boys spewing out the bus. They were all over the road in an instant, squawking zigzags through the mass to clobber each other round the head with their bags. Next were the little girls, slower, mingled in with the big-belly boys who weren't so partial on chasing about. And then the older ones. The girls kept separate from the lads, paired up tantling down the road with a snitter of talk kept close between the two as if all they had to say was secrets, meant for the hearing of nobbut themselves. I couldn't spot her. There was a lad stepped off, looking back smiling into the bus, and I scoured through, pressing closer to the hedge, but it was another lad came off the bus talking to him. They walked on together and got in the back of a Land Rover.

Then I started thinking, maybe I'd imagined it up. Maybe she hadn't talked to me at all, I'd just dreamt it, my brain had been flowtered by those gommerils in the car. I'd been drinking and all. God knows what came out the pipes in the Tup. Just take a look at Seymour.

I bristled along the hedge, but they couldn't sense me, they were too busy with their secrets. There were two pairings of lasses who'd joined up at the back of the crowd, bundling close together as they walked toward town. I eyed them, checking I'd not missed her – girls weren't marked so different from each other when they were wearing the same uniform and you were viewing them through a hedge. And these all had wet hair, too, damp straggles clung over their shoulder tops, showing dark against the white of their shirts. She wasn't there.

There was a fair gap opening up between these last and the rest. They weren't mooded for hurrying, they were having a fine time laughing about, until a car came past and they giddied off to the side the road, where I was creeping alongside.

Eeeuw! Not likely.

Yeah, imagine kissing him.

I scratched my ear trying to get a listen of what they were saying.

That beard. It'd be like kissing your dog, or something.

They giggled. One of them jumped up at another lass, pawing at her shoulder. Woof! Woof! Her skirt flapped up as she jumped, and I stooped for a snatch underside of it. Woof, woof, my eyes swarmed up the flesh of her thighs, busting for the soft curve of her backside. She stood laughing a moment, clearing the hair off her face, where it had stuck to her cheek with damp. Then they were all at it, woof, woof, their feet padding up, down on the marbled floor. Do you want to stroke my beard? Woof! Go on, give it a stroke, just a little one. They were all shivers, arms folded, rubbing the goosebumps on the backs their arms. Then one of them turns and dives in. Come on, she waves, bobbing up and down, and then they're all in, the splash of water jinnying round the walls with their laughter. Beardie beardie weirdie, beardie, beardie weirdie. I watch the glimmer of their swimming costumes slipping through the surface of the water as they chase up the pool.

One of them gets out. Her feet squilch-squelch on the tiles as she walks off, the sound of the others swimming and giggling fading away behind. Aye now, where are you off, then? She's going at a fair crack, and I lose her behind a pillar. Hello, where've you gone? Time to switch on the X-ray eyes, lad, she's smart is this one. Then I realise she must've gone in the changing rooms, and I go toward the entrance, pausing outside a moment as I feel queer going in, no matter I know it's only her inside, it still feels queer, like going in Father's bedroom.

I go in the entrance, a proper soaking for my feet in a footbath, but when I turn the corner it's not all ties and bras hung from pegs and her stood naked in front of me – it's a car park, and she's walking through it, singing to herself. I steal between two lines of cars as she reaches the open portion in the middle. She stops, looks ahead both sides, hmm, which way shall I go, and I gain on her, silent as Mr Fox after his chicken dinner. At the end of the line of cars I bide a second before moving into the open space, and copping that I've lost her. She's disappeared from sight, and the singing has stopped. Well now, you're a crafty one, I'll give you that, I say, looking about the place for where she's gone. It's quiet this side of town, just a few grey houses round the car park, and I still my parts, listening. I can feel the sting of blood racing through me. I follow on, same direction she'd been headed, toward a narrow street leading out the car park, but she's tricked me, the bumblekite. I turn round and see her stand up behind a car. Then she runs off back toward the high street, a proper flight she gets on, I don't bother going after her. I stand flat-backed against a vehicle and listen to the sound of her feet on the road, dying eventually to a patter.

7

We sat quiet round the table, chewing our tea. I was thinking to myself, the garage days were over – there wasn't use trying to talk with a girl just because of something she'd said to me in a dream. She didn't come past that way, it was clear enough now, that proved I'd imagined it up. I was thinking on all this, when Father spoke, talking through his food.

Aye. We'll sell them pups to any as'll take 'em.

The way he said it was like him and his brain were having a discussion inside his head, but the last part had spilt out.

We'll keep one to work t' farm wi' Jess.

There was a glob of gravy on his chin, slipping down a cleft toward his gullet. He didn't notice it, kept on eating, silent. He'd said his piece.

I bided a moment, until it was right to speak.

Which'll we keep, Father?

They're all t' same size. I aren't bothered.

Can I pick one, then?

No. Buyers'll take what ones they want.

It went quiet again while we mopped up our food. After we'd done, Mum stacked the plates and took them to the sink. He took his sleeve to his chin and wiped it, the skin scraping against his cuff. I studied out the window.

Tha's lucky they're too old for t' bucket, lad, he said, and he pissed off out the room.

I kept my glare on the window. It was beetle-black outdoors already, and I watched Mum in the glass, washing pots at the sink. He was right, course. If Jess had dropped a bigger litter, we'd have drowned most straight off. We hadn't need for the spares. Every summer started with that bucket, stood in the yard, brimful with cold water. Normaltimes it was kittens, as we hadn't need of any –

they were all spares. Mum would bring them out in a cardboard box, and I'd fetch a dinner plate, and a log from next the fire, before Father pulled them out the box two or three a time and floated them gentle in the water, like a bairn with a toy boat. I'd be on plate duty, resting it over their heads with the log weighted on top, pushing down until their lungs filled with water.

Father would go off then, see on his other jobs. I'd put the log and the plate back, and Mum would chuck the bodies, picking them from the bucket like wet socks out the washer.

He put a sign up soon after, down by the road turning at the end of the track. DOGS FOR SALE. THREE MONTHS. WORKING OR PET. There was a smear of paint at the bottom where he'd wrote £15, then his brain had ticked over and he'd blotted it out, scheming that towns would likely pay daft prices. They'd pay a fair pocket for Sal, I knew. Father was right about the others catching her up for size but he knew sod-all about the nature of awther one and Sal was easy the conniest. She had a fluff of brown, both cheeks, that was how to tell her apart, and that was what'd make her the most saleable, unless it was a farmer came buying – what did it matter to them the colour of cheeks? They'd not give a shite if she had two heads and a hump so long as she could work a flock.

The first buyers weren't farmers, though, they were towns. They were leaving by the time I bolted in from the fields, the car trembling off down the tractor-path avoiding the potholes. I shot a look over the stable door, but it was empty so I went in the kitchen, where Mum was shushing five-pound notes between her fingers. The whelps were scratching at the insides of a wooden box. Sal was still there. They were down to three, mind, one of them took off to become a town dog – a life of slipper-carrying and dried-up biscuit food.

Mum slapped the notes on the tabletop. Thirty pound, she said. Then she picked them up and counted again, all concentration, the one eye squeezed tight as a Scot's arsehole.

Thirty, it is. She laughed. And they chose the runt, they did.

I was in next day when another pair came round. I stepped down from my room and the first I saw of them they were inside the kitchen door, wiping their feet on the mat. I wouldn't fuss with that, I thought, you're best doing it on the way out, the state of our floor.

Oh, what a homely kitchen, the female was saying to Mum, but that wasn't what she meant – what a muck-hole, she was thinking. There were two of them, a young couple, in matching coats – these mighty, blown-up, red affairs. They couldn't walk through side by side, they'd have knocked all the trunklements off the walls, you go first, no you, oh, will you look? Little sweethearts. Look at them. They're gorgeous. I stood by the fire watching on, burning the backs my legs. They both knelt down aside the box and the whelps scraffled up the side to have a study what was going on, three small heads peeping over the top – fucking hell, have you seen this? There's two giant tomatoes here, blathering at us. Mum stood over them, her brass-counting face on her. She was chuntering. Oh, it's a bonny one, that. What the hummer did she know? She thought her budgerigars were bonny and all. Right characters, she always said about them, and she was right, if humping yourself in the mirror all day told for character.

The man held Sal up to his face and shook her so as her haunches waggled.

Is it a boy or a girl, this one? he asked, rubbing the back of his finger up, down Sal's cheek.

Mum glegged the underside Sal's belly. Oh, she's a girl, her.

Rub, rub, with the finger, you'd best watch yourself, feller, or she'll have it – she'll chew on anything these days, now the teeth have come through.

The giant tomatoes gave each other a look. We'll take this one, the man said, holding Sal into his body. Then they chose a second, picking it out the box as I sloped out the kitchen and went upstairs.

I traipsed further into the Moors. The cold weather had begun setting in, past week or two, and it was a brittle afternoon – all still, save for the heather crackling under my boots. Most folk, such as Father, weren't partial on the darker months, but they suited me rightly. The heather had gone through pink and purple to russet, the blare of gorse quieted, and folk on the Moors scarcer than ever.

I drifted on, an hour, two, lost with myself – where was I, on the Moors? No, I was on some other planet, a vast of barren space all round and me the only person there. I stopped and viewed about.

Hello! I shouted. Hello! Any other bastard there?

Course, there wasn't, and my voice belted over the Moors, nothing to echo it back. It'd reach Whitby in a minute or two, pricking up the ears of some grizzled old fisherman – ey up, bastard, what? Must be the sea playing tricks again.

I crackled onward. I was close by the border where Danby High Moor turned into Glaisdale Moor. There wasn't a real border between, never had been, only the heather spreading on, but I knew the line of it sure as if there was a wall or a fence all along. Further on there was a slack in the ground – Tumbale's Rest – called after a giant back in ancient times who sat his backside down there and sunk the ground in. Father had told me that story when I was a sprog, and I'd bricked it all the way home, thinking Tumbale was going to come and eat us, until Father said that he was a friendly giant most times, and only ate sheep, so I could shut up sniffling.

As I walked down into the slack I marked a Land Rover parked up past the lip of the other side. A body was moving about aside it. A man, fiddling round in a shooting butt, tending it. I kept on. I wasn't capped to see that. This part the Moors was blotted all over with horseshoe-shaped walls, for the Trilbies to cower behind and slaughter grouse by the barrowful. They were out every weekend now, huddles of them knelt with their guns propped over the wall. Got one! How many's that? Must be a hundred by now, some feast we're going to have tonight, except we're not going to eat them, we're going to string them up a while then throw them out. Land management, the Trilbies called it. Seemed the grouse were on the wrong team, then.

Bugger if I knew how he'd pierce a bird from the air, if he couldn't heed me from two hundred yards. Now then, Trilby, shall I cackle about like a grouse, would you notice me then? Cackle,

cackle, that's right, I'm a grouse – a big lanky one, why don't you point your gun at me? I'll fucking show you what we think of your land management. But he'd not spotted me, he was away in the Land Rover, belching off over the Moors.

There was still light left in the day when I got back to the farm, so I went for a sit on top my rock. They had a fire going again. I wasn't mooded for looking that direction, mind. I looked otherways, and marked Father hadn't took the sign down yet, though I didn't much fancy gawping on that neither, so I hunched my knees into my belly and shut my lids. I could hear the sheep bleating down below, a couple of fields away, and Father bawling at Jess, Get by! Get by! I thought about the whelp that hadn't been took away. Good luck, lad, I thought, some life you've got ahead – Father bawling himself ragged at you, until you die.

I fell asleep, but my brain was riddling with me, for the picture hadn't changed. The valley was painted on the back my lids – the smoke slurping out the chimney, the sign jutted up next the road. There was no hiding from anything, not in my dreams or anyplace. I trailed up for the skyline, and that was more viewsome, a dark, clear line, it seemed all the world ended there. I rested my gaze on it, but it wouldn't keep steady, it started fogging up, darkening, until I realized the whole skyline was turning red. A blood-coloured band was seeping over the top, moving down the valley side – it was like one of them films on Sundays where the villagers are working away building a wooden shack, all these women in loin cloths scrambling round after a chicken, until suddenly the barbarian army shadows over the hillside and they're charging down to kill everyone and burn the village. These weren't barbarians, mind. I could pick out the front ones before long – it was towns, in giant tomato coats.

Are you okay?

The tomato army reached the town, covering it until it disappeared in a sea of red, and they were still coming over the skyline, there must've been a million of them piling onward, filling the valley, moving toward me.

Hello, are you all right?

Her again. Mind, she made a gradlier dream than the giant tomatoes, so I looked her over. She wasn't in her uniform this time, she had on jeans and wellingtons and a mighty green jumper. You were . . . you were . . . but she didn't finish, she stood back, fiddling the ends of her sleeves. I looked down at the valley. The tomato army had gone, retreated back over the skyline. You probably think I've eyes in the back of my head and all, do you? I said. She looked at me queer. I was on a walk, but I saw you on the rock, and . . . She went quiet. She looked like she was going to set flight. Even in my dreams I couldn't make her stay put. I tried to remember the next part my conversation, something about mushrooms, but I couldn't find it, so I said, you're walking, are you? Yeah, I – there's a path on the other side of that wall. It's okay, isn't it, like with the sheep and everything? I thought you might be hurt or something. Me? No, I'm fine, just being yonderly, is all. I was rolled over on my side, my knees still hunched into my belly, looking like a babby, so I sat up. She said, it's a good view from up here. The town looks funny – it looks like a toy town or something. She looked out at the valley, fiddling still with the sleeve-ends.

She had a hair clasp on the side her head – a big yellow sun with a smiley face and firebrands twirling off losing themselves in her hair. Talk to her, you doylem, the smiley face was saying. She'll bugger off, if you don't. And another thing. If this is a dream, how is it your side's aching from lying on the rock, eh? Do you think you'd feel that in a dream? I stood up, brushed myself off. He was right, that hair clasp, it did seem real. There was no telling, though, not for certain. He might've been codding me. Just bleeding talk to her, he said, a grum look on him now, replacing the smile.

We've a puppy, if you want to see it, I said.

She smiled. Okay.

Well done, lad, the hair clasp said. That's more like it.

I was fair nervous, walking her to the farm, no matter I wasn't certain yet she was real or not, I still had the collywobbles. I thought she'd be all talk about the puppy – how old is it? Why's there only one? – and the rest, but she kept her peace. All you could hear was my breathing. I took her on the path round the fields toward the back the farm, as I didn't want getting spotted. Mum was in the kitchen, and she'd certain come waddling out with a face on her, what's our Sam up to, then? Hello, love, do you want a fatty cake?

Is that your dad down there in the tractor? she said.

It is. Sour-faced bastard. I meant it funny, but she didn't laugh. She hadn't remembered. We quieted again.

The sky was getting dark, clouds clenching together further down the valley, deciding which way to go. Hmm, shall we druft off over the tops there, or shall we go to Marsdyke's and piss it down? I sped up some. I was itching for a gleg across at her, to get a look at her face, but we were too close so I looked down at her feet instead, bugger knows why, they were only feet. We were stepping together, I marked. Our legs moving forward same time, like we hadn't four legs but two between us.

It's going to rain, isn't it?

It is, yes. Best be quick about it, I said, as I unsnecked the back gate and shunted it open, following behind her after she'd gone through. Her backside was hid underneath the jumper. There were splatters of mud up the back of her jeans.

He's through this way, I said, and I took her into the yard, keeping clear of the kitchen. There were marbles of sheep shite everywhere.

In here.

There was only one bulb in the stable, hung over the door, and I couldn't see where the pup was through the dingy light. We stood a moment, still as stones, until he poked his nose out the straw, here I am, Marsdyke, selling me too are you?

She picked him up. Hello, little man, hello there. He looked like a bagpipe, with his belly bulging through her hands and his legs all angles.

What's his name?

Not got one. He's the runt.

She didn't like me saying that, I could tell. She moved off, other side the stable with him, to where a weak shaft of light jabbed through two bricks missing out the wall, bouncing him up and

51

down, babbling into his big sock ears. You're not the runt, are you, baby? No, you aren't, are you? And he wasn't and all, the runt had gone first, I didn't know why I told her that.

You can name him, if you like, I said. But I couldn't have said it loud enough, for she didn't answer, else she was blanking me. I watched as she moved next the hole and the light showed her face, pale, soft, the hair pulled back, tucked behind her ear. The clasp had shut up now, minding his own business, smiling away.

She looked toward me. Is he for sale? I saw the sign.

No, he's not, I said. Father should've took it down by now. The others are sold already. Outdoors, it was shuttering down, I didn't know how long since, I'd not marked the start. He's not the best of them anyhow, I said. There was another I'd named, was bonnier than this.

She set the pup down. Why did you sell it, then?

The pup bounded over to me and went at biting my boots – great lumping articles with balloon toecaps, like a pair of clown's shoes.

I didn't. Father sold her.

You should've told him you wanted to keep her, she said, staring right at me.

I did.

I looked away, out the door, at the fields misting up with rain. He was still out there, Father. I couldn't hear him, but I knew he was there, clagging wet. Rain! Fuck rain. We made of sugar, eh? He'd be out there until the sheep were penned before he came indoors, not bothering to change his clothes, and sit down by the fire, steaming like a plate of spuds.

You don't like your dad, do you?

That froze me up. I didn't know what she was saying that for – I'd never talked about Father or anything like that before, not to anyone, except for doctors. I made like I'd not heard her, the words drenched out by the rain. I just gawped out the door.

We had to sell her, I said after a while. I turned and looked at her. She was knelt stroking the pup, a patch of light in her hair. You don't know how a farm works.

Smart, that was. I hadn't meant to say it, but it was out now, the words spinning toward her, into her head, there was no getting them back. She stood up, and I thought she was going to walk off into the rain, but she kept still and looked at me. Who did you sell her to?

New people, I said, for I didn't want to tell her it was towns, and nettle her even more. From the city, in these red, puffed up coats. I thought she'd say, oh, which was it, was it Jim and Jilly? or something like.

Snobs, she said instead, making a study of her feet.

The pup had scurried back into the straw to hide himself, a scratching, rustling sound coming from underneath, and one portion of the bedding quivering from his movements.

I know what you're thinking, she said.

That wasn't so likely. I hoped not anyhow. I was thinking what a queer, bonny article she was.

You're thinking, I'm a snob too. And I am, I guess, but the people round here, they . . . She stopped there, so I didn't know what she meant, all I knew was I'd stoked her up and now I hadn't a clue what she was saying all this for.

We could get her back, you know, she said.

Eh?

Your dog. Steal her.

I didn't rightly know what she meant at first – Sal was gone now, there was no finding her, she was off with the giant tomatoes someplace, carrying slippers.

Look, I should get home. Mum'll think I've drowned. I'm not kidding, though. You should think about it.

We walked through the far side of the yard, and I opened the gate for her.

See you later, she said, and ran off down the field with her jumper pulled over the back of her head, slipping once further down and almost falling over, then carrying on at a jog until I lost her in the mist. Groups of sheep were clotted together against the inside of the pen, piss-wet through. I wasn't worrying about them, mind, they weren't made of sugar neither, and I had better things to think over. I turned for home, a great daft smile on my chops. I'd not dreamt all that up, I could be sure. I didn't need my old charver the hair clasp to tell me that was real.

8

The mud lasted out the week. Our fields, which had a cold, dry crunch previous the rain, were turned to soft, slimy blutherment, keeping the sheep to their pen and Father to the yard, stalking round kicking at a bucket. After a couple of days, and more rain, he said the weather had beat him, and he made me help get the barn fettled up with a bedding of straw and troughs of water and feed. He was riled, having to do that. He usually waited a while yet before housing them up, until it was biting cold and every final patch of grass was grazed up. It'd cost him, he said, housing this early, before tupping week had even come. That was why I kept other side the barn from him, and why the yard bucket didn't sit straight on its arse any more without keeling over.

It was lucky that next time I saw her, Father wasn't about. It was lucky, too, I wasn't curled up on the rock like a babby – I was in the tractor, off down the track to fetch the sign. She was on one of her walks. She asked me if I'd thought more about getting Sal back. I thought she'd have forgot about that, but I told her I had, I'd give it a try, no matter I couldn't see we had chance of doing it. Don't worry. Leave it with me. Let's meet here at four o'clock tomorrow. Then she had to be getting off, like always.

I went up to the stable after I'd got the sign. Well, little feller, you ready to be a snob, are you? I said quiet to the pup. He was pressed into a snug he'd made in the straw, tearing at a plastic bone with sharp, new teeth. A champion slipper-carrier, I thought, laughing, even though I had something of an ill feeling about the affair. Not much, just a griming, though it clung over the hubble-shoo I felt for getting Sal back, and stealing from towns, and seeing her again.

*

The sky was glistening like a mighty slab of steel as I watched her coming up the track, bright enough the ramblers needed their sunglasses.

All right? I said, when she got nearer and I could see her smiling. Fine day, eh? She didn't hear me, I said it too early.

Hi, Sam, she said as she got to a few steps away.

All right? Fine day.

She stooped to where the pup was laying between my boots, and fussed him up some, ruffling his coat so as it stood all ends and he play-growled back at her through his fangs.

Are you ready? She looked up at me.

Yes, I am, I said, stepping back.

The way she had it planned out, you'd think she was military, not a schoolgirl – this is who they are, this is where they live, this is when they'll be out. It wasn't even her dog. She said her dad had known right away when she'd asked who it was that wears the matching Puffa jackets. Emily and Ian Rea. Sounded like an ailment, to me. More on, it wasn't careful, asking her dad, as he'd certain snout us out if the tomatoes started investigating, but I didn't say that to her.

We set off toward the far side of town, for that was where they lived. We'd be there by five, she said, which would give us an hourish to find a hidey-hole and suss the house out.

How do you know when they'll go out, I asked, all curled eyebrows like Watson with Mr Holmes.

It's Friday night, she said, early doors in the Fleece. All the snobs go there tonight. Even Mum and Dad have been a couple of times.

The Fleece. Ramblers' pub other side of Felton Top, I should've known that was where all these new towns met up. The type of pub with brass pots hung off the ceiling and foxes' heads growing out the walls – my stars, that looks like a tasty dinner you've got down there, I'd be after a bite of that, if they hadn't nailed my head on the wall and stuck a fish tank round it.

We walked down the hillside toward the town, and once we got there we sided round it, past the back the store, where there wasn't anything save for a few old beer cans and an army of brown thistles busting out the tarmac. We didn't talk much, we just carried on, all business, taking turns carrying the pup, then letting him down to scuttle ahead when he got too heavy.

Your dad friendly with them, is he? I said, after we'd not spoke for a time.

What? No, well, he knows them. They all *know* each other, of course. They're like, proper ex-pats round here, aren't they?

They are that, I said, turning to look at the hills so she couldn't see by my face I'd not understood.

She bent to pick up the whelp.

You must really hate us, mustn't you?

No, I said, flowtered, I don't hate you. She was silent. I don't hate *you*, I should've said, but I'd missed it now, she wasn't answering, and we carried on walking. We were on a lane, minding boggy pools left over from the rain, and we trod upward as the hill bent steeper up the other side the valley.

Further on, there were two old cottages to one side, both of them mighty postcard, with red tiled roofs and iron lattice criss-crossed over the windows. Indoors they were empty and dark. I could see from the bare grate in one of them that no fire had been lit recent. They were second homes, these, the owners still in London or York or wherever, jam jar shopping. They'd sit empty most the year, except for a couple of months in the summer, and Christmas, when the whole area started teeming with towns, bumping into each other in the store buying firelighters, yammering two hours about swallows' nests, without marking the shopkeeper chuntering to some old cloth-head at the counter, glowering over at them.

I think it's awful the Fat Betty's closed down, she said.

It final, is it? I'd not heard. I followed her over a stile. They'd be riled in town, then, proper upshelled, for at least as long as it took until the new place opened.

I put my name on the petition, she said, and I made Mum and Dad sign it. It's stupid, anyway. They think they're moving with the times, but they've got it wrong, because the snobs won't go there. Those bars are so for the Pinot Grigio crowd.

Right.

It's killing the local culture. I think it's awful.

I kept shut. I couldn't likely tell her I didn't give a stuff about the Betty, or that these new towns weren't any worse than the tosspots that lived here in the first place. They could all get leathered together for all I cared. She let the pup down, and we walked on in quiet.

The house was set a way off from any other, in a knobble of small hills. I'd not seen it before, but this wasn't my side the valley, mind. We put usselves down behind the top of one of the hills, bellied on the grass with the pup ligged out between, powfagged and sleepy-eyed from the walk, not knowing what we were about to do to him. We had a decent view of the house from there, and the valley past it – the mirror of my own view from the rock – with the fringe of moor up top in the distance. I had a spy for the farm, but I couldn't see it, owing to the glower of dark getting in.

This house had been a barn once, but now it was all roof-windows and a curved glass outhouse stuck on the side. There were lights on in most the upstairs windows, but nobody in sight.

I bet they're getting changed, she said, hushed.

What for? They're off down the pub.

She laughed, for I'd said something daft, but it gave me chance to snatch a look at the soft lump of her backside.

Look, quick. She pointed at the house. The female walked past a window. She hadn't the coat on, but it was her, certain.

That's them, I said, and we kept still, waiting, near on ten minutes probably, until the little feller between us woke up from his dog dream with a yap and scuttled forward toward the house. We dived for him, same time, and I caught hold his leg, dragging him back. I propped my elbows and snugged him under my chest, stroking the top his head until he quieted. I wondered if maybe he'd seen Sal.

I don't think they heard, she said, as we scanned the windows, halfways expecting one of them to appear with a pair of binoculars, but nobody showing. She was closer now, it felt like she was whispering in my ear. We might have to wait here the night, Sam, at this rate, do you mind if we cosy up? That wasn't what she said, what she said was – brr, it's chilly – and I was fain glad, for she'd flinch off if she cosied up to me, unless she liked umpteen bones jutting at her, it'd be like cuddling a sack of firewood, holding my body. She was closer, though, certain. I could feel the warmth off her, muddling my sides and my legs so as I hadn't the knowing of my borders and I wasn't sure if we were touching or not. I had a bell-ringer of a stalk on and all.

Next thing, the tomatoes were at a downstairs window, coats on, talking. I shifted forward an inch.

Careful, don't move, she said, thinking I was after a better look, though I wasn't, I just needed to budge my stalk because it was jipping like hell, rooted in the ground like that – bloody hell, the worms were saying, what the fuck sort of plant is that?

They disappeared again, but a moment later they were opening the front door and she was pressed up even closer. They were on their way out, the front door shutting and the man putting a key under a plant pot, the gawby. When they'd drove off, she stood up and lifted the pup. Easy peasy, she said, and I followed crooked after her toward the house, my joints all crammocky from lying still so long and my stalk only half bated.

The house was sorted neat and tidy inside. It wasn't like our house, with mould sneaking up the walls and raggy cloths laying about the place that'd been there fifty years. Here it was racks of newspapers and the carpet all fluffed up like they'd gone over it with a brush. What undid me, though, was the pictures. Everyplace I turned there were breasts – in the hallway, the front room, rising up the stairs, all these naked lasses flumped over settles or hiding in a flower bed. I couldn't take much of a look, mind, in case she caught me gawping. She didn't seem to think it was queer, all these pictures, she was moving on ahead, going between rooms with the pup under her arm, mighty casual as if she was in her own house.

We went up the stairs and I tantled behind while she looked in a room on the left, came straight out and went other side into another. After a moment, when she'd not come out, I followed in. The bedroom. She was stood next the window, spying out.

I thought I heard something, she whispered, but she must've changed her mind soon enough because then she was back at poking round, checking through a side door that went into a small bathroom. I was waiting by the entrance, listening for noises, when I saw the slippers. They were next the bed, two pairs, matching, fettled up in a line, perfect straight. Sal had learnt fast, then, how to carry slippers and pen them up. I went over and tried a pair. A snug fit, champion soft, I wouldn't have minded some of these myself, it beat traipsing round the house in boots or holey socks the whole time. She came out the bathroom and walked past me out the door into the corridor, not marking the slippers. You don't mind if I take these do you, Mr and Mrs Tomato? You'll be missing a dog when you get back, a pair of slippers isn't likely going to cap that. But I didn't take them, I shook them off and lined them up with the others, careful I didn't get them aslew.

I've found them, I heard from the corridor.

They were asleep in a little room full of towels. I went toward Sal and she woke up and looked at me with her head still rested on a towel. I thought I'd be filling my boots, seeing her again, but I wasn't – it felt queer, like she didn't want me to take her, she was happy here carrying slippers, she didn't much fancy going back to sleep in a damp stable and getting kicked for barking at cars. She gave a great yawn as I hunkered down to pick her up, and I marked how heavy she'd got. She was heavier than him we'd kept. Must've been the science diet. If I shook her she'd rattle like a tin of biscuits. All right there, lass – I squeezed her into my chest, all the while not looking at the pup we were dumping, which she was now setting down on the towels, to have a sniff at the other we'd sold.

It wasn't anything to her, mind. Creeping round someone's house, stealing a dog, you'd think she did it every week, to look at her, the mighty grin on her face. Come on, she said, and she was off. She picked a grape out the fruit bowl as we left the sitting room, and I glegged a last look at the breasts when she wasn't watching.

We ran most the way back, trying to carry Sal and laughing and a thousand thoughts clattering about my skull, think about me, think about me.

9

Course, Father didn't mark the dog had got a size bigger, and got brown cheeks, and become a female. All he saw was she had the right portion of legs and she was ready to be worked. I let her watch on, firstly, stood up top the field by my leg, viewing Jess as she moved to Father's whistle. I didn't know if she was learning or not, but she was all attention them occasions, watching the dart-halt-dart of her mother rounding the sheep. Afterward, I'd take her up the Moors and practise her to bide at heel, stalking slow beside me until I shouted, rabbits! and she could bolt off over the vast, no matter there was a real rabbit to chase or there wasn't, and a moment later she'd come panting back to me, her great pink lollicker flapping out her mouth.

He'd taken bad, Father, maybe that explained for him not noticing her. He said he hadn't, he was bruff as ever, but he only said that because he didn't want Mum making a palaver. I'd heard him through the storehouse wall, coughing in judders like an engine that wouldn't start. He was going in the storehouse regular, and between the bursts of coughing I heard him chuntering, fuck off, or something like, no matter there wasn't person else in there with him – I figured he was talking to the ailment, as if it was a body lived in the storehouse Father went to fratchen with when he got angry.

It was likely on account of him taking bad that he had more work for me. I wasn't fussed, mind. What do you want me to do today, Father? and he'd eyeball me all wary, thinking, is he being smart, shall I belt him? But I wasn't being smart, I'd have mucked out the whole barn if he'd wanted, not a grumble. He didn't want that, though, he just wanted help getting the sheep fit to see out winter.

Towns don't have much idea, but there's a mighty amount of

work farming sheep. It's not all fluffy lambs in blankets suckling milk from a bottle in front the fire, such as they think – it's being a veterinary, a dentist, a knacker, mending ruptures and rotted teeth, cutting dags of shite off their backsides where it clumps in the wool. The maggot fly was still about, and Father had me dagging in the barn each morning soon as my tea was slurped, for he didn't want his flock riddled with mawks, clogging their pipes and nibbling at their workings. Sal sat quiet in the corner, and I kept a watch on her as I snipped, so that she didn't steal off with a dag from the floor – there's nothing pleases a dog like chewing on a piece of sheep shit. Some are more partial on it than a fresh, juicy bone, but I wouldn't let her, for I didn't want her taking bad. The storehouse was full already.

After I dagged their backsides, Father dealt with the front end, dosing and vaccinating against ailments, parasites, the paste gun jammed in their mouths, aimed down the gullet. Forget ramblers, or Jack – a sheep's the most half-baked article around, that has to have its feed put out, its arse cleaned, its feet trimmed, else it'll get sick or go lame. Bugger knows how sheep got by before farmers came along. Not so gradely, certain.

It was owing to the daft nature of our sheep that we got another visit from Chickenhead. The afternoon was near sliding to dark by the time I'd done in the barn, and I was about to clear off on to the Moors with Sal, when I saw her marching into the yard.

Excuse me, she said, coming at me with a grum face on her. She must've found out about me and the girl, I thought.

Your sheep is blocking my car.

Ask it to move, I said, looking over her shoulder to see if she'd come on her own. She didn't like me saying that, old Chickenhead, not a bit. She stepped forward and I thought she might clonk me one over the head, but she didn't, she just stood rooted, the hair trembling in the breeze.

Your sheep is stuck in the cattle-grid, blocking my car. Kindly remove it, or I shall drive over the top.

I tweaked a smile. She thought I cared what she told the girl. Sour-faced cow, she could say what she liked, she could say I'd kicked her out the yard if she wanted, I know what the girl thought about Chickenhead. I didn't want her running over the sheep, mind, and she had a look in her eyes that said, I'm a loopy old spiceloaf, don't think I won't do it.

We walked through the fields toward the cattle-grid, and she didn't speak a word to me. She thought I'd put the sheep there myself, probably, just to piss her off. I could see the car up ahead, but it was too far yet to gleg inside. She'd give me the smile, when she saw me, or a wink, that'd be enough. Course, Chickenhead wouldn't see, it'd be too slight for her, but I'd know what it meant – sour-faced cow, she's too busy getting riled to notice anything, she doesn't have a clue about us.

When we got near, though, I could see she wasn't in the car. Just the kid. He was fidgeting on the back seat, his snout squashed to the window.

Stupid animal, said Chickenhead, it would die there if no one pulled it out.

I couldn't argue with her on that. It'd happened before. Poor beast was having a champion struggle against its plight, the great lump of its body pressed against the rusty bars of the cattle-grid, four matchstick legs kicking away underneath.

You could've tried giving it a shunt, I told her.

It's your sheep, she said, not looking on me, you can pull it out yourself.

I wasn't mighty upskittled to hear she wasn't helping. Fetching sheep out of cattle-grids wasn't on the adverts when they'd decided coming here. And it was midweek, anyhow, welly weekend was days off yet. I took a look at her, glowering on with her hands on her hips, as I balanced round behind the sheep. You know what your daughter was up to last week, do you? You know we've been meeting up in secret? Course she didn't. She hadn't forgotten the mushrooms, her anger was still glowing, stoked up each time she saw me, and she thought the girl felt the same.

The sheep gave out a weak noise as I straddled over her. All the struggling had taken the banter out the old lass – a rannock, I knew, for she hadn't more than a couple of teeth left. Her time was mostly counted. I took hold her haunches and hefted her up, but she was too heavy, she wouldn't lift. I hardly shifted her, and she wriggled out my grip. It wasn't so easy as all that, lifting an old rannock like her while you're balancing on slippery poles and there's a grum-looking female giving you the death eyes. I stood straight and had a think what to do.

Perhaps you should get your dad, said Chickenhead.

I looked at her, and saw behind that the simple article in the car was goating about, knelt on the seat, singing, his hand shaped into a big nose pressed on his face. I couldn't hear him – the glass was eight foot thick, to protect from all the robbers there were round these parts – but I knew what he was saying. Bogeyman! Bogeyman! Bogeyman!

Will you get him, then. She still had her hands on her hips. Your dad, will you go and find him?

I'll manage myself.

I took another hold the back-end, facing otherways this time, looking away from them two staring at me. She's a bonny one, you know, your daughter, she doesn't much take after you. You wouldn't picture her with me, would you? Wouldn't picture her with the Bogeyman, with a bastard-looking rapist farmer, shows what you know, eh?

Go on, you almost had it then.

My forearms were smeared with muck, and I'd done my back. I decided to try the head-end.

You'll have to help me here, old girl, I cuttered soft into the sheep's ear as I bent down to her head, fixing a look ahead of me. Bogeyman! Bogeyman! I heaved her up by the neck, and it seemed she'd understood me because she started scrabbling her front legs and one of them popped out. Bogeyman! Bogeyman! I pulled at the other leg, and when that came free I shunted her forward and she clambered off the cattle-grid, hobbling into the field.

Finally, said Chickenhead. Thank you, and she turned off to get in the car. Thank you, now I can get home and put tea on, and blatherskite about that rude Marsdyke boy. As they drove off, the kid upped his Bogeyman dance, braver now the vehicle was too far away for me to do anything to him. Oh, you'll never believe what he said to me, that boy. Ask it to move, he said. I've never known anything like it, can you believe that? No, Mum, he's awful – shaking her head, a great frown on her – you must be very upset, Mummy, you sour-faced cow.

The ram arrived not long after, ready to tup our ewes. Me and Sal watched on while the truck parked up, and he stepped on to the walkway Father had made, leading to a holding pen in the field. He paraded down it like a boxer, all eyes on him. Hello, I'm here to rut the women, so of course I'll be needing my supper soon, I've a big week ahead.

It was Norman's animal. Each winter, he got hired out a week each to Turnbull, then usselves, then Deltons, so we had him a week early this year, on account of Turnbull clogging it. Deltons always got him last, after us, when he'd passed his fettle and was lagged and spent. It was a fair champion job he had, mind, that tup, rutting all the females in the area, and you could tell it'd got to his head. He was always scratching his great curly horns on walls and fenceposts – look at me, look how fine I am, no wonder I have such a way with the ladies. You could be certain he didn't need the shite cutting off *his* arse.

Father had built a small house out of old wood and tarpaulin for the tup to sleep in, with a holding pen all round that took up half the first field. We always kept him there a few days before letting him into the flock, to get him mooded right. And we always kept him company with No Bollocks, the wether, for he got too frothed up if he was left alone. He steadied up when he was with the wether – poor castrated sod who kept himself pot-of-one the rest the year waiting for his charver the tup to come and stay, though I didn't know what the bugger it was them two had to talk about. Been up to much lately, oh, you've been rutting have you, that's nice, I don't much go in for that myself these days, not since my knackers were sliced off.

Sometimes I went to the pen and watched him. He took no notice of me, even as he stepped through my shadow, he just paced round the rim of the pen, while the wether stayed indoors tidying the hayrack. After a few minutes of pacing he'd stop, sniff the air, figuring where the ewes were. Then he'd belt his head against a post and glare at the barn, as he knew they were other side that wall, going about their business without heeding he was outside and they were all about to be bred – them that wanted to, and them that didn't, it didn't much matter to him.

I stood leant over the pen one afternoon, long enough I had pink grooves on my elbows. I was watching him pound at the turf with his front hooves. He'd made a small hole by the fence, trying to dig his way out, or bating his lust.

Come on, Sal, I said, nudging the warm lump by my feet, and when she'd shook herself ready we set off on a wander.

A few months later these fields would be full of lambs pestering at their mothers' teats, a hubbleshoo of bleats filling the air mixed in with the cuckoo and the chack-chack of fieldfares. Now, though, everywhere was hushed and cold. Not an item of life anyplace save for me and Sal, and a mawngy crow sat in a tree gawping into space. We kept on until we reached the new fence, and I framed up the house. She'd got back from school a half hour before, I'd seen the car. I bided at the fence, watching for when she'd come out with the coal scuttle and walk to the outhouse.

We'd be back with the secret meetings soon. She wasn't daft. She knew it'd look aslew, the two of us together right after we'd stole Sal back, specially as her parents were friendly with the tomatoes. She was waiting until it was safe again, so I was fair content to know her from a distance, for the moment.

I stared at the spot of wall that was her bedroom, the small black square of window too far out of range, and I pictured her inside, going about her business, changing out of her school clothes. Music playing, singing along to it, looking at herself in the mirror, a fug of soaps and sprays and the smell of her body floating through the room.

I was so lost in her bedroom it was a few seconds before I heard the sound, the coal scuttle clanking as she came outdoors and walked round the front of the house, until she came into view, with a boy. He had the school uniform on. They went into the outhouse together, and even from inside there, where I couldn't see them, that laugh of hers came dancing up the hill toward me, jinnying and teasing round my ears – you again is it, still watching her, are you? Anyway I must get on, oh it was a funny one, that, a real funny one – and it danced off over the Moors.

IO

We stood watching through the trees. The curtains were shut, course, but I didn't move my eye off that top window. Sometimes I thought I could hear voices laughing, but it was likely just the leaves chuntering with the wind. I couldn't tell anything from the outside, the curtain kept shut, nobody coming outdoors except Chickenhead, once, to fetch something out the car. She had a blue apron on, she'd been scouring the cookbooks, well now, what shall I cook them? Best wait till they come down, I wonder if he's heard the one about the cattle-grid yet?

We fucked off from there before long. Ran down the hillside chasing rabbits and kicking at thistles all the way down until we got to the river. It was low again, since the rains had left, rocks poking out all the way across. Well, Sal, looks like we're done for now. Only thing for it is to swim across, the tomato army's gaining on us, they're not far behind now. I threw a stick in the water and she jumped after, splashing across with it clenched in her mouth until she got over and looked back, the head cocked, befuddled. You aren't coming too? Course I am, I said, and I stepped my way over the rocks, slipping a few times into the water and wetting my kecks up to the knee. There was a glishy blue stone near the other bank, and I picked it up and rubbed it between my fingers. I'll be having that, thanks, and I snuck it in my pocket. Then we made our way up the other hillside, an itch creeping up my thigh from the sog in my kecks. We kept upward, passing near the House of Breasts, but Sal didn't notice, she was too busy jamming her head down rabbit holes to care about that.

It was back-end the afternoon when we got to the top, peeping over the other side at all these cars parked up and chimney smoke curling out the pub, come in, come in, warm your bones by the fire, why don't you?

We angled toward the pub, close enough we could hear them laughing inside. The Fleece. We hid usselves behind a four-by-four and minded the place through the car's mucky windows. There was a sign jutting over the door with a black and white picture of a man straddled behind a ewe, a pair of clippers in his hand, and the both of them with mighty smiles, oh there's nothing beats the shearing, we're having a grand old time of it, so we are.

Coo up, I shunted Sal and when I looked down I saw she'd pissed on the ground, trickling under the car. It made me laugh, that did, and I opened my flies and pissed up against the tyre next hers. We made a fair puddle between us, steaming up the underside of their vehicle. Darling, I think something's leaking, there's oil coming out of somewhere, oh, no, it isn't, look, it's wee – someone's weed on the Range Rover!

It was warm inside, that was the first thing I marked. The fire was going a belter, and a group of towns were sat aside it, playing at some game with a board on a table. We stood in the doorway a moment, framing the place up. The clink of cutlery, ramblers arfing and barfing about cuckoos and the like. Not a place Lankenstein was welcome, this. But in we went anyhow.

The barman had clocked me already. He was leant forward with his hands set on the counter, his eyes flicking from me to Sal as we walked toward him.

She's well behaved, I hope, he said to me. He had yellowish skin, like he'd been part baked from standing too long in the heat.

She is, I said. I'll have a pint of Theakston's.

She was on her best behaviour, Sal, for there were a few other dogs in the place, but she wasn't taking up. She kept close by my leg, and I could feel the warmth of her belly and the deep, slow press of her breathing through my damp kecks.

I took my pint and found myself a big leather settle near the fire. Sal lay down between my boots and fell right off to sleep with her chin on the ground. She'd be thirsty soon enough, so I got up to fetch a bowl of water – they couldn't likely deny me that, for the other dogs had them – and I spied Norman through the doorway to another room. He was supping with a town, the both of them sat there in Barbour jackets – so I saw these lovely jam jars in town the other day, proper gradely, they were, I'll have to show you. My arse. When did Norman become the sort for buying jam jars, was what I wanted to know? Put a few things in order, mind – seeing him here – such as his shabby cows, and the broken tractor that'd sat in his field a month past. Father was right. Turning, he'd said. He's turning, the old cloth-head.

I didn't want to walk past the doorway, so I took a big, clean ashtray and went otherways to the toilet and filled it up. I was on my way back, about to steady the ashtray on the floor, when a dice rolled over near my feet. A man got up from next the fire and came for it, creeping toward me, acting at tiptoes, all of them grinning behind.

Sorry about that, he said, bending over for the dice. His face was niggled red with blood, blotching over his cheeks and his forehead. He picked it up and sat back down, laughing as he handed the dice to the man aside him. Sal opened her eyes a moment, then closed them when she saw nothing was doing. I took a drink, smoothing my thumb over the cool, round stone in my pocket.

There were six of them round the table. Each time it seemed there was some quiet, the thrum of the pub settling, lulling about my ears, one of them'd sudden holler out and they'd all be craning over the board like it was a sheep at market. I didn't know what they were so flowtered about. When we went on a trip to Scarborough once, me and Mum had spent most the weekend playing at some game like that, but only because it was sputtering rain against the window and there was sod-all else to do.

I picked up a beer mat and fingered the frayed edges, tapping it on the rim of my glass. Win a holiday for two in Australia! it said. Champion, that – who was I going to go on holidays with? Mum? Father? Her? Not unless I fucking dreamt it.

One of them was looking over. A big lad with rolled-up sleeves, butcher forearms and spindly black glasses. I glared him back but he took no notice, for it wasn't me he was looking at, it was my pint, and the beer mat in my hand, tapping down. Ting. I'd gulleted near half a pint by now, so it sounded out nice and clear, and after another sup of beer it took a higher pitch. How was he supposed to concentrate on his game with me sat here making all this racket, poor sod? I could've laughed, the face he had on him, screwed into a scowl like the arse-end of a fencepost. Ting. The others were still at the game, jolly-jolly – they'd not marked this poor sod all twined up aside them, until he stood up and came toward me, my hand tightening around the beer mat as he stepped up.

That's a lovely dog, he said. Can I stroke her?

I nodded, something taken back.

He squatted down by my feet. He's got a beautiful coat.

She.

Oh, sorry. Well, it's in beautiful condition, whatever the gender. He kept looking at her, stroking. Is she a sheepdog?

She's training up.

I see. She's very well behaved, aren't you girl? He stroked her head again.

Sal took no bother of him. She was flopped out, head brewing dog dreams, not mindful of this town touching on top her head and talking about her gender.

He said, are you a farmer?

A rapist. I'm an ugly-bugger rapist whose only chance with a female is when I've got her pinned on a schooldesk. I looked down at him. I am, aye, I said. His eyes widened like barn doors when I told him that, he thought he'd found some rare breed – it was almost as good as a cuckoo, this. They all came clambering round then – slow, quiet, for I was a rare breed and they didn't want to frighten me off. I could've laughed my arse off, but I let them blather on while I sucked my pint, all thoughtful, well now, gather round, gather round, and I'll tell thee t' tale.

Is it hard work being a farmer? Do you farm sheep or cows? Do you think sheepdogs are more intelligent than other dogs? I had to laugh at that.

Only one of them didn't join round. The blood-blotched one stayed in his seat by the fire, fiddling the dice in his hand, staring out over the board and the plastic cars and houses left lined up round it because they'd all come to talk to me.

We should let you get back to your pint, anyway, him with the glasses said.

Yes, sorry, went another, you were enjoying your drink before we barged in. He shifted in his seat and bent down for a stroke of Sal.

You been walking? I asked.

Yes, we thought we'd get out of town for the day, before the kids break up next week. We're from York, most of us. We come here quite a lot, though.

We don't see many farmers in here, normally. It was the blotchy one. I hadn't marked he'd come over.

One of the females said, no, they didn't, and he said, not really a farmer sort of pub, is it?

But I said nothing.

Another group of ramblers had come in, they were tantling round the fireside table, muttering at each other, are they sitting there? I think it's free.

Sorry, it's taken, one of these said, and two of them went to sit back at the table.

Where do you normally go for a drink? said Blotchy. Farmers, I mean.

Different places.

Him with the glasses got up then, said he was going to the toilet, it had been nice talking to me. Blotchy got in closer, sat down where the other had shifted off, next to Sal. She was still sleeping. He started rubbing his finger down her snout, wrongways to how the hair grows.

I don't imagine you very much like us hill-walkers, do you? he said. Tramping over your land, leaving gates open.

She doesn't like that, I told him, and he stopped.

She's got a very wet nose. That's a good sign, so they say.

But he'd not listened. He waggled his finger behind her ear, no matter any bugger knows you don't touch a dog rough round its ears as they're gentle there, so course she woke up and snapped at him.

And he hit her.

He belted her round the mouth hard enough a gob of drool splattered on the floor. I leant forward, some of them were still at the game, the big lad with the glasses was moving his car round the board, hopping it square to square until he landed on one with red houses all round it, oh would you believe it! He didn't see Blotchy wiping his hand on his kecks, gawping at me with big eyes, he knew he shouldn't have done it, but it was too late for that, my hand was already out the pocket. I heard his nose crunch, a daffled look in his eyes, he didn't know what was happening, it was all too quick. I just stood there a moment, looking at the stone, a film of red glimmering on it like it'd been painted, and a noise swelling up all around – chairs scraping, the clatter of plates, folk shouting – then I bent down to clout him another, but someone pulled me off before I could get a swing and I stumbled against the chair.

I knelt up, there were hands on me, I tried to get hold of Sal. He's nuts. He's nuts. She'd slithered under the chair, and when I went to touch her she slunk back further – thought she'd done wrong, too young to know it wasn't her fault. Even clever dogs needed learning sometimes. Someone get somebody. I hooked her collar and pulled her toward me. Good girl, I shushed, good girl. I turned round and the barman was stood over me, Blotchy on the floor with his hands covering his face, floundering about like he'd gone under a tractor, the towns all stooping round him. Get somebody, someone get somebody. The barman had his hand on my shoulder so I stood up and threw it off. Now, please, he said. Now, what? I didn't know what the fuck he was talking about, I closed up on him and walked him back with my face edged to his, and I could tell he was bricking it from his eyes and him not marking Blotchy on the floor behind, he tripped and fell backward over the table, flooring glasses and upskittling the board game. One more under the tractor! A crowd of folk were having a gleg in from the other room – what's going on? Can't see any tractors here, can I get back to my dinner now?

76

Sal was barking now at the hubbleshoo all round.

Rabbits, I hissed.

She cocked her head on the side, the ears pricked.

Rabbits.

Stop this, stop it. She yelped at a chair, scratching underside of it, she took no bother of the other dogs yapping themselves daft. Rabbits, Sal, rabbits. He's psychotic, they both are. There were rabbits jumping about all over the shop now, she didn't know where to look, there were so many, so I pointed her behind the bar, for I could see one hiding behind the counter, but he ran off soon as I did. Get him, Sal, rabbits, go get the rabbit, and she chased him other side the room where he picked up a chair and held it up jutting the legs at her like he was being attacked by a crocodile – all these rare breeds, they must have had a bust-in at the zoo. Sal was frothed up now, so I whistled her and she came straight to heel, the tongue flapping out, and I'd have left right then if it hadn't been for Norman stood at the door.

What you playin' at, lad? He was looking at me, angry. I could hear a female sobbing someplace. And what're you playing at, Norm, mixing with these? That was what I should've asked him.

Yer father'll bray you if he hears on it.

He will, I said, and walked out, Sal towing after.

I knew I was in for one if he found out, but I didn't stew on it, treading back to the farm. My brain was cleared of thinking for the time. Sal seemed the same way, as she followed quiet by my heel through the car park and up to the hilltop, where we rested usselves a moment.

Come here, lass, let's have a look at you. I sat myself on some tufty ground by a rock, and pulled her close, using my thumbs to ease the sides of her mouth up over the gums. It was smarting some, clear enough, for she gave a simper when I did that. There was some bleeding, showing bright where it had run on to the teeth, so I damped my sleeve with spittle and padded it off. It was just a nick, she'd be right enough.

Back on our own side the valley, we swerved a mile or so west of the farm, to a part of the moor boundary I didn't much come to.

Sal ran off on to the Moors and I traipsed after. Before long, the land sunk to a wide spread of rough marsh. The grass was long enough I lost sight of her for a while, until she panted back up to me from nowhere, the hair on her belly draggling with bog. Off to one side of the marsh was forest, a great swaddle of it, river-bottom green. On the other side, the direction of the farm, a mass of moor dipped and swelled, all colours, depending how the weather had got at it. This boggy land was yellow and life-lacking, poked with thistles, but further on the land turned russet, where it had been beat with wind and wet and all else as lambasts a piece of open moor. We trod about a couple of hours before we got hungry and set back for tea, and I didn't look down at the house so I didn't know if he was still there or not.

II

There was a bike outside the house. Its frame glinted in the morning sun. All else was normal – the vehicles gone from the drive, the air still and quiet, the curtain shut. Only this bike, rested up against the back the house, and an expedition of ducks waddling out the coop, off down the beck.

I sat in the kitchen while Mum shuffled about baking parkin. She was yammering about Father's ailment.

He's riled he can't shake it. It's that has got him i' this state.

She spooned a large dollop of treacle into a bowl filled with oatmeal and whirled it round.

Janet thinks it's bronchitis, but course your father won't go to t' doctor's – he's behind enough already wi'out wasting his time at the bleedin' quack's. She lifted the spoon out the bowl, twiddling it round to catch a dangling gloop of treacle, then put it in her mouth and sucked loudly. She was making the Christmas parkin – I didn't know why she bothered still, it was only for Deltons. Tradition. They swapped tins a fortnight before Christmas, wary, like two crooks doing a deal. Course Delton didn't make parkin, she made fatty cakes. Best fatty cakes I'd ever ate and all, she'd not have made better if she was baking them for the mayor, just so as she could get one over on Mum. I watched as she poured the mixture into a tray.

I'll take them down to her if you like, Mum.

She fixed me a look, shaking the last drops on to the tray.

Why's that, then?

Don't know. Might as well.

She was flummoxed, clear, but I could tell what she was thinking – that she'd not have to go herself.

All right. They'll be ready tonight. I'll put 'em in ' tin and you can take 'em down in the morning. And you can take a tin for them down the hill and all, get 'em right side o' us. No mawks in parkin, eh?

There was a griming of snow over the fields as I set foot for Deltons'. Too cold to snow a big dump, they'd be saying in town, whatever the bugger that meant. Too cold? – you didn't see a mighty load of snow in summer, did you? It was there again. Same place, but leant up slacker against the wall, like he'd been in too much of a hurry to get inside for fettling it up proper. I carried on to Deltons', kicking at frozen humps of molehills, explosions of soil scuttering on to the snow. She'd have a turn when she saw me at her door, old Delton. Good morning, Mrs Delton, Mum asked me to send you her best – here, she baked you some parkin, you crozzled old trull.

I got to the top of Deltons' land, and I laughed out, but there was no one to hear me, not even Sal, as I'd left her behind dozing in the stable. I opened the lid of the tin to sneak out a piece of parkin, but Mum had layered it neat as a crop field and I didn't want to spoil it up.

I snecked open the gate to her garden. I could tell somehow just from the sound of my feet on the snow-cleared path, my sort wasn't welcome there. Even the gnomes were pissed to see me. Would the lady of the house be at home? I asked them gnomes, but they weren't going to answer me, they had a munk on because I'd scared all the fish away, they just looked down at their rods drooping into the snow.

But she was ready for me. The door opened and she was stood there with a cake tin snugged under her breasts.

Morning, Sam.

Mrs Delton.

It was the same tin as always – a square, red article with a gold edge and a picture of a robin pecking at a nut.

Your mother sent you down, then. She's keeping well? I hear your father's taken bad.

He has the flu. He'll be 'right.

A cat slipped round her ankle and sat looking at me from next her foot. You aren't coming in here, Marsdyke. I'd get gone if I were you, I don't know what you were thinking coming here in the first place.

You'll send our best, will you?

Yes. Here. I offered the tin toward her and as we swapped them over I glegged indoors of the kitchen. There was a newspaper on the table with a pair of glasses weighted on top. She was hoarding up her gossip for the day. Bogeyman buggers ramblers' board game in pub. She'd glut on that for weeks, if she found out, but it must've been they'd not called the police, and Norman hadn't told, neither, for Father hadn't been near me since.

They're a decent sort, the family moved into Turnbull's, aren't they? Delton said then.

I've not seen much of them, I said, but that was daft because she knew it was a lie, and the gnarly smile came out soon as I said it.

Oh, they are, too, lovely family. Daughter's a pearl. She turned to go in. Give your mother my best. Parkin, is it? Tell her thanks. The cat slithered in through her legs and she shut the door.

She knew about the boy, she'd seen the bike come past, that was why she said it. Daughter's a pearl. She knew I'd made a gawby of myself over her, it wasn't hard to find that out, she didn't need to read it in *The Blatherskites' News* to learn it. I fucked off for home with the fatty cakes, readying up for my second delivery.

There was a damp patch on my arse where I was sat, owing to the snow melting away, past couple of days. The tops had a covering still, other side the valley, and there were dollops of white along the wall bottoms, but most the land below was smeared with grey, half-thawed slush. It was clagging his wheels up, that was why he was going so slow. Most the week he'd raced along the tyre tracks Chickenhead and the dad had ploughed leaving the house, but he wasn't mooded for that today – he didn't want slush spraying up his backside.

I bolted another piece of parkin. Then I picked out another for Sal and let her scraffle a feed out my hand. She was partial to sweetmeats, cakes and the like, toffees – she'd eat the wrapper and all if she snatched one up Mum had let fall on the settle. We sat on the rock there, the tin between, eating their parkin.

Eleven o'clock he always came, when the house was certain empty. Mind, I didn't know why they had to keep it secret – Chickenhead would likely fall over her arse to know her daughter had copped on with a boy from the school. A decent sort of boy, all shiny teeth and rugby muscles. Why keep that hid? She had a lust for secrets, was why.

He cycled on, steady, closer. No head down, arse in the air today – here I come! Here I come! Hope you've got the fire ready – he got off by the trees and walked the bike the rest the way. She didn't come out. He cocked it on the wall, usual place, and went round the front the house, bold as brass, like he'd been coming round for years and not just this past week. Nothing happened then for a while, except for Sal was sick off the edge the rock, until a half hour later smoke started spilling out the chimney.

They kept the fire going into the afternoon, a smudgy coal-cloud seeping around the house as I finished off the parkin, then finally he strode out to the bike, still I couldn't see her, and he stole off before Chickenhead got back with the kid brother.

I left then, fettling Sal up comfortable in the stable, for she had the collywobbles, and I took the empty tin up to my room and hid it under the bed for safe keeping until after Christmas.

12

The ram was fit for tupping. Next morning, Father opened the barn and let the sheep in the field, and they soon enough got wind of where he was, frothing and stamping behind the fence of the holding pen. Some of them walked close past, brushing up to the fence, letting him get the smell of them, sidling for his attention, and he heeded each one go by, a mad glare on him and the foam building round his mouth. Sackless article the wether kept indoors, as Father went in the pen and fastened the tupping harness round the ram's neck, and the gate was unsnecked. He didn't bolt out for them, mind, he trod slow and steady into the field, looking round, now, who's the first?

Father stayed for two breedings then he pissed off someplace, satisfied his hired goods were in decent order. I didn't shift. I watched him climb a third, and a fourth, without letting up, he certain wasn't fussed about a nice cosy fire to fuddle up aside – nithering cold in a shite-filled field and all the rest looking on was fine with him. After he'd done a fourth he took himself off to the side the field for a munch of hay, and the sheep bunched up in groups around the place to chelp about him, what a man he is, that was the best yet, don't worry, it'll be your turn soon.

Hi, Sam.

I looked round and saw her other side the wall but I stared off otherways pretending I'd not seen her.

Just thought I'd come up and see how you and Sal were getting on, she called out. I'm on holidays.

I glegged at her then – she was in her wellingtons and a tattered coat. She let herself through the top gate without asking and came toward me.

We're fine, I said, no matter Sal was ligged out retching in the stable.

I've not seen you about much, she said. What you been up to?

Working. I didn't look at her, I watched the ram, to show I was working still. It's tupping week, I said.

She laughed. That was mighty funny. Course, I wasn't going to let on I knew why she was laughing.

Tupping? Is that what you . . .

Sex, I said. She went quiet and I got a fair tingling through me, saying that to her, and I thought she might get gone, maybe he was at the house, waiting for her. That's the ram, there, I said, and I pointed him out. He was prowling about, choosing his next.

What on earth's that thing round his neck?

A tupping harness.

He's that big, is he?

I knew she was smiling, but I didn't look on her.

It's for marking off them he's bred, I said.

How do you mean?

The red part on his chest is chalk. It marks off the ewes when he rubs on them.

That's romantic.

Just then, like he was listening in, the ram mounted another and went at her while we watched on, silent. After a time, she stopped looking, and gawped at her feet, then off toward her house. I studied her a moment, then I turned back to the ram tupping the ewe, hefting the whole of her body forward with each welt he gave her. The ewe just let him, not a sound, not a sign she was liking it or not. I knew she was, mind – no matter she was sore from his clobbers, or that he was bruising on top her neck. She'd have tried to move off if she didn't like it, she'd have struggled at least – she didn't do anything, though, except one point she gave out a small noise, quiet, but enough, and I knew she was liking it because her hand tightened into a fist, not gripping anything, just closing tight on itself so as the flesh went white round the knuckles and there was a chain of half moons across her palm when he'd finished and the hand went limp.

I should get going.

Next thing she was halfway down the field, the top of her head bobbing up, down over the wall, she didn't look back, far as I could tell. The ram had wandered off for the hay tab, and the ewe was still stood same place as the breeding, nosing at the dead, brown grass, bored-looking, stalled. You'd think nothing had happened, but for the dark, red stain in the middle of her back, small and neat like it'd been marked on with a stamp.

I watched until she got to the field bottom, then I went up to the rock for a better sight, watching her go in the chicken coop a few minutes – egg-collecting, from the seems of it, for she was holding something when she came out. She walked round the side the house, past the back wall, and disappeared. There was no bike there today, I marked. She'd come up to see how me and Sal were getting on, had she? Had she, shite.

The sun was belting, it had cleared the last the snow and slush, and he was cycling off at a fair crack through the trees away from the house. I had to get a shift on else he'd be gone, racing down the hillside back to wherever it was he lived – some old farmhouse, likely, same as her, unless he was a boarder, going home to a room full of rugby muscles arm-wrestling in dressing gowns and making mucky words on a Scrabble board, gosh, you've trumped, you rotter, no, you've trumped, anyway listen up boys, I've got one for you – tupping – she heard Lankenstein say it yesterday. I came down the field and over the stile. There was a muck-lather of sweat on my forehead that I wiped off with my finger. I took the paste gun out my pocket and tested my thumb on the plunger again, so it spat a tiny splurt in the air. The Cyclist went out of sight behind a hump of ground the track coiled round, then he appeared other side, stood on his pedals, face lifted to the sun.

Further below, the Christmas decorations in the town were glimmering all down the high street. Proper sparkly it was, this year. Most years they had mangled wirings of blue and red light bulbs and a half-dozen grubby Santas that spent the rest the year in the storekeepers' office, hid with toilet rolls and tins of beef, and got fetched out for Christmas and strung off the lamp posts – by gow, it's a fair view from up here, you can see the whole world, what a muck-hole. Not any more, mind. There was brass about the place these days, and the rambling class went in mighty for Christmas. So it was lanterns the sun was reflecting off now, and small, glittery lights round most the pub signs, and baubles on the miniature Christmas trees that were pinned on the walls above each shopfront – save for the gaps where they'd been stolen off by tosspots.

Even from where I was I could tell he was pleased with himself. Couldn't wait to get back and fill his boots telling what he'd been up to – how they always got a fire going first, to make the place nice and snug, then they had all the afternoon for it and the best thing was, there was no one around to bother them. Fifty mills of blowfly vaccine and he'd be telling a different story. The shits, sweating, sped up heart rate, not so snug and cosy now, eh?

I was breathing heavy coming down the last field, and I near tripped over a stub of rock jutting out the ground, stumbling forward all over the shop until I righted myself. They'd have liked that, Lankenstein flat on his face and the paste gun all smashed up under him, they'd have liked that just gradely.

He didn't mark me, stood on the thin belt of grass that ran down the middle the track, he was too busy sunning himself when he came round the corner. He near clattered into me, swerving off last moment and braking to a halt with one wheel on the field. He looked at me, riled I'd got in his way.

You all right? he said. His face was brown from being cocked at the sun the whole time.

Lovely day for it, I said.

Right.

We've had snow up here till just recent.

Yeah, I know.

He was big, like I'd thought – broad shouldered, with thick, strong forearms that tensed and corded as he clenched on the handlebars. I could see the chimney puffing away behind him, though it was too far off to see the smoke cloud moving, it looked perfect stilled, like a photograph. It was so peaceful everywhere it didn't feel real, like the world had stopped, except for a faint hissing noise that sounded like the rasp of a goose someplace in the distance telling someone to fuck off, this is my patch, this is. I knew it wasn't a goose, mind, it was the Cyclist spinning his pedals backward. He was looking past me – can I get round him? Is there room enough? I don't want to stand round yammering about the weather all day.

You've had snow in town, then, have you? I said.

What town?

That one, down there, I said, pointing down the valley, with the Christmas trees growing off the walls.

He spun his pedals some more. I don't live there, he said.

Right. Where you from?

Ampleforth.

Fair ride from here, that.

It's only half an hour. He toed his pedal into position, straightening the front wheel.

Know her from school, do you?

What?

The girl. She goes to Ampleforth. That where you know her from?

He looked at me in the face then, instead of looking off past me.

Do *you* know her? he said.

Yes. I'm learning her about farming.

A smile tweaked on to his big, square face. Right. He spun the pedals again. She never said. What's your name?

Sam Marsdyke.

No. Never mentioned you. Then he trapped a pedal with the flat of his foot and pushed off. I stepped aside as he came level with me – see you later – he didn't even look at me when he said it, but that was fine with me, I was taking the paste gun out my pocket at the time. He was moving past me and I kicked at the front wheel, but he'd set off too quick and I missed, and my foot jammed under a pedal, sending a great welt of pain up my shin. The bike keeled to the ground with him falling on top of it and me somewhere underside the both. The pedals were at their hissing again, louder now, as they were next my ear, and somewhere up the tops I could hear a tractor chugging along – likely Father filling the troughs,

fuck this, fuck that, oi sheep, get out the way, you fuckers. I felt a
wallop then, as the Cyclist kicked me in the kidneys. He was stood
over me, looking down. There was a scrape of skin ripped red out
of his suntan.

What the hell's your problem?

I fumbled about on the track for where I'd dropped the paste
gun. What was I going to do, stab it in his foot? I cracked up at
that, the picture of him stood there with a mighty syringe sticking
out his trainer, agh, my foot, my foot, now I'm going to get the
shits. Course, he didn't think it was so funny, and he kicked my
hand away like it was some rat scuttering at the rubbish bags. What
did you do that for, you bloody inbred? I laughed more, I couldn't
stop it by then, a gaspy, spluttering laugh, for I couldn't breathe
right well owing to the kick. Fancy her, do you? There was a dribble
of blood on the end of his nose, jiggling each time he breathed out.
Lucky for you, she's well into whack-job farmers, she told me. I
just lay on the floor, laughing. Lovely day for it – who'd have
thought we had snow until yesterday? But tell me – are sheepdogs
more intelligent than other dogs? He smiled, his lips snarling up as
he tightened his eyes, like there was a pulley-string between. You're
fucking psychotic. That just got me going again with the laughing,
the tears running sideways down my cheek. You show symptoms,
Sam, of a clinical psychosis – perhaps some schizotypal form of
personality disorder. I recommend a period of rest and recuperation
and ten apples a day. That wasn't what she'd said, sod knows what
she did say, I was too busy gawping round the room at all these
mighty-sized books and a wall full of certificates in gold frames, as
if she had a prize herd of Wensleydales she showed at weekends.
Dr M. Neeves MDF, winner of the North Yorkshire mental bastard
fair, November.

Yeah, she's crazy about you, you know. I should give in now,
really. Beauty and the freak. We were both laughing now. The
dribble on his nose stretched and quivered, I'm going to fall, I'm
going to fall – and it dropped to the ground. He picked up his bike
and brushed a hand over the seat, then he swung his leg over the
saddle and turned round to look past me back toward the house,

and I marked his face freeze up, like he'd spotted the barbarian army coming over the horizon. His leg hung suspended over the bike an instant as though he was going to piss on it.

What the fuck's going on?

The first I saw of her she was knelt aside me with her face right up next my own, and I closed my lids, for I didn't want to gleg the look in her eyes. Jesus, Sam, are you all right? I wanted to get up, I'm grand, thanks, pick something up off the floor – the paste gun – oh, there it is, I knew it was someplace round here. But I couldn't move. I just lay there like a babby with my lids shut. Why are you laughing? What is it? What are you laughing at? He's a psycho, that's why. He fucking attacked me. I heard her get up and crunch toward him. No, he didn't. I saw what happened. She'd seen, then – watched me pinned to the ground gibbering into the grass. I pictured her up, looking out her window like the girl from the fairy story, watching after him until he was a tidgy pip in the distance. Just because you're pissed off with me, it doesn't mean you can take it out on just anyone. I'm *not* pissed off with you, I told you. You so are. I opened my eyes and watched a wisp of cloud druft behind a tree. Yeah, well, I'm hardly going to Whitby with you now, anyway. He attacked *me*. He's a psycho. Oh, shut up. I was watching, remember? You rode into him then you kicked the shit out of him. I should've told her that if I'd not caught my leg under the pedal it'd have turned out different, he'd not have been able to do it to me. He'd be having the shits all night and I'd not be a half-baked lump blithering on the floor.

It went quiet then, and the cloud came out the other side the tree. I thought a moment, maybe I can crawl off round the corner without her noticing. I bellied along the belt of grass using my arms and legs to push me along, like a giant pond skater. I'd not got more than a yard or two when there was a hand on my shoulder and she said, Sam, what are you doing? I sat up and she was bent toward me. He'd buggered off. I couldn't even see him.

I'm fine, I said, never mind my leg ached and my senses were daffled and out of kilter like when the power's back on after a shut-out and all the articles in the house are spinning and beeping, boiler lighting up, alarm clock flashing midnight, the freezer whirring.

You're not hurt that badly, are you?

No, I said. I got up, and even though she was looking off down the track now, I could mark she was crying. I put my hand toward her, to touch her on the shoulder. Sorry, I said, then I backed off without touching her.

What do you have to be sorry about? She said it so quiet it didn't seem like a question. It's me who should be sorry. She walked off without saying anything else, or looking at me, which was probably a gradely piece of luck, owing as I looked like I'd been dragged arse-uppards through a badger set. I stood a time and watched her disappear round the corner, then I picked up the paste gun from where it was hid in the grass, put it back in my pocket, and trod for home. It must've broke, because the blowfly vaccine, all warm and syrupy, started leaking through my fingers, pooling and seeping into all the other stains rotted into the cloth.

13

Mum was twined at me spending so much time holed up in my room, because Sal was always up there with me and she wasn't fond on dogs in the house. They trod muck and hairs through the place, was her opinion, which was a daft rule, to my mind, considering the other stinking articles she allowed indoors, such as Father and the cat. She didn't bother us, mind, so we kept up there hours each day, just staring out the window or flipping, blank-eyed, through the farming magazines that'd been piled up next the kitchen fire. European subsidy cuts, supermarket margin increases, liver fluke risks – none of it was any interest to me, except sometimes for the pictures of walloping new tractors I'd never get the use of. Sal just kipped aside the bed, fain pleased to be out the cold.

I still had the sheep to see to in the afternoons, housed up now in the barn until they lambed. Sometimes, while I was checking on them and sorting their feed, I went out to slip a look down the hill, but I never saw her, I didn't even know if she was there or not. Didn't see the bike neither, mind.

Christmas came. A proper belly laugh, like always – the three of us clinking and scraping dry humps of turkey around us plates, each while Mum making conversation. Janet has family come by this year, I hear tell, not brought a scrap wi' 'em for to help her with t' meal, miserly tykes. We'd not had anyone round usselves since Pa Leggott died, except for Janet, when she didn't have family to cook for and she came up ours to moan about how they'd been previous year. Father's brother lived in Helmsley, so we didn't much see their lot, and Mum had a cousin, moved south years ago, who I'd not seen since I was a babby. We never made much of a fuss over Christmas anyhow, for the farm still needed working same as normal, so there wasn't time for trees and holly and decorations and the like. I did get a present, though, off Mum – *Concise*

Encyclopaedia of the World. She always got me something like that since I was thrown out the school, and she'd marked me collecting up the newspapers from the garage, she said, she could see I was taking interest of what went on in the world.

When it was done and new year over with, Mum went and fetched the tin back from Deltons'. I could tell from her mood after she got back that Delton had got under her skin – ee, we had a time of it this year, the whole family round, you should've seen the goose I cooked, I could've fed an army. Anyhow, thank you ever so for the parkin, you have a good one yourself did you, just the three of you, was it? I'd told her I'd go down the new family's place for the other tin, and I waited until she'd left before I went upstairs to pull it out from under my bed and put it on the kitchen table for her. They enjoy it, did they? she asked me later. They did, yes, they send their best. Aye, well, I'm fain glad someone appreciates it, and she chuntered off to the cupboard with the tins.

Father's ailment had shook off, and he was busy about the place seeing to all the jobs he'd been too ill to get done and hadn't trusted me with. Guttering the yard drains, mainly, and fiddling with the tractor engine, although he had a new occupation took up much of his time the rest the winter – letter writing. After the subsidies had dried out from quarterly, to half-year, to once a year, he'd been waiting on his Single Farm Payment since back-end. It should've come September, and after he'd spoke to the authorities asking where it was, just before Christmas, they said it'd arrive first week of the new year, but it hadn't. So he decided he'd write them and keep on at it until they sent his cheque.

I'd never seen Father writing before, I didn't know he had the learning of it, except for signpost writing, but each couple of weeks he sat himself at the kitchen table, fettling all his equipment neat around him – pen, authorities letter, envelope, stamp, a letter pad he'd bought at the store – and he'd write, careful, his forehead furrowing up, one slow word after the other. I didn't sit close by when he was at the letters. Most times I went to my room, or I sat other side the fire, and I never got to gleg what he'd written, because he stacked it all up and took it upstairs when he'd done, but I could see they weren't ever more than half a page. He chewed his tongue while he wrote, he didn't even know he was doing it. It reminded me of the half-brains at the school who sat at the back and when they weren't throwing rubbers at my head they were hunched over their desks gurning concentration faces at the paper, like project hour at the nuthouse.

The big livestock farms over at Glaisdale had got their payment already, he was certain, though I didn't know how he knew that, now he didn't go down the Grouse any more. It just riled him further, them getting the money, because he didn't see why they needed it anyhow – they were the ones got all the sales, for all buyers wanted now was constant supply, and they could afford to sell for cheap. One day, when it got to February and he still hadn't word back from the authorities, he went off spying in his tractor to Glaisdale. They'd had it, no doubting, he told Mum when he got back, they had roller shutters on the barns, and new feed silos, and a humming great Massey Ferguson sat in t' yard, not even used. All he needed for was cladding sheets for t' barn roof, but he hadn't t' money for half. I just smiled, when he'd gone out the room, imagining him hunkered behind a wall, spying through the cracks. By! – them's roller shutters, them is, the bastards.

She never came up. I wouldn't hardly have known if she was still there or not, except for sometimes the curtain was open and sometimes it was shut – she had it closed some occasions for more than a week at a time, sod knows what she was doing in the dark there. Moping, probably, else she was growing mushrooms.

I only saw her once. It was afternoon, and I heard the cattle-grid, she must've been coming back from school. I wasn't fussed for looking, but my head was drawn round as I listened to the vehicle coming up the track, I was like a bull tethered by the nose. I followed the car along, watching the dark squares of its windows as it drove on until, quarter of a mile from the house, it stopped. For a couple of minutes nothing happened, it just sat there in the middle of the track, and I started thinking maybe there was a sheep stuck in the next cattle-grid, before I remembered they were all shut up in the barn. Then a back door opened, and the girl got out. I heard the thud of the door closing just as the car started moving off. She stood a moment, it seemed she wasn't sure what to do, and I got back to unfastening the hay bales, in case she might walk up the hillside toward me.

When I looked back, though, pulling the cut string off a bale, she'd started down the track for the house. I watched her spidering along avoiding the puddles, glad when she didn't slow up at the spot where it'd all happened with the Cyclist. She walked slow, down the dip into the trees and through the gate at the entrance to the farmstead, slamming it shut behind her. She didn't look up at ours anytime, far as I could tell.

I got on with the bales, cutting the string and gathering up huggings of hay to take for the barn and load up the feeding racks. The sheep watched on, their jaws grinding side to side with cusps of hay sticking out all angles. They were eating double portions now, their bellies swelling with the young that were growing inside. The best part the year was coming up – a barnful of sticky articles stumbling about the place on tidgy twig-legs. That'd be more viewsome for her than showing how the mothers got tupped. One of the ewes was pulling on a mouthful of hay caught on the rack, snagged by a piece of string, so I went up and loosed it off for her, then I sat down on a full bale and looked about the barn. Do *you* know her? She never mentioned you. Well, she wouldn't mention me to *you*, would she, Cyclist? You're the last she'd be telling, you and Chickenhead.

I pictured her up – I imagined her there in the barn walking about studying the newborns with their bodyguard mothers, her great wellingtons flapping against the backs her legs.

The ewe will start to get flowtered first – bleating, pawing at the ground, that's how you know she's close. She'll keep coming back to the same plot of floor and laying down, then she'll get up again and pace about.

I stood up, listening to the words echo round the barn, and I went to check outdoors that Father wasn't about before I latched the doors shut and sat back down again.

A birth can last three or four hours, if the lamb doesn't slip out easy first time. She'll need assisting, if there's nothing showing. One of us holding her steady while the other slides an arm in to feel for the babby. Not rough, for it'll hurt her if it's too fierce, but gentle, nursing your fingers around it to feel if there's a leg stuck, twisted wrongways, or if the whole body's turned end on. It doesn't need much pulling, just until it starts to show, then she'll do the rest the job herself.

I thought I heard a noise outside the barn. I stopped and got up for a look, but when I examined out the door there was nothing to be seen, only Mum through the kitchen window other side the yard, so I left it by and closed the door again.

Normal presentation, the front feet will come out first, then the head, the eyes half-lidded, then next thing there's a steaming lump on the floor, slipping and tripping over its legs to get at a teat. If the ewe doesn't fancy licking it, likely if she's a one-shear and she doesn't have the knowing what to do, we'll have to put the lamb under her nose, so as she can clear off the birth fluid, dry its fleece, and get the blood going. Gets them familiar and all.

That'll do for now, I thought, and I left the barn and went in the house to my room, thinking it over. It'd need shaping up some, but it was good, it was better than the tupping – but I'd not been ready then, was the problem, she'd come out of nowhere. I'd likely need to change the part about the assisting, though, she might not be too partial on the sight of my arm up a sheep's back-end.

Sal was close on full size now. The tan smudges on her cheeks she'd had as a whelp were now grown down her neck, meeting at the throat. She had a fair coat on her and all, soft, thick and glishy, and muscles building around her haunch from all the rabbit chasing and sheepdog training I had her at. She was getting better at working the flock. There was still plenty to learn her, mind, particular when a ewe came loose from the rest – she didn't have the nous yet how to get it back, she'd more likely square up to it, teasing, shaping to spring toward it then flumping to the ground, until the ewe was all aflunters and it tore off otherways from the pen.

This part the calendar, I made sure she got a gradely amount of walking, because the dogs usually turned fat round this time, while the sheep were housed up and there wasn't work for them to do. Most times we went straight up top the Moors, but one morning we followed along the edge of them, valley one side, heathery tangle of vast the other. The direction of the lower ground, the land had started to soften and stir – the brown patches fading from the fields, and yellow spots of primrose scraffling through the hedgerows. Over the next few weeks the thaw would move up the hillside, field by field, warming the air and waking the squirrels, until it reached up the top and met the Moors. It took a fair amount of warming before the Moors took any heed of the season turning, though. They had their own calendar. A month on and you'd still be nithering cold if you came up there without a coat, never mind only a couple of miles down folk were scraping the cack off their barbecues already, shaping up for spring.

We passed by Deltons' and kept on, curling round the hillside until Norman's farm came into sight, considerable lower down than us and Deltons', spread out flat at the bottom of the hillside. That was part of why Father had never been too warm on Norman, I knew, because he could keep cows on that flat, green land, and there was more money from dairy than from a flock of half-brained sheep. The other part I'd never been right sure – I only knew that sometimes, when Father was oiled or just when he was twined up tighter than normal, he'd gristle on about Norman. Spilt a ton o' muck over ' town road, he has, sloppy bastard.

There was nothing flash about Norman's cows today, mind. Most the herd weren't to be seen, just a couple of old girls plodding about by a wall. The fields were in bad fettle, I marked – mud-sumps around the gates, rips of blue plastic sacking hopping about in the wind, and a portion of wall which had sagged over, leaving a mighty hole. He was slipping, certain enough. We walked along a field and through the hole into another field, to say hello to the cows. They didn't look too happy. Their udders hung huge and swollen under their bellies, mighty sore-looking. He not been milking you, eh, ladies? They just stared at the wall. They were a state, the pair of them, puffy-eyed and their backsides all slathered with shite. I'd seen more viewsome cows, truly.

After we'd done talking to them, we moved off toward the farmhouse, sod knows why, as I wasn't mooded for meeting him, not after the last time. There wasn't danger of that though, I understood soon enough, because when we got near I could see there was no one about. Kitchen light was off and the yard was bare. I couldn't even spy a tractor anyplace. All that was there was a great signpost stood next the yard gate. It was sideways on to me so I couldn't see what was wrote on it, and it started spinning through my head – puppies for sale, working or pet – and course that made me think about the night in the tomatoes' house and that made me think about her. She wasn't easy to blank out. Soon as I'd closed off the part my brain that was thinking about her, she'd pop up in another part – hello, here I am, there's some strange things in your head, you know. You still doing the pond skater impressions, are you?

I walked to the signpost. It was made of half a tree and all shiny in the sunlight, probably the only item about the place that wasn't band-end condition. WHITELOCK HOMES. Norman must've been putting another building up, else he was selling up. Either way, there wasn't nothing else to see round there, so we clogged off.

We went direct over the Moors this time, Sal wandering off investigating for rabbits. There was a bird singing somewhere, a peewit, I could hear him close by, pee-wit, pee-wit, but I couldn't see where he was, bunkered up in the heather. I had a look round, but he was too well hid, and I left off my search and started thinking on something else – the tomatoes' house, and all them pictures of naked females in flower beds. There was one I was thinking about, particular, she was lying frontways over a settle with her feet propped in the air. She was bare, mainly, the skin white as anything, just a green cloth – a scarf or such like – covering over her backside, draping down in a slump on the floor. All you could see was the slow valley between her shoulders one side, and the rise in the cloth other side. She looked drowsy, but closer in I could see she was awake and I marked it was the girl. Her eyes were closed, but she was crying. The skin on her top lip was damp, and she was chuntering to herself – leave me alone, she was saying. Under a shroud of hair, her chest was shuddering with the force of the sobs. Leave me alone.

14

She was sat up against a wall, reading a book. I hadn't caught on it was her at first, I'd thought it was a rambler, but when she stood up and paced about I knew the uniform and the shape of her. She was a mile away, toward the forest, and it might've been a magazine, I couldn't rightly tell, but she was certain reading. She had a scran with her and all, because she ate something one point, and she stayed there, reading and eating, until early in the afternoon, then she made off to the house.

It wasn't long after that, I learnt the proper meaning of the signpost down Norman's. Father came in the kitchen and sat in his chair, and I knew straight off he was grum for he didn't fix his look on anything and there was a quiet about him. He was mostly quiet, Father, but there were different sorts. This was a brown study, certain. Mum mashed a pot of tea and I sat at the table listening to the budgerigars chattering bollocks at each other in the next room. After a time, when Mum had set a mug aside us each, he said, I hear tell Norman's putting t' farm up.

Me and Mum just drank us tea in silence.

Sold the whole plot, he 'as.

I almost told him about the signpost, but I stopped myself when I looked at his face, all worn and sagged – he'd likely take it as I'd hammered the signpost in myself, if I told him that now.

Two hundred acre, he said, and took a drink from his Greengrass mug. I'd gave him that mug as a bairn, it was the one he always used, with a big face of Claude Greengrass off *Heartbeat*, a champion daft grin on him. It looked something queer now, when Father lifted the mug to his lips, seeing them two faces brought next each other – Greengrass grinning, Father grum as a miner's arse. I didn't understand what he was so bothered over. I thought he'd be glad to see the back of Norman.

What's he done that for? said Mum.

Father glegged up at her, a look on him that told he'd never heard anything so stupid.

For t' brass, he 'as. He's sold up t' same as built Amblebrook.

That capped it all, that, another Amblebrook, at Norman's. I knew the place well enough – I'd passed it on the valley road, and from a certain spot on the Moors I could see it off in the distance, a development of houses further down the valley toward the coast. That was what they called it – a development – because it was developed up from nothing, just a scratch of ground next the river. Off-comed hole, I called it. Twenty or thirty red houses, all bright and glishy like a piece of flesh with the skin torn off. Probably that was what the town used to look like, way back, before it started to snarl up and scab over.

Norman's would likely end up the copy of it, as there wasn't anything local about Amblebrook. All pebbly drives and great squares of garden, front and back, never mind the Moors were wrapped all round. It looked like it'd been designed in a matchbox, with a looping road and tidy figures of children playing football, and a fat babby angel pissing in a concrete fountain in the middle of the roundabout.

Father took another glug of tea. Old Greengrass wasn't bothered about any of it, the bone-idle nazzart. Certain he'd have some scheme or other to trick these new Amblebrook city folk out of their brass. I imagined a pair of coppers chasing him down the matchbox street, shouting after him – Greengrass! You put that angel back, you hear. Greengrass shuffling along on his gammy leg, losing them in a shrubbery bush. Father had always been fond on old Greengrass, laughing at his calf-headed schemes – guided tours for towns of a haunted barn, two pound entry, only the barn was never haunted, course, it was just creaky with subsidence.

He sat now, churning his thoughts. Norman was a different type of nazzart all over. His family had been working that farm best part of a century at least, but he was happy to sell it fast as a rabbit's fart, just for a quick pocket. Norman's father never had much brass, no matter the land was gradely and he could keep dairy, for he was a doylem. And no doubt Norman wouldn't manage all this brass he had coming, properly enough to pass it on to any son he might get, for Norman was a doylem too. Clogs to clogs in three generations. But that was his own problem. Amblebrooks all over the shop, that was ours. Seemed the whole county was teeming with folk out to steal a pound from the land.

Not far from us, further into the Moors, some smart tyke was tricking money out the ground – out the air, more like – at Goathland, because that was where they filmed *Heartbeat*. In summer it was teeming with the pink and green hats, come for a sight of Greengrass. They came in by the coachload. Never mind Greengrass wasn't there and neither was the southern copper, and there wasn't a thing to see except for a couple of bare fields and a van selling bacon butties. A coachload of tourists gawping at a field – likely old Greengrass himself had scammed that one up.

Mum came over and sat herself in a chair near Father.

Won't trouble us, not up here, she said.

Aye.

It's three mile off, is Norm's, and our land don't border. Won't trouble us. Most we'll see is a few more ramblers. Might bring some more brass int' area, an' all.

For who, t' brass?

For t' area.

For us, eh? Think we'll see t' brass usselves? He was looking at Mum now. No. More brass they bring in, the more of them'll come.

He stared into the fire. Both his big scabby hands were clasped round the mug as he took the last of his tea.

Place 'as gone to rot, he said, quiet.

There were other changes too, course. Further down from Norman's, they were fettling up a drinking hole for the new Amblebrooks, as work had started already on the Fat Betty. There was a mighty, yellow skip in the car park, slowly filling with manky articles of furniture – pictures and trunklements off the walls, chairs, tables, bar buffits reeking with fifty years of smoke, spilt ale and stale farts. And I had to laugh, what they were calling it. Betty's Sister. You could imagine all them brewery authorities sat round their office in York, thinking that one up. That'd make up for the town's favourite pub being dumped in a skip, they reckoned. Champion – fat old Betty would be proper chuffed her more viewsome young sister had took her place, certain.

I stared into the fire with Father, picturing builders working all round the hillside below us, clouds of dust and lugger-buggers losing their tea about the place, and slow, steady, the dust creeping uphill choking everything until all that was left was our farmstead peeping out the top, with me sat on the rock, watching.

15

It was always the times I wasn't watching for her, she appeared. I wasn't even thinking about her, I was too busy studying at a sheep's foot. It was a fine day, so I'd took a batch of two-shears into the first field to get started on the foot-trimming, and I was knelt examining inside a hoof when I heard her calling at me.

Hi, Sam. Her face showed itself over the wall, smiling. What you doing?

Foot-trimming, I said, and I carried on looking at the hoof, I couldn't likely just stop and kneel there staring at her. I took hold the paring knife and started carving off the rough overgrow of the hoof, and a quiet settled. I glegged an eye up and she was stood watching, all interested. I finished the one foot, letting the horny cutting drop on the ground, then I rested the leg down and lifted the other front foot.

It's so they don't get clogged with muck between the sole and the horn, I said. Else they'd go lame.

Looks like she's enjoying it, she said.

The sheep was propped on its arse, pregnant belly rested on the ground, and she was right, I wasn't struggling for a steady hold, which was something queer, for normaltimes they struggled like bastards.

I'll do yours too if you like, I said, and straight away I wished I hadn't, but when I darted a look she was laughing, I'd made her laugh. Next thing she was climbing over the wall. She mounted up until she was stood near the top, scouring for the best way down. I searched up her legs as she came down the near side, testing for footholds in the stone joints, but she kept one hand pressing the skirt against the back her thighs, guarding. She lowered herself slow to the ground, without jumping, and I fixed my look back on the foot as she turned round and knelt down other side the sheep from me.

How long before they give birth? she said, looking at the sheep's belly.

A month yet, first of them.

She hitched up her sleeve cuffs, keeping them from getting mucky resting on the ground.

You finish school early, did you? I said, because I thought she must've, I didn't say it to nettle her, they probably ended early for orchestra or something.

After a time she said, I didn't go.

The final hoof was trimmed enough now, but I kept on paring it finer so as my hands were busy. After a while of her staring off someplace and me paring so far I'd have half the leg off if I didn't stop, she looked at me and said, I hate it, Sam.

What, school?

Yeah, school, everything.

I didn't know what to say to that. The sheep righted itself and walked off, so for a moment we were knelt there looking at each other, or, more rightly, I was looking at her and she was looking blank at the place the sheep had just left.

I hated it and all, I said.

I near told her I got thrown out, until I thought better on it. She lifted her head, looking at me in the face, smiling. I turned away, and as I did I marked a body, stock-still, spying down at us from the farm. Father. He stayed put a moment, then he went into the yard.

I should get about it, I said, standing up.

Of course, sorry, you're working. She got up and brushed at her knees. Sam, I'm sorry, you know, about before. For a second I didn't know what she meant but then I remembered the track and me the pond skater.

We split up after that, she said. She looked daffled then, she'd told more than she'd wanted, so I said, I'll be off, then, and we left away.

He copped on to me the same afternoon. I finished trimming the rest the sheep I'd took in the field, and when I brought them back to the barn he was there, up the ladder, fixing sacking over the holes in the roof. He didn't say anything right off, he made like he'd not marked me, and when he did start, he still had his attention on the roof.

What's that girl want, coming up 'ere, then?

I was learning her about foot-trimming.

He hammered a nail through the sacking into a wood joist. What's she care about that?

Don't know, I said, which wasn't glibbing. She's not like you'd think.

He hammered in another nail, so as the sacking hung down limp, like something strangled.

What I think is you're not to be mixin' wi' her.

He nailed in the other side the sacking and came down off the ladder. He must've had other things on his brain, he'd normaltimes be sharper than this. Probably it was the Single Payment – he still hadn't got it. He came toward me, but I could see I wasn't in for, what'd I told you, Nimrod? What'd I told you? He didn't look angry, so I didn't back off.

She shouldn't be coming up 'ere. Then he said, remember, lad, you've not always t' owerance over your doings, and he went to put the hammer away and write another letter.

Course, I didn't take Father's heed – I heeled to her closer than ever.

She was wagging school plenty often. What I didn't understand was why it was only me knew it. Type of school she went to, they likely wrote a letter or they telephoned up soon as you weren't there – Chickenhead, your daughter wasn't at orchestra today and, quite honestly, we're all worried. It wasn't the same as for me. No one telephoned when I wagged, fortunate enough, though I never did it so often as all that, mind, and most times I did I was in the building already, tantling along the corridors, or in the bog, because I couldn't be fussed going into class. Wetherill drating on about clouds feeling sympathetic and a pair of girls behind me wafting their hands in front their noses, making all these puffing noises as if someone had stepped in a bucket of shite.

She was wagging most days, though. She had a routine – half seven, she'd leave in the car with Chickenhead and the brother, but an hour later and there she'd be, end of the track, walking back. Then she'd go straight for her spot – a hollow in the ground a mile up the hillside, next the forest, and she'd stay reading books until she had to go home, before Chickenhead got back.

Men started coming to Norman's. It wasn't builders, not yet, it was men with clipboards and wellingtons and a big wheel on a stick they went round measuring the fields with. Most times there were three cars, arrived same time, and the men would stand about in the yard, Norman with them, then they'd go in the house a while before they came out and examined round the land. They walked about the fields in a group, each while stopping to prod the ground and scribble on the clipboards. The cows had all gone now, I marked. Norman strutted round with the men, big-headed as his ram, he was that pleased with himself. Let me show you this, let me show you this, have you seen this molehill yet? Let me show you. I wondered where the ram was now. Sold off someplace, a new hillside of females to tup.

They spotted me one time, and they stopped their examinations to stare up at me and Sal, so I gave them a wave. Hmm, who's that up there, Norman? It's not Greengrass, is it? We'll need to make sure the angel's secure in the fountain, then – and up come the clipboards, all the men scribbling away. They took no more bother of me after that, they were more interested in how deep the stream was and what the view looked like otherways over the valley. After they'd done with their measurements and scribbles they'd gather in the yard again, and set off all together, the line of cars worming off toward town.

She'd been in her spot a couple of hours, sitting mainly, except sometimes she got up and walked around, or she went in the forest, disappearing a few minutes, until she reappeared and sat down again, back at the magazines. I checked round the yard wall that Father was occupied with sheeting the hay bales, then I went to fetch Sal. We kept along the walls, so we couldn't be sighted that easy. Sal wasn't partial on walking so straight, she'd rather be off thundering over the fields, and I had a job keeping her to heel until I tricked her there might be rabbits living in the walls. She couldn't get close enough after that, stalking the foundation stones for the smallest sign of movement. She didn't find any rabbits, course, though she did snout a tiny skull hidden in one of the joints that I had to pull her away from in case she tried to eat it. I picked it out the wall – it was smooth and clean, unharmed, and shaped like a funnel, with miniature eye sockets either side the size of raindrop spots in the snow. A mole, far as I could tell, though bugger knows how he'd got there, halfway up a wall. Took a wrong turning someplace, else a bird had got him, plucked him out the turf soon as he'd surfaced and flown for a perch in the wall to have a feed. I thought on it as we walked toward her, rubbing the top of the skull with my thumb before storing it in my pocket.

We came into the field other end from where she was, ligged out on the slope of the hollow. Sal clocked her and sprang off to say hello, not fussed about rabbits any more. She didn't know who it was, probably, she was just friendly-minded. Other side the field, I could see her skiffling for her bag, but she must've recognised Sal then, for she stay sat and started patting the ground. I bulled myself up, and walked over. When I got near, Sal was bellied in front of her, frozen, chin on the ground. The girl was feeding her bits of scran from her lunch box.

Stay. . . Stay . . . I could hear her now, she must've seen me. Sal stayed like she was told, until the scran was tossed up and she caught it out the air.

All right, I said.

Hi, Sam.

I sat myself next to Sal, who was poised flat to the floor, waiting on more titbits. I could tell it wasn't just Sal was enjoying the game – she had a great smile on her, dangling a half-sarnie. You couldn't picture old Lionel staying put like that. He'd have ate the lunch box by now.

You wagging school again, then, I said.

She didn't say anything, just looked away. I gave Sal a firm stroke, from the top her head to her back-end. Sorry, I said, I meant . . .

It's all right. What about you, anyway? Shouldn't you be farming?

I'm done for the morning. Not much work till they lamb.

She threw another piece of sarnie. Sal left it where it fell, not sure if she was allowed to get it.

Good girl, she said, and Sal slotched it up. We went quiet, and I started the stroking again, ruffing the thick hair around her neck. She was having a champion time of it, Sal was, all this stroking and titbits.

Mum'll freak when she finds out.

I nodded. She had that right.

What's she going to do, though? she said. Move me to another school? Send me back to London? In my dreams, she will.

You from London, then?

Yes, Muswell Hill. She looked for some other food, as the sarnie had finished. Where did you think I was from?

Don't know. South someplace.

She smiled.

We sat looking over the valley for a long time. I wanted to tell her she could read her books if she wanted, for she was glegging at them where they lay on top her bag – I wouldn't have minded, I was peaceable just sitting quiet with her looking out. Sal didn't understand the game had finished, she still had her eyes locked on the lunch box.

Why'd you move up to the Moors? I said.

She paused a second. Because Devon's reached saturation point, she said in a queer voice. She was taking off Chickenhead, I thought. And because the Lawrences have had such a hard-on since they moved to the Dales. Mum and Dad are probably too stupid to know that the Moors and the Dales are different places.

The Dales aren't so rough as here, was all I could think to say. It's more postcard-looking over that way.

Yeah, that's why there's even more snobs there than there are here.

We stopped our chatting for the time, and Sal gave up waiting for food and went on a wander. She had that blank look on her, when I couldn't rightly tell what she was thinking, though likely now she was thinking about Chickenhead, or school, and how she hated everything.

Here, I said, I found this. I took the skull out my pocket and held it toward her with my hands flattened like a plate.

She jerked backward. What the hell's that?

A mole's head.

She laughed. You're a strange guy, Sam. She didn't mean it unkind, though.

I started to put it back in my pocket, but she reached forward and took it from me, bringing it near her face to look inside the cavities.

They've wanted to move to the country for ages, she said, but they didn't because I was at a crucial age, apparently. Like, as though once you get to fifteen, you're not crucial any more.

I nodded, watching her study the skull.

You can help with lambing, if you want, I said. I'll show you.

She smiled. Thanks.

We walked off together, when it was time, and I told her we should keep tight to the walls, but I didn't tell her it was so Father couldn't spy us, and she didn't ask why, she probably thought it was something to do with farming, and not damaging the land. Mum and Father were in the kitchen when I got back, and I knew from Mum looking at me queer they'd been talking about me, but they didn't say anything on it.

16

It was mighty early, before the sun was all risen, when the first ewe dropped her young. We'd been up hours already, waiting for the start – me, Father and the help, sat lined up on the kitchen chairs against the barn wall, passing a flask of tea as we watched over the bloated articles pacing their pens.

Course, Deltons had the whole family round to help with the lambing, but we just had the one same help as we'd got last year – a lad from down the valley, had his own vehicle. Mum thought he was something special, for he was training to be a veterinary, and he was always thank you this, thank you that with her, but all I saw was he wasn't much use for anything but tidying the racks and cleaning out pens. If there was a proper job to be done, Father had me on it. When it started to get light outdoors, we herded them into the field so as they'd have plenty enough room, and soon after we'd done that there was one ewe took herself off to a corner and began to paw the ground and gurn her lip, showing the teeth. Tha's first, Father said, and we stood a respecting distance off to watch the babby drop, a steaming bundle on the grass.

By midday we had six, all settled in snugs of straw in the barn. Most of them came natural, only two needed assisting – me steadying the front end while Father coaxed the lamb out with his hand and the help dawdled round the field yammering, she's ready, this one, I'm sure this one's ready. We just ignored him. Father hadn't time for paying heed to him, or for gristling about Norman, or subsidies, or the weather, with all the work needed doing. He didn't ease up until evening, though he let me and the help take us lunch in the kitchen. I ate mine quick, not bothering to listen as the help blathered on at Mum about his college and how many years he'd got left and what they got fed in the canteen. I was straight out to help Father – assisting the breached births, persuading the stubborn ewes to nurse, housing them with their lambs once they'd dropped.

In the afternoon I went round the field, with the help, collecting up afterbirth into buckets. We walked opposite ends, shovelling up the sluthery piles before they started attracting any scavengers who might get their jaws on them, such as the crows, or Mr Fox, or Sal. I'd half-filled my second bucketload before he'd done his first. He was more interested gawping at the Moors. I wasn't fussed, though, he could idle all he liked as far as I cared, until I marked he was looking over toward the forest, and even though her spot was empty that day, I didn't feel comfortable with him looking there, so I told him he'd better go back in the barn and see if Father wanted anything doing, I'd finish up with the afterbirth.

Father stopped at tea, and after that we took it in shifts so that there were two of us minding the flock any particular time, day and night. That went on the rest the week. A hubbleshoo of activity, it was, the flock growing and the sound of bleating ringing in your ears, chasing all else out your brain so as all you could think was lambs. And centre of it all was Mum, cooking up endless plates in the kitchen. Every time I went in, there were pots hissing and bubbling on the stove, or a growler of a pork pie on the sideboard. Here, she'd say, onions and bacon and potato razzling in a skillet behind her, stop five minutes, will you, I've panacalty on the go. The smell of food got everywhere – the barn, the fields, my room – so as it drufted into my head while I was asleep and I'd wake up with my mouth juicing because I'd been dreaming dumplings.

Things got better yet for Father. No deaths the first week and then his Single Payment came. Soon as he got it he went in the tractor to put it in the bank, then he came back and ordered cladding. I heard him on the telephone, talking to the man about how the spring was come early this year and it was welcome, for it'd been biting cold that winter, eh? I'd not heard him like this for a fair time. The grum days were certain over, for now, he was like a pig in trough. One afternoon, I was on with the help, and when I came inside for a piss there was a rocking sound coming from upstairs someplace. I went up to the landing and I could hear him with Mum, not a noise from either of them, only the bed creaking and the frame knocking against the wall. I listened for a time, then I went to piss and returned out to the barn. Father didn't keep indoors much, though, not to start with. Even when it wasn't his shift, he was too het up checking and double-checking the babbies, and wandering about the field like a travelling quack, the insides of his jacket stuffed with syringes, tongs and lubricating fluids.

At the start the next week, the help left. Most the flock were lambed, so he packed up his sleeping bag from where he'd been camped in the sitting room, and went off back to his band-end canteen dinners. Mum looked like her world had fell through, kissing him goodbye – you'll be back next year, I hope – but me and Father were glad to see the back of him, and start on six hours a turn.

Now I wasn't with them two the whole time, it meant we could start with the meetings again. She hadn't been in her spot since the lambing began. The first couple of times I was on my afternoon shift I looked out to see if she might be back, or if she'd moved to a different place, but I couldn't sight her. It seemed she'd stopped wagging, for the time – but then I started thinking, maybe she was just coming mornings now, and I was missing her because I was in my bed from six until midday. I couldn't be sure of it, so I decided I'd leave her a message for if she did show up. I wrote it in paint on a piece of wood, so it wouldn't dribble off in the rain:

IF YOU WANT TO HELP WITH LAMBING THEN COME ROUND THE BARN BETWEEN HALF MIDNIGHT AND HALF FIVE.

I ran out to the hollow when I was on a night shift and I knew Father was asleep, and I wedged it under a stone.

She didn't come. I left the message there two nights, then I thought I'd fetch it back, for she clear wasn't wagging school any more, and I was worried someone else might gleg the message. A rambler, likely, getting the time wrong and showing up when Father was there – hello, we're here for the lambing demonstration, are you Mr Greengrass? Before I had chance to get it back, though, she appeared.

Hi, Sam. She stepped in the barn, looking round because she couldn't see me. She'd picked a champion moment. My head was behind a ewe's backside, slopping her vulva with lubricant because the lamb was jammed. She sighted me, and walked over.

Can I help?

No, it'll be right.

She stood near and watched on. I had my hand indoors of the womb, slubbering for a handle on the lamb. The ewe was bleating with pain, stamping her front feet. This wasn't how I'd pictured it. The way I had it, the ewe was licking straw off the lamb's back and I was explaining her how it was important the lamb started suckling straight off. But she'd been there five minutes without us speaking, and when finally I did pull the lamb out it didn't start suckling, it lay on the floor with a film of fluid clung round it, dead. I stood up and we both looked down at the body.

Is it all right? she said.

No. It's dead.

Oh. She bent for a closer look, like she didn't believe me. Is that normal?

Happens that way, sometimes.

The ewe was licking at her babby, clearing off the birth fluid. She was a one-shear, so this was her first, and she didn't understand yet it wasn't alive. I hunkered down and picked up the sticky body, the one side of it matted with straw, and the mother bleated at me, confused.

What are you going to do with it?

I couldn't likely tell her that normaltimes we took the skin off and bagged the body in the rubbish. Bury it, I said. I left her in the barn while I went out for a shovel, then we buried the poor little bugger quiet by a wall in the corner of the field.

I thought she'd not want to be coming back after that, but I was wrong – it was like I'd told Father, she's not like you'd think, I'd said, and it was true, a dead lamb wasn't going to stop her visiting me.

★

It wasn't the change in the temperature, or the heather spreading pink, that told me the calendar was turning, so much as the sound of it. Spring belted out everyplace. All manner of creatures were waking up, dropping young, returning home – the lot of them yammering at each other. Hello, here I am, been asleep this past few months and, by, I'm hungry. These towns, they moved up fancying the peace and quiet, the stillness of things, but you'd have to bury your head in the ground if you wanted some quiet round here, and even then you'd hear the moles chuntering.

The best of it was the birds. Swallows, wheatears, snipe – great flocks of them flying back from Africa or someplace a million miles off they'd been since back-end, and fetching up to their old nest the same week they had the year before. Same day, sometimes. Sod knows how they did that – it wasn't like they had an alarm clock to remind them, ee, that the time is it, we'd best be off, then, leave all this sunshine behind and fly a million miles back to the Moors. They just shared a gumption it was time to go. Some viewsome sights on that journey. Vasts of desert, and mountains, and great forests too dark and grum for folk to live, save for the tribes, spearing fish out a river. They passed over the cities and all, viewing down on swarms of people maggoting about like they had been the last year, and the year before that.

They'd have passed over the girl, last year. Crossing London looking down on all these houses big as barns and someplace amongst it all a small green hump that was Muswell Hill. That was back in the days when she was happy, and she didn't hate everything, and she was probably sat on top the hill next to some great muscle of a lad – you can see the whole world from here, he was saying. What was he talking? The whole world? All they could see was streets of barn-sized houses and a mighty clock next the river. She didn't know anything else in them days, she had no choice but to follow Muscle down the hill holding his hand until they came on to a street thronged both sides with people, it's this way, he was saying. Then he was taking her into a house, and upstairs to a door with a picture of a flash red car. It was fast as anything, no doubting, but you could tell no one ever used it in case it got a scratch or stopped being so shiny. The door was shutting and all I could see was the car and the door closed in front of me, and through it I could hear the steady rocking of the bed as he held her into the pillow and bred her.

The swallows had missed her this year, mind, for she was in our barn helping with the lambing, listening to me. She came up regular, she was there almost every night since the help had gone. I learnt her about foot rot, roundworm, fly strike; and most times she listened in close and I stared at the floor, but sometimes she was more interested in talking about this bitch and that bitch at school, who'd put her bag on the bus seat so that there was nowhere left to sit.

Mum knew about her visits. I didn't know how she'd found out, as I'd been mindful we were quiet, but she'd learnt it somehow. She came in my room one morning when I'd just gone to bed after my shift, and she started jabbering about it being a good year for the lambing this time, and how Father was pleased at me for I'd been working hard, staying up these nights. She'd marked the girl from down Turnbull's up here a couple times, she said. You're friendly on her, are you? That's fine, it's time for that, she said, it's long enough now. She stayed sat on the bed a while, smoothing the spread with the back her hand. She was thinking how to say it, but she couldn't shape the words. Then she looked at me – Sam, you'll be careful of yourself, won't you? It can't happen like the other time again. I will, I told her. I'm learning her about the farm, is all. She kept looking at me, like she was testing if I was glibbing her or not, but then she patted the bed, smiled, and left out. Fine, that's fine, that.

She'd sat there before, something similar, after I was thrown out the school, only there'd been no smiling and bed-patting then, her eyes all puffed up, set on the window, like she couldn't bear sight of me. You've to promise me, Sam, it'll never happen again. Your Father'll have shut of you. You've to promise me, Sam, you hear? She was proper choiled up a long while, after the school. She wouldn't go into town, them days, for she thought the whole valley was chelping on about it – eh, you hear what the Marsdyke boy's done this time? Fair luck the teacher came back when he did, then, hell knows what he'd have done else. I didn't much go into town, neither, because I knew they were all on at it, aside from Father had banned me anyhow. I had the Moors, though, but Mum wouldn't much even leave the house, because she'd have to go past Deltons'. She stayed indoors most the time, on the phone to Janet each five minutes – hadn't I always spoke up for him, Janet? How many times? Them cats of Delton's he killed, and each time I'd spoke up for him till I was blue in t' face. Codded meself it couldn't have been him done it. Codding meself now he'd not rape a girl. But the bruises – there were bruises all up her arm, Janet, how'm I to speak up for him with that?

It was one of them days, when I was getting back in from the tops, sneaking through the house up to my room, I heard her in their bedroom, sobbing. Father was far off in the fields so I stopped outside the door and listened. I could hear her shutting drawers, each while a quiet settling, until it'd come again, a faint, jolting sob. I stood there a long time, and I knew it was best leaving her peaceful, but she didn't stop, she'd probably been on at it all afternoon, and eventually I went in and sat on the end the bed. She just carried on with what she was doing, putting socks away. We didn't neither of us say anything, but she wouldn't stop her crying, she was doing it worse now, fixed concentrating putting the socks away. I'd never known Father had so many socks, I remembered thinking, all of them brown. I didn't plan doing it, I told her. But she wouldn't look on me. She finished doing the socks and put the empty basket under her arm and I knew I should've let her be, but I didn't, I just stayed put. Then she did look on me, and I saw she'd stopped crying. If a person's got bad in 'em, she said, it'll leach its way out, no matter if they plan it or other. She picked up a sock that'd dropped on the floor, tidying it away with the others, and went toward the door. Janet says I'm not to blame meself. I couldn't have done different. You must've came out backward. Then she left out the room and went downstairs to the kitchen.

*

I still kept her visits to the night shift, never mind Mum'd said it was fine. Father wasn't so freethinking, I knew. It suited her, too, she said, because she couldn't risk skipping school any more, and it was easiest waiting until her parents were asleep, so they wouldn't find out where she was going and give her a load of grief. She stayed about an hour, most nights, though sometimes she stayed until two or three o'clock, then we'd say goodbye and she sneaked off down the fields to let herself quiet back into her house. One of them nights, when she'd stayed late, she stopped before she went out the barn door and said, Sam, we should go for a drink sometime, you know, in the town or somewhere.

17

People were looking at us. There were a fair few about as we walked down the high street together, and they all made sure they got a good stare before we went past. She wasn't bothered, though, she didn't even mark any of it, she was occupied with talking to me.

My parents pretty much freaked, they were so pleased I was going out, she said, as we got nearer the pub. They think I've made a friend at school, called Catherine, and I'm going round to her house – which is pretty funny really, seeing as Catherine's a complete bitch.

I smiled at her, and watched ahead at a couple of towns going in the pub. I'd not seen Mum or Father as I'd left. Father was in the barn, and Mum likely thought I was out walking, so they'd not eyed me dressed in my good shirt and my old school shoes when I slipped out. It was her idea to come to Betty's Sister – it would be funny, she said. We could go snob-watching. I didn't feel right comfortable going into the place, mind. I kept thinking, they'd know me from before when they wouldn't let me in, and I'd have to take her down the Tup, or worse, she'd want to know why I was barred and then she'd find out everything.

There were round wooden tables outside, each spiked with a furled-up red umbrella, and either side the door were two great metal furnaces on poles, for heating the outdoors. A blast of noise escaped from the door as we went in – not the woollen muffle of conversation like normaltimes when a pub was busy, but a hard, bouncing sound, jarping off the walls and the planed-down floorboards.

Come on, she said, going ahead of me, I'll find a corner. They won't serve us if they see me, because I'm under age. I trailed after, looking downward at my school shoes. Most the drinkers were crowded in groups near the bar, stood in circles yammering at each other – the men laughing, slapping each other's backs, and the females all lipstick and shiny belts and a smog of perfume as we pushed our way through. I touched her on the arm, in front of me. What do you want to drink? I asked her. Bacardi and Coke, she said, and she disappeared through the crowd. As I approached the bar I started to feel easier, because no one seemed to be looking at me, and I didn't recognise the barmen or any of the drinkers thronged round the bar. Except for one. When I got to the counter, sat next me, hunkered over on a metal buffit, old Jack was staring grimly into his pint. A calf-lick of hair was stood proud above his forehead.

Jack, I said, and he looked up, daffled, squeezing his eyes to see who it was.

Oh, he said. He gawped at me a moment and I thought he was about to say some more – hast-ta seen t' place, lad? I can't understand they done it. I took meself two lines on t' petition, you know. But he didn't say anything, he turned back to watching his pint. The barman gave me a queer look when I ordered the drinks, but that was owing to I looked a sight in my good shirt and my hair brushed – he didn't know me, so he couldn't refuse serving me. He poured my pint and I marked the tops the pumps were shaped into the head of a smiling female – Betty's sister, no doubting. I took the drinks when he'd done and went to find her, without speaking again to Jack, still staring into his glass.

She was parked on a mighty, brown leather settle in an empty corner of the pub. I set the drinks on the table and sat opposite, on a low seat about two miles away from her.

You can come sit here, you know, she said, smiling. There's a better view.

What of?

The snobs, she said.

I shifted over and lowered myself on to the other end the settle. I couldn't likely turn to face her while we weren't talking so I looked out at the crowd, same as she was doing. Sometimes I'd snatch a piece of talk from the noise – a man beldering something out and the circle busting with laughter. It was too noisy to hear what they were laughing about.

They're repulsive, aren't they? she said.

Least they're kept to themselves in here, mind.

She turned to me and frowned, as though she'd just caught me having away with a cow.

Sam, they shouldn't be here in the first place. This pub used to be the heart of this town.

For some, it was, the heart, I said. I left it at that, and she didn't ask what I meant, she went quiet again and I stared at the chalkboard on the wall aside us. Soft and luscious, with characteristics of elegant strawberry, it said on it, about a wine, like that might make you want to drink it. She'd curled up into her side the settle, her knees drawn up on the cushion.

What do you think that is, then – an elegant strawberry? I said.

She didn't know what I meant firstly, but I nodded at the sign, and she laughed.

You see her over there? she said. The fat tart in the red top – I'd say she was one, if it wasn't for the fact she's about as elegant as a pig on ice.

We both laughed at that, then she said, we're being watched, look.

I looked out, but I couldn't see anyone watching, they were all too busy at their yammering.

It's the Burridges. They're friends of Mum and Dad.

Should we leave, then? I said, no matter I still couldn't see them.

No. I don't care.

I'd near finished my drink. There were rings of froth dried down the insides of the glass. I glegged the board again, for something else funny.

They're going to come over. Look, they're coming.

She was right. A pair of them were shuffling to the edge of the crowd. They stopped there, talking with their heads close together, twice giving the eye over in our direction, then they started toward us with big blank smiles.

Jo, the female said, how are you getting on? Are your mum and dad here? They both had smiles fastened on, and I thought they were going to sit down on the seats opposite, but they didn't, they stood next each other smiling down at us.

Mum and Dad are at home, she said.

Oh, right. Do tell them we said hi.

I could tell she didn't want a palaver, she wanted to get back to her yammering, she could blatherskite about this later. But the husband wasn't going to let it by so easy. He supped his drink and leant forward. He had a pewter tankard – it was one of them that never got used before the place was done over, they were all hung off the roof back then.

Just a Coke in there, I hope, he said, laughing.

She didn't answer him. She took up the glass and drank a slow glug of it, the white of her throat coursing up, down.

Coke, and rum, she said, setting the glass down.

He didn't know what to do about that. We all watched him, waiting for what he'd say, but all he did was he laughed again. He was making like he thought she was joking about the rum, but he knew she wasn't – he kept darting his eyes at the glass, as if the rum might show itself if he looked at it enough.

Are you a friend of Jo's from school? he said, turning to me.

Sam's a farmer, she jabbed in.

Oh, he said, and for a moment I thought he was going to ask me something daft – tell me, is it true that cows can foretell the weather? – but then he fixed a look all over me and I knew he wasn't thinking anything like that, he was thinking – what are you at, bringing girls in here, getting them puddled? His wife was pleading at him with her eyes. Please let's go back to the group, dear. We don't want a scene. There's a fortnight of gossip from this, already.

He took another slug out the tankard, backing away.

Do mention us to your parents, won't you. And don't drink too many Cokes. He wasn't laughing now, though. We watched them make their way back, in discussions. We should phone Chickenhead. That boy's got the devil in him. Did you see the way he was dressed?

Do you think they'll tell your mum? I said.

Of course they will.

It was only as we were walking back a short while later, my feet jipping from the bastard shoes, that it came to me maybe that was the reason she'd wanted to go there in the first place, because she'd wanted to get spotted.

I glegged another look at my watch. It was past one in the morning. The barn was peaceable – only the dim wheeze of fat, tired ewes and sometimes the rustle of a babby too full of dander to sleep. She wasn't coming. I stood up for an inspection tour of the barn, limping some because my toes had blistered from the night before. No matter of that, mind, I was fain pleased the way it had passed off, never mind we only stayed for one drink, or that she'd been quiet walking back, or that Chickenhead would likely be banging the door before long. I kept thinking about the joke with the strawberries. There'd have been more of that, certain, if them two hadn't shoved in.

Toward the end the barn I marked one of the sheep ligged out between the wall and the back of her pen. She was on her side, breathing fast and heavy into the straw. Each few breaths the whole her body would jerk as she tried to right herself, but she was proper rigwelted and she couldn't get up. I knelt down by her and touched her head with the pat of my hand. She was shivering, no matter she was hot as coals, and I knew right off it was pneumonia and she hadn't much wick left. I fetched a blanket and covered her over, then I sat aside and made sure she didn't throw it off with jerking too violent – she was too far gone for me to do much else besides fettling her comfortable now.

I was sat there with her, when I marked a pair of eyes watching us. Half-hid in the dark of the pen, her babby was looking on, too boggled of me to come out any further. Poor little bugger wasn't more than a few days old, didn't understand anything of the world except for where milk comes from, but it knew right well its mother was ailing. Even so stupid an animal as a sheep has a nous for death, and danger, from the day it drops. I went over to scoop it up, and it struggled some against my chest as I carried it to a free pen other side the barn – there wasn't sense in letting it watch the mother die, and anyhow, it'd need fixing on to another ewe soon enough.

Just as I was carrying the lamb through the barn, the door slid open and she stepped in.

You're here late, I said.

She came up to me without speaking.

Here. I offered the babby toward her. You fancy holding it?

She took the wriggling lamb and pressed it tight into her. Hello, little man, she said, quiet. There were red patches round her eyes, I marked, owing to the hour.

Sorry, it's late, I know, she said, talking fast, like she'd spied my thought. Just I saw the light was on and I knew you'd be here and . . . I don't have to stay long, obviously, just tell me when you need me to go.

It's fine, I said, I'm here while six. Stay until you want.

I went to close the door. As I started sliding it shut I noticed there was a blue rucksack just outside, she must've brought with her. I set it indoors by the wall and went back and showed her where the pen was, to put the lamb. Then she followed me over to the mother.

She got flowtered when she saw it, and flinched back.

What's wrong with it?

Pneumonia, I said. I went in closer, and I saw that the ewe had passed off. That was her lamb, you were just holding, but it'll need a new mother now – this one's dead.

She walked away. I'd been too rough about it, she hadn't the habit of seeing death so close up. I came after her. Sorry, I said, but she didn't seem she was listening. She was at the lamb's pen, picking it up, then she went to sit on a bale with the babby on her lap. I stood watching her stroke on top the lamb's head as it bleated and bassocked at her to let go. They have a fair nous for death, sheep do, but they've even more nous for not liking being held. I left her at it while I heaved the dead ewe out the barn and lay her in the field, covered with an upshelled wheelbarrow weighted down by an old tyre, making certain it was secure. Father would deal with the body in the morning – probably he wouldn't want to pay for taking it down the knacker's, so he'd burn it on the Moors. That was another item I didn't need to tell her. The stink of scorched flesh seeping into the air, catching on the druft, until the place reeked of death for miles round, turning your innards each time you went outdoors.

I went in the storehouse, where we'd hung up the hides of the dead lambs – four, so far, which wasn't such a bad loss as other years. I picked the biggest – 14, wrote on it in red pen – and found a pair of scissors. She was still on the bale when I got back, the lamb rested something quieter in her lap now. I sat a distance off from her, for I was worried she'd think it ugly, watching me snip leg-holes in the dead hide, but she was so lost with herself she didn't even mark what I was doing until a few minutes later. When she did notice I was at something queer she looked over, half-curious, without remarking on it.

It'll need to wear this now, I said, holding up the skin. Jacketing. It's to foster the orphans on ewes who've lost their own.

She wasn't much impressed.

It's best, I said. Sheep are daft articles, you know – the ewe'll think it's her own from the smell. And that lamb would die if it wasn't fostered.

She let me take the lamb from her and I returned to my place, wrapping the jacket over it to measure the other leg-holes. It was a size bigger, the live one, so I had to cut them right in the corners. I pushed the left legs through their holes and clung the hide round tight, stretching until I could slot in the right side legs. It was a snug fit. I let the lamb down and it skiffled about in the straw – what the bugger's this, then? Haven't you anything bonnier, a Barbour or something?

The barn was well sorted into rows of pens all numbered up, so it was easy enough to find number 14 and set the lamb aside it. After a while of the lamb bleating outside the door, the ewe poked her head out and they looked on each other. I glegged round to see if she was watching, but it was hard to tell, she was on the bale still and I couldn't heed where her eyes were focused. The ewe nosed up to the strange creature outside its pen and sniffed at the jacket, while the lamb stood stone-still like a criminal under investigation. I thought for a moment they might not couple, the ewe would cop she was being tricked, but I shouldn't have worried for next thing she was licking it all over, my babby, my babby, you're alive, where've you been this week past? The lamb seemed happy enough and all, finally getting some attention, it's grand you're well again, Mum, and you've done with the jerking, but just let me at the teats would you, I'm starved.

They were taken to each other, certain, and as I returned to the bale I thought she'd be pleased but when I got closer I marked she was bluthering. The patches round her eyes had reddened, and the lip was going.

They're happy, I said. I promise. They don't know any different.

I know, she said.

Come see – they're like Darby and Joan over there.

She smiled, she thought I was a proper nimrod – Darby and Joan, who the fuck's that? She got up though, half-smiling, half-sobbing, mooded like a rainbow.

See, I said, as we both looked down on the ewe feeding its new lamb, but the sight of it made her fill up again and she was soon wiping the tears off her cheek.

I had a big argument with Mum, she said.

That pair told your parents, then?

She nodded. She'd so kill me if she knew I was here now. She thinks I'm on drugs or something. She just doesn't have a clue about anything.

I hadn't much of a clue, myself, but I kept that lipped up. She looked me in the face. The hair in front her ears was clagged to her cheeks.

You think I'm such an idiot, she said.

I thought she was a picture, never mind her hair was messed and her skin was damp and red, all I wanted was to touch her. I didn't need to worry about that, though, for my wish was met soon enough, she was moving toward me, her hands touching my back, hugging me. There was a damp spot on my neck I realised was her nose, she was breathing in great lungfuls of muck and sweat, but I didn't care much, I had my own nose pressed on top her head taking in the smell of her hair, I could've held her there all night if it wasn't for my bloody stalk stiffening up down below. I shifted my crotch back so she wouldn't mark it, putting a hand on her waist, gentle, and even through the coat I could feel how soft the flesh was underneath. She was sobbing into my neck, I patted her on the back with my free hand, then I moved it other side her waist so as I had a grip on her and I could hold her off my loins. I was stiff as a pole by then, else I'd have pulled her in close, don't worry about Chickenhead, she's a sour-faced cow, what's she got to do with us? Nothing, that's what.

Sam. She pulled off and stood facing me. I'm leaving. I want you to come with me.

A tear dripped off her chin and splashed on the lamb, suckling milk next the edge the pen. It stopped feeding a moment – eh up, it raining, is it? Just as well I've this new jacket on, I suppose, then it started up again at the teats.

She wasn't crying any more, mind. She had a serious face on her, waiting for what I'd say, though I didn't rightly know what she meant, come with her, she'd left here before when it was this dark, and she hadn't needed guiding back then.

I'm going across the Moors, she said.

I remembered the rucksack, propped by the door. You're running away? I said.

Yes. I need you to help me.

The house was mighty quiet, only the muffled sound of Father snoring. I was sure the budgerigars would start chattering and give me up as I snuck upstairs to gather my clothes. They were asleep, though, perched at the top the cage rested against each other, they didn't even wake when I clicked the kitchen door shut behind me.

The queer thing was, it didn't feel anything strange. It was like we were off on one of our walks, me guiding us along, thinking for something to say, and her keeping silent alongside, lost with herself. The only thing different was the darkness and not being able to see the paths through the heather once we were on the moorland. Unseen scratches and prickles cut at our ankles as we scraffled through, it was like we'd intruded on The Night Assembly of the

Hedgehogs. I asked her where she wanted to go to, but she said she didn't know, and that was all we spoke, so I just led us south, straight across the Moors. It was a champion moon at least, he was something helpful, looking down, guiding us on. I could see all the marks on his face, lit up gradely. You do know you'll half freeze to death, once you go to sleep, he was saying. But I didn't even know if she wanted to sleep at all, she might've wanted to keep going all night, make some ground before Chickenhead discovered she'd gone. Hmm, well, I recommend you head for some shelter nonetheless, rather than walking all the night – I hear tell from the cows that we're in for blashy weather tomorrow. They're never wrong, you know. I just winked up at him. Don't you worry, Mr Moon, I'll keep us right, there's nobody knows the Moors well as I do, but he was ignoring me now, he'd spoke his turn.

She wasn't mooded to walk through to morning, though, we walked an hour, then she said she was tired, we needed a place to lie down. We carried on until we came to something of a slack in the ground, it wasn't much shelter, but it was the best we were going to get, and we settled down near each other, covered over with coats and jumpers. I laid awake looking at her back, trying to tell if she was asleep or not, and thinking about the dead sheep under the wheelbarrow, and Chickenhead coming into her room in the morning, seeing the bedsheets all knotted into an escape rope dangling out the window – she's gone! He's taken her, it's that boy, he's taken her.

18

When I woke up, my body felt as if it'd taken the bastard of all brayings. My neck, back and legs were all jipping from stones and heather tangles that'd dug in where I'd laid, and I had an itch on my forehead where I'd rested on my rucksack. I rubbed my finger over the skin-grooves pressed in by the plastic emblem on the front the bag. FORAGER was branded on my head now. I smiled at that. Seemed about right and all – two foragers escaping across the Moors, Chickenhead and Father and the tomato army on us tails, getting closer and closer, until they think they've caught us but when they pull back the covering of gorse it's not us after all, it's a Trilby with his gun – do be quiet would you, there's a beauty of a grouse over there and you've probably scared her off now, dammit. I sat up and felt the blood flow back into each the aching corners of my body. Forager. I liked that. It could've said worse. Bogeyman. Lankenstein. Rapist.

She was still asleep. From the looks of her, it seemed she was laid comfortable, her face was that restful, she might as well have been in her bed slumbered on a great plump pillow with all her teddy bears round her. I stood up and looked back where we'd come. It was a fair distance, considering. Some three miles to the dark horizon at the start the Moors, and a mighty thickness of heather and bracken and jutting rocks we'd stumbled through in the dark. Father would be up by now. He'd not mark I was gone yet, he'd not learn that until midday, when I wouldn't come into the barn to start my shift, and he'd fetch Mum to go wake me up. She'd knock before she came in, so as not to gleg anything foul I might've been doing inside. Then she'd open up and see I wasn't there, and she'd tidy up the room some before she had to go back down and tell him. Likely she'd think I was on a walk, firstly, until it got to tea and I still wasn't back and she'd know something was aslew. And the puffy-eyed days would start all over again. Steering clear of Delton, never leaving the house. I'm not to blame meself. It's not my fault. He came out backward. Best get on with this washing, then.

I didn't know what would happen once they understood I was gone. All I knew was we had most the day to crack on, and get a start on all of them following us.

We should've got going right off, truly, but I didn't want to wake her, she looked so peaceable, so I just sat looking over the Moors instead and it must've been a rabbit running about up ahead, set me off thinking about Sal. I couldn't have brought her with us, course, there wasn't question of that, she was too young yet. I wouldn't have been able to feed her proper and she'd make it easier for them to spot us. It still jarped at me, mind. It was daft but I started worrying she'd think I'd forgot to take her, as if a dog might be pissed at you for something like that, even a sheepdog. Father would likely work her too hard now, because he'd be grum about having to do all the tending of the new flock and not getting time to clad the roof as he'd wanted, she'd probably be an empty sack of an animal like her mother when I got back.

Course, I didn't know when that would be. Or if she planned coming back, even. She certain didn't much seem to like what she'd left behind, there was no doubting that. But however long she wanted to hide out on the Moors, that was fine by me, for I knew them well as anyone, a fair portion anyhow, I knew the holes and the forests, the streams, the burial sites, military installations, the lot. They could search all they liked, they'd not find us. We could hide out long enough they forgot about us, or thought we were dead, and then, when it was safe, we could go to the coast and settle usselves – another chip there, dear? Oh, go on, don't mind if I do – or we could go south to the other end the Moors. To London. To Muswell Hill, sat looking down on the world. Is that Muscle down there, punching that tree? Oh, don't worry about him, he's just jealous.

The first I knew about her waking, she was laughing to herself. She was lying there still, but her eyes were open, staring straight up at the sky.

Shit, we really did it, then? she said. Then she started laughing again. Where are we? Do you know?

Glaisdale Moor, I told her. Next one on from Danby. I knew that was where we were because I recognised the tumulus stone up ahead. We've come a decent stretch. Three miles, I'd say.

She sat up and scanned round.

What now, do you reckon? she said. She had a griming of muck over the side her leg.

Don't know. Go to London?

She laughed.

Well, I definitely don't want to turn back, that's for sure. Let's just keep going, I say.

I directed us south over Glaisdale, deeper into the Moors. The cows had it wrongways – it was a proper gradely day, not even a smudge of rain cloud off east to the coast. We made some good distance, our rucksacks propped behind us, a person could've took us for a pair of ramblers, we were in such spirits, nattering what a fine day it was and spotting for rabbits and grouse skittering through the heather. There were no people about, though, to think that about us, for we were getting too far in.

We kept on, an hour or so, getting slowly higher as the Moors sloped upward, mounting until the tumulus that marked Glaisdale's highpoint, Flat Howe. We stopped there, and took a viewing round. Further south, as we'd been walking, the vast of pink-brown carried on endless, steeping and slacking, darkening, for twenty miles, but off eastward the land dipped, furrowing into Glaisdale valley and a small beck glinting, dribbling away to the sea.

Shit, Sam, it's beautiful.

It is, I smiled. Muscle punched his tree.

She took a seat with her back against the stone, and fumbled in her bag a moment, then pulled out a bottle of water and a couple of foil parcels, handing one of them to me as I sat down opposite. A picnic. We were proper ramblers now.

When did you make these? I asked, grinning.

Yesterday. Are they all right?

Gradely, they're gradely, I said, unwrapping mine.

They were and all. Pork and apple sauce, there were even strips of crackling inside, which had gone something chewy but were tasty no matter. After a couple of mouthfuls, I took the crackling out to eat separate, and I saw she'd done the same, as it wasn't easy biting through it. They must've had a joint yesterday, and this was the leavings. I pictured them up, sat in the kitchen, the dad carving up the meat yammering what a splendid beast she was, while Chickenhead ignored him and the kid slipped spuds under the table to Lionel, parked by his feet.

They'll likely be missing you by now, your parents, I said.

She kept her gaze over the Moors.

I don't know if *missing* is the right word.

What will they do? I said.

Nothing much, I don't imagine. They'll probably assume I've sneaked out for a walk, to avoid another lecture.

Right. Then what do you think they'll do, later?

She looked at me now.

I don't know. Argue. Complain how selfish I am. She smiled at me. Come on, let's get going. Which way do you think? Let's go towards the coast, shall we?

We balled up the foil, putting it in my bag, and I led us forward. I didn't understand why she didn't rightly know where she wanted to go. She wasn't fussed where she was headed – but it seemed, though, that she'd planned the escape. She'd even made sarnies. We'd need to plot it out more orderly before long, once they got our scent.

Is this the right way for the coast, Sam? she said, for we were continuing south. I thought it was over that way. She pointed east.

This is right, I told her, which was glibbing, a little. We weren't on a direct path, she'd marked correct, we were moving deeper in, but I wasn't ready for going to the coast, it was too parlous yet.

We carried on over Glaisdale on to the next moor, Rosedale, and all we could see from there was nothing – flat, brown and similar-looking all around, so that a person who wasn't familiar could turn themselves in a circle and lose all their bearings. On a sudden, she shook out of her rucksack and took off, running zigzags over the moor with her arms in the air. I didn't know what she was at, I thought an instant as to running after, but I didn't, I watched her, the heather shushing against her jeans as she went. Then, dump, she tripped and fell to the ground. I ran toward her. When I reached her she'd turned over on to her back, and she was all giggles. I knelt down aside her, smiling.

You all right?

I tripped over, she said, jiggling with laughter. There was a centipede on her leg by the ankle, not moving, trying to fathom why the ground had turned blue, until he decided it was safe enough and he sped toward her knee, a hundred legs light as eyelashes treading in perfect step so as it slid quick and smooth like a spill of gravy. She hadn't marked it, she was too busy giggling, I followed its advance up the soft of her thigh, curving round and disappearing through her legs. I was looking to see where it had gone when I heard a voice not far away. Two voices. People, I said, and I ligged out on my belly aside her. She turned over. Where, she whispered. There, coming by that way, I pointed. I watched them, they were fifty yards off, going same direction as usselves, they'd pass fair close by, the line they were taking. Ramblers. They must've been able to see us already, the covering wasn't deep enough to hide properly. I watched them through spriggets of heather, getting closer, until their voices took shape.

. . . not too bad, really.

Sure, sure. What, even without the kids?

Oh, they'll be off soon enough, anyway. Becks is seventeen now. She starts university next year.

Two thin men with beards and rambling sticks. They were almost level now, not more than twenty steps away, but they'd not marked us.

And they don't, well, they're fine with you now, are they, the kids? After your, you know, the relationship?

They side with their mother, of course, but they've always done that.

Sure, sure.

They went past and the conversation faded off. They hadn't spotted us. Or, if they had, they'd not paid any notice. Likely thought we were birdwatching. We kept low, watching them traipse off prodding their sticks at the ground. Slowly, they disappeared from sight, shrivelling into the moor. I didn't know what it was they needed them sticks for, they could walk well enough without. They only had them so they could screw great glishy badges on to show all the places they'd bogtrotted over. Turnbull used to have one in his kitchen, next the fire, that he used as a poker. There were all manner of badges on it – Snowdonia, Dartmoor, Cotswolds . . . there was one I remembered with a drunk-looking eel, eyes all askew, wrapped round a beer tankard, that was the Norfolk Broads, and another near the bottom that was probably the Lake District, but it was all sooted up from the fire and it might've been the Peak District. I didn't know where Turnbull had got it from. He'd certain never been to all these places. He must've stole it off a rambler, who'd rested the stick up against his gate a moment to admire the scenery.

We got up from our hiding place.

Like a couple of convicts, aren't we? she said.

We are, that, I said. They'll have us guilty for everything now. Murders, robberies, the lot. No turning back now.

I looked round and she was smiling.

Ee, I'll tell thee what, one of my gnomes went missing the other day – it was Delton, she had her down perfect, I near bust my sides it was that good – I'll bet that was them, ooh yes, it was them all right.

We were having a fine time of it, as we carried on south, I told her any story that came in my head about the humdingers I'd had with Delton. It was the funniest thing she'd ever heard – I told her about the time I knocked into her car with the tractor and the times she'd accused me of shooting her cats. I told her about all that, then I told her about rambling sticks, and she thought that was funny and all, Turnbull using one for a poker. She wanted to know more about Turnbull too, and what his farm was like before they moved in. I'd been daft, before, thinking she'd listen to anything Delton told her, she knew Delton was a liar. Devilry? Shut up, devilry, you don't think she's going to believe you now, do you?

It was middle of the afternoon when we got other side of Rosedale Moor. We both had gleamings of sweat over our foreheads and I had a fair hunger on. If I'd planned it better, I'd have brought my shotgun with us, that way I could've caught us a feed – a rabbit or a grouse or something – but I never thought about that and it was left in the storehouse propped up aside Father's. Mind, even then, we'd still have to cook, somehow. I couldn't likely serve her up a raw, fleshy rabbit – there you are, lass, get your chops round that.

The land lowered just ahead, there was a small valley running across, a crease in the ground lined with trees, before the Moors rose up again. As we walked down into it, a railway track showed itself through the tree-gaps.

That's random, she said.

Used to be for taking coal. It's for tourists now.

What, they still use it?

Aye, it's proper postcard. There's a restaurant on it and all.

She was quiet a minute, looking down at the track, wondering if she believed me, or if I was at the jokes again.

Do you know where it stops? she said.

Nearest's Newton Dale, probably, I said, pointing down the track. It goes to Goathland.

Come on, she said, smiling. You hungry?

We shuffle-footed down the banking and started along the gravel sides of the track, the coal dust turning our shoes black before we'd even gone twenty yards. It took near an hour until we got to the station, though that wasn't rightly the correct word for it, as it was just a small wood platform in the shade of an oak tree. There was a gate leading on to a narrow road curling past, but there wasn't any traffic to be heard, the day was perfect still and untroubled. She walked over to the timetable pinned to a board on the tree. There was one quite soon, if it was right, she told me, and we sat waiting under the tree. I didn't ask her what she'd got plotted, or if we were going to disguise usselves to throw them off the scent, I was minded just to follow what she wanted.

The train pulled round the corner with a hoot and a puff of dirty black smoke. There was an old boy cocked out the front cabin, he hopped on to the platform as the train eased up. Newton Dale! – sod knows who he was shouting to, there was no one else there, and he'd not even heeded us, sidling out from behind the tree as he walked down the platform, stepping into the first car while he still had his back turned. It was dark inside, it took a moment for my eyes to tune in. It wasn't busy – the only folk as I followed her down the aisle were an old couple both asleep with their arms folded, and a family with two small girls stood on a seat jumping up and down banging their hands on the headrest. The parents were too occupied trying to quiet them to notice us going by. One of the girls gawped at me, though, yoghurt or something sluthered round her chin and cheeks. I bent my head down as I passed, the face she had on her, she looked like she might start into the Bogeyman dance if we didn't get by quick.

There was a sign for the Pullman Restaurant, further down the train, this is the way, she said, and she took hold my hand. She was leading me through the next car, there was an ancient fire extinguisher hung on a wall, probably didn't work any more, and she was giggling again, there was no stopping her these days. A husband and wife, both in glasses, glegged up an instant from their crossword puzzle. Look, it's them, the Moors convicts, I've heard they can't be caught, you know. We came to a door with a curtain in the window so you couldn't see in, except for a snicket where it wasn't drawn fully. She was peering through, her breath misting up the glass. I felt something nervous about going in, but she was set on it and I wasn't hardly going to leave her now, I'd have followed her into a miners' piss-hole if she'd asked.

The door clunked shut and she let go of my hand. A fug of food wrapped round us – a Sunday smell of gravy, spuds roasting, and thick, gloopy stew bubbling away all the day. She parked herself in one of the booths, and I slid in opposite.

It's like a museum, isn't it, she said.

She was right, it was, all these tassled lamps and faded photographs of the train in old times, pulling containers of mighty coal heaps, blackened miners sat on top grinning for the camera.

It is. There's a couple of antiques sat just there, I said, quiet, nodding at an old pair in the booth across the aisle. She laughed at that. They were a proper Darby and Joan, dressed up smart in brown wool jackets, they must've been mafted, but you wouldn't guess to look on them, staring blank-faced at the empty table, the old lad's foot shaking underneath, his trouser-leg halfway up to the knee. We were still laughing about it when a sweating man with flabby jowls came up the aisle and stood over us.

Can I see your tickets, please? he said. He had on a blue apron with umpteen pens hooked in the pocket.

I waited for the signal we'd have to make a run for it now he'd asked that, I watched her face for when she'd throw me the look. I was tensed ready to run, but she turned to him and gave a mighty sweet smile.

Mum has the tickets. She's down the train in another carriage. We'll pay separately, thank you.

He studied us over. He was thinking, hmm, is she glibbing to me? Maybe I should make them fetch the tickets. The girl's bonny enough, but that lanky article sat there, that's her brother, is it? Hmm. He turned it over a while, then he said, are you ready to order?

I could see he wasn't too sure still, glegging an eye at me over the top his pad as he scratched down the order. Steak and ale pie for me, roast chicken for her.

We'll have to be careful of him, I said, as he walked off.

I wouldn't worry. What's he going to do? She stood up and pushed open the panel at the top the window, shunting it stiffly along, her stomach skin stretched taut under her shirt as she leant over.

The waiter arrived again, pushing a cart down the aisle, the old pair's dinner on it. They came alive then, knife and fork clenched ready, you'd think they'd not ate for days, the amount of food they had racked on the cart, maybe they were a pair of convicts themselves, had to cram up when they got the chance. He placed two walloping beef dinners in front of them and arranged bowls of spuds, carrots, cheesy cauliflower and a basket of thick, buttered bread around the table. I started getting a proper hunger on, looking at that lot. He'd not even trudged away with his cart and they were tucking in, chewing away gummily with the next forkful hovered at their lips, lining up the next dribbling slab of meat.

Do you think that'll be us? She was leaning over the table, whispering at me.

What's that?

Those two, do you think we'll be like that when we're old, getting all dressed up and going on day trips?

·I got flowtered then, I didn't know what to say to that. I'd not thought about day trips and what we'd do when we were old, I'd not studied any of that properly yet, all I'd thought was we needed to hide out until they stopped looking for us. Right, maybe, was all I said and she must've got flowtered too, for she went red and said she needed the toilet.

I watched her walking off. Day trips. That was a good one. Course, we'd need to steal Sal back, she'd be partial to a day trip – great long walks, new rabbit kingdoms to explore. Us two old codgers bumbling after, where d'you fancy going today, love? How about Lindisfarne, eh, we could get the boat out, go see the puffin islands and the crumbling abbeys a thousand year old, looted and tumbled by the Vikings. Another badge for the stick. I looked over at the old pair, troughing their dinner. One thing I did know – we'd not last so long as them, not last a day, if we went back. They'd not let us together again. Chickenhead would have her away right off, someplace she'd not escape from or get in trouble, London, probably, she'd not cause any bother there, with Muscle looking after her, showing her the sights. I gave a look through the snicket in the curtain to the closed toilet door.

The other end the car there was a pair of Chinese in shorts, drinking tea. Tourists. They were the only other table except for them across the way, polishing off half a cow. I didn't understand it, why they wanted to come here, arse-side of the world from home, to sit drinking tea on a train to Goathland. Wasn't there else better in between, or had they seen it all already? Mind, it might've been they lived somewhere nearer. There was a Chinese family in Addleston, owned the takeaway. I didn't much understand that, neither – travelling a million miles to serve up foil cartons to a herd of nimrods spewing out the pub at closing. I peered through the snicket, but the door was still closed.

It'd be a while before we could start with the day trips, I'd probably need to explain her that. She was too full of dander, sometimes – when she had it in her head to do something she'd just get doing it, but we'd be found out if we didn't act steady a while. It wasn't sensible, truly speaking, that we were on the train now, even. We'd be lucky if someone didn't tell the authorities, probably this jowly bastard rattling his cart up the aisle.

The pie, he said, setting it down before me with a crafty look on him – gone to see Mum, has she? Or has she escaped you?

She'd been gone a fair while. I waited until he fucked off, then I got up. I was at the end the car when I saw her through the curtain, coming out the toilet, and I hurried back to my seat. The old lass was eyeing over at our dinner. Bugger, he's back, look, we weren't quick enough.

It was a champion feed, great hunks of meat soft enough they pulled apart with a fork, and a slow, thick gravy I wiped up the last of with bread and butter. She lotched hers down and all, a pile of chicken, she had, she was finishing up the last of it as the train pulled into Goathland.

Come on, she said. Let's go.

I wasn't minded to argue with her, I got up, collecting my bag with a look round to see if the waiter was about. He was in the kitchen or someplace, so we walked out the car, bold as brass, the old lass looking up at us – what, you're not having pudding? We clicked the door shut behind us. The old boy in the cap was stood on the platform. Goathland! There were plenty for him to shout at this time, though, a fair crowd out for the afternoon, getting an eyeful of *Heartbeat* country. He nodded at us as we went past. He hadn't a clue he was looking at a couple of crooks. Folk didn't expect that kind of thing, not on a steam train. We walked past him and I pictured him coming in his house, folding his cap up, well dear, he says to the wife, rotting in an armchair, you'll never guess what happened today. A pair of young 'uns got off without paying their Heartbeat Pullman. The buck of it, can you believe the like? I was so busy thinking about the old boy, I didn't heed the waiter shouting at us from the far end the train. Excuse me! I turned, unthinking, and he was on the platform next the car. They've not paid, Andrew, they've not paid. He started coming toward us. We stepped on, faster. The old boy stood there, betwaddled. I clutched her hand and started a jog, tugging some at her arm a moment until she was running too, our hands gripping together.

He's chasing us, look, she said, the muscles in her neck tightening as she looked behind. He was clodding after, his jowls bouncing saggily under the chin, he'd only gone ten yards, but he was spent. We turned through an open gateway at the end the platform, and down a snickleway between a house and the back the station, past a fat ginger cat licking its paws on a doorstep. He wasn't going to catch us now, but we kept running, no matter, still holding the other's hand, coming out on to a bigger road thronged with bodies. Goggle-eyed tourists tottering about the place with mighty great cameras dangled off their necks. Searching for Greengrass. We were clattering along the road through Goathland now, cars, minibuses, coaches strung down the one side, and tourists gawking through the windows of the post office and the empty police station. I was laughing by then. He'd be proud, himself, at the trick we'd just pulled, old Greengrass. He'd be filling his boots at that one.

We barged down the road, arms swinging, scattering the tourists, I started imagining it wasn't the waiter chasing after us, it was the southern copper off *Heartbeat*, holding on to his policeman's hat bumping into all the goggle-eyes. Greengrass! I shouted. Greengrass! The tourists were staring at me, but that just made me say it louder. Greengrass! Get back here, you old nazzart. She was laughing so hard she near undid the stitching, the whole affair was that daft, the crowds parting to look at us – bugger me, they were thinking, get the camera out, he's here, it's Greengrass.

We were nearing the end the line of coaches and we slowed up, our Heartbeat Pullmans slopping and slapping inside us stomachs. We rested up against a wall on a quiet stretch past the mass of tourists, laughing like ale-partners.

Greengrass! She said it the same way I had, drating *graaass* all slow and drawn out. Sam, you're a mentalist – what was all that about? Greengrass! I just laughed, and we carried on out of Goathland, walking slow as the crowd thinned and our breathing steadied to normal. There was a souvenir shop on the side the road, all manner of trunklements in the window – model police cars, records, tea towel displays of Greengrass and the policeman, even one of James Herriot, sat in a field with two hundred dogs on his lap. Tourists weren't fussed this wasn't Herriot country. They'd buy anything. Then I saw, at the bottom of the window, lined up on the sill, the mug I'd got for Father. Exact same mug, it was, Greengrass grinning away with his red neckerchief tied aslew. Probably this was the same shop me and Mum had come in that time, I wasn't sure, it was so long back, all I remembered was we'd searched through every article in the place for something to give him.

We trod on, past a row of houses with viewsome gardens, flowers bouncing out of hanging baskets and chimney pots. What did he care if I'd run off over the Moors and wasn't coming back? He couldn't care a shite, was what, except there'd be more work for him. He didn't think I was any use anyhow. He was probably up on the tops now, burning the dead ewe, if he'd not seen to it earlier. Wheeling it up the path, mawnging each time the barrow jammed in a rut, until he got to the charred patch of ground we used for the burnings, where he'd soak the wool with fertiliser and set it ablaze. He likely thought it was my fault. Not paid heed early enough when it took bad and now he'd lost a decent two-shear, fuckin' boy's even done a band-end jacketing on t' lamb, that'll need doing again.

The houses were spreading apart now as we made for the Moors, and there weren't hardly any tourists about. There was only one left, coming otherways down the street, a man with a babby perched behind him on a rucksack seat. He gave me a queer look as he came past. Probably thought I was going to steal the babby. He had a gleg round once we'd crossed, checking it was still there. I just laughed, the tosspot, and I looked round at her, she was smiling away, lost with herself. He could give me all the queer looks in the world, for all I cared, I felt so bruff my innards were near bursting their pipes. He was a mentalist if he thought I was bothered about him.

We walked another hour or two, until it was getting late and we were powfagged after our adventures. The sky had dimmed to dusk and a giant shadow spread over the Moors, turning them russet to dark brown, like a mighty beer stain soaking through a carpet. The train had took us east and it was more populated these parts, with small villages and hamlets hidden in gullies winding through the moorland. The sea was closer now. It was clear visible, bearing down on the coastline five or six miles off, craggy islands of rock specking black in the far ocean. Then, when the light got too weak, all you could see was a great black band brooding under the sky. She wanted to doss down anyplace, she was that tired, but I kept us walking, because it was fain important we searched out the right spot. It wasn't too dark when we found one – a small wood, set apart on a plain of barren, quiet moor, no people or farms or villages around. I found us a dry plot between two trees and we settled for the night.

19

I slept a fair time, not waking until the sun was high above, bawling at us to get risen. I stood up and paced crammocky circles around her, getting my legs working as she slept on, balled up, her elbows tucked behind her knees and what seemed like the mention of a smile on her lips. Greengrass! Greengrass, get back here you nazzart! I had a little smile myself, watching her from above, then I strode off into the deep of the wood for a piss.

She was still asleep when I got back. She was like a whelp, gathering her energy with a mighty deep slumber to get herself full recharged, ready for more adventures. I stepped soft toward her, and lowered myself next her body. She didn't stir, so I inched up closer until we were lying aside each other, snug as chicks in the nest, and I could feel her breath touching against my face. I stayed like that a time, watching her. What was queer – it wasn't the times she was away from me, like before the lambing when I hadn't seen her for weeks, it was these times, cosied up, or laughing together like barmpots, that my insides frammled knots from wanting to be closer still. Course, there was time yet, we had a whole future of day trips ahead, once we'd done with being convicts. All we needed was to think how to steal Sal again, then we'd be set. I looked at her a moment longer, then I edged away and sat a yard off, perched on my rucksack, until a few minutes later she stretched out with a yawn and opened her eyes.

What time is it?

Past eleven.

Is it? She sat up, rubbing the side of her face. I'm hungry.

I smiled. Come with me.

I waited for her to get up and follow, and I tried to take her hand but she wasn't fussed for any of that yet, she was still half asleep, and I led her into the wood.

Where are we going?

Breakfast.

I brought us to a small clearing where the sun poked slats of light through a gap in the trees. She stood observing as I stooped into an old, dead tree stump that a bunch of tall nettles were growing inside. With my jacket sleeve pulled over my hand, I pinched hold a nettle leaf, and with my other hand I teased off the flowers underside of it. When I'd collected a palmful of the tiny, white petals, I held them up to show her. She thought I'd lost my brain, the face she had on her.

Suck one, I said.

She took a nettle flower, unsure, and held it up to her mouth, tightening her lips as she sucked on it.

Mmm, that's sweet. She took another. Thanks, Nature Boy.

I shared out the rest the flowers between us.

They're not going to fill you up, course, I said. Just tickle your belly some.

We finished our crop and went collecting some more from the nettle bushes growing round the edges of the clearing. She studied me, the first few pickings, so as to learn how to get them without being stung.

Sam, where did you go to school?

I plucked a flower and moved over to a new bush.

In town.

You didn't like it either, did you?

School wasn't so bad – it was the bastards in it I wasn't so partial on.

She didn't say anything else and I thought she'd let it by. She went on picking flowers in quiet as I trod off a distance, going behind another tree stump, but after a while she followed toward me, searching the nettle growths other side the stump.

Did you have a girlfriend at school? she said then.

I glegged over the stump top at her, lit up by a shaft of sunlight. She was concentrated on the nettles, waiting for what I'd say.

Yes.

I sucked a flower, the sweet tingle of nectar disappearing on my tongue. Someplace in the wood a bummelkite was buzzing away, searching out his own flowers to sup a drink from.

They weren't all bastards, then, she said.

No, we got on fine.

She laughed. Well, that's lucky, her being your girlfriend and everything. What was her name?

Katie Carmichael.

The drone of the bummelkite filled my brain – it sounded like it was inside my head, no matter it was really a way off in the distance, head jimmied up a flower bell, like some floppy white bonnet. That and his stripy black-yellow jumper, he was fetched up proper rambler. Katie Carmichael. I'd not spoke them words out loud for a fair time. I focused myself on the sound of the bee, blanking out all else, imagining him going from flower to flower, well, here's a fine day for it, summer's here, for sure, pity someone's had at all the nettle flowers already.

Sorry, she said. You don't mind me asking, do you? I was just interested.

No. Fine. It's been three years anyhow.

She was looking at me over the stump. Is that when you left school?

Yes. I lobbed an empty flower case on to the ground, avoiding her eyes. The bee had drifted further away, I strained for a listen of him, but he'd gone too far off.

We used to wag school together, I said.

Did you ever get caught?

Sometimes. We'd get put on detention.

The shaft of sunlight switched off like a light bulb as a hump of cloud passed over, slowly drifting through the clear sky as I watched it through the window, lost with myself, until Wetherill's shout jarped my attention. Marsdyke! Stop time-wasting. You have an essay to write, I don't need to remind you. I took up my pen and looked at the sheet in front of me – The Value of Education. All I'd wrote was – Education . . . and a picture of an alien with its nose drawn out of the E. I sneaked a glance sideways to look what him next me had wrote. Almost a page, was what, though I couldn't read it – they didn't let you sit too close in detention, to stop you playing up. I wasn't heart-sluttened about that, mind, owing as it was an arsehole called James Trott sat next me, who was on detention for writing – Conway's a spastic – on to his desk, and spelling spastic wrong.

Where to now?

She was back at the entrance of the clearing.

Come on, I said, walking past her toward the bags. You're still hungry, are you?

Starved.

Come on, then.

We collected up the bags and returned on to the moorland, adjusting our eyes as we stepped outdoors of the wood into the bright. I was heading us east, toward the dull blue frame on the horizon, because that direction, about a mile away at the end this stretch of moor, was Garside – a village big enough there was a pub, and shops, and articles to steal. I didn't tell her my plans yet. I was waiting until it was time, and she wasn't in such a quiet study. She'd lipped up, thinking on what I'd told her. Imagining me and Katie Carmichael sneaking behind the back the school, kissing and holding hands and giggling at bollocks. Might've been she thought me and Katie Carmichael were still warm on each other, even after so long. She should've tried the picture I was thinking – of Katie Carmichael pinned to the desk and the flesh bruising up her arm. That'd cure her.

There was a bridleway we came to, led straight across the moor toward Garside. I wasn't right sure of my plans yet, but I knew it'd need us both, one of us would likely have to be the distraction, knocking over a pile of tins or something similar. Oh dear, sorry about that, and the shopkeeper coming over to help, all smiles, don't worry, love, it's no problem just leave it to me – and all the while I'm stuffing my pockets with punnets of sarnies. She was tailing behind a yard or two. She hadn't so much dander as yesterday, she was hungry, was why.

We're going to steal us some lunch again, I said, over my shoulder.

Oh. Is that a good idea?

You want to eat, don't you?

Well, yeah, of course, just . . . I've got some money, you know.

She'd not told me that. She'd not been so qualmish about stealing the day previous, neither. I thought for a moment whether we should use the money, to buy our lunch, but then I realised we'd be best saving it for the time. We'd have more need of it later.

We won't get caught, I told her. You don't need to spend your money. Come on.

As we neared the end the moor, a great, flat plain came into sight down below. Garside was settled in the middle, and the land all round it was coloured bright yellow with fields of oilseed rape, so as it seemed we were looking on some mighty daffodil, the village as its centre. The bridleway took us down the hillside to where the oilseed fields began, and we walked along the edge a while until we found a snickleway path through the yellow, and waded through, the tops of the flowers reaching up to our stomachs, a butter-coloured mass for miles all about us, bulging and writhing with the breeze. I picked the head off one. I wanted to show her how they split open with a squeeze and poured out a spew of greasy, black seeds slippery enough you couldn't hold a fistful, they fell out your grasp as soon as your hand gripped. She was still in a study, though, and I didn't tell her. They'd be harvested and ground to oil in a few months, all these crops, bubbling and spitting in skillets from this coast to the other as folk fried up their bacon and their panacalty. I'd learn her about all of that later, after we'd had a feed and she'd got her energy up. She'd see soon enough there was nothing to worry over, we'd be running out the shop with a bagful of food and the shopkeeper chasing after, holding hands and laughing like monkeys, she'd see.

I led her through the oilseed until the path met with a narrow, winding road that took us into the village. Garside wasn't much – a scatter of houses along a single road, fair similar to Goathland, with a post office, a grocer's, and a church aside a small graveyard. People who lived here didn't want for much else. They could live and die and be buried a gobspittle from the house they got bred in.

There was nobody about, luckily, as we followed the bend in the road on to the main part the street, from where we could mark the whole place, deserted, peaceable as a fluffed fart.

That's the grocer's, look, I said, pointing her the village store, with its neat boxes of onions, potatoes and fire kindling lined up on a trestle table. All we have to do is you distract the shopkeeper while I get some food. I was talking fast, I knew, getting flowtered because we were about to begin the next of our adventures.

I'm not sure. What if we get caught?

But I didn't answer her, I started for the shop, and she followed on. I could hear her footsteps behind me.

It was fettled tidier than any shop I'd ever stepped in, you'd think we were the first customers had ever come in the place. Down one side was all stacks of newspapers bound with string, and down the other was drink – a wall of green bottles most the length the shop, that turned white near the counter end where the drink ended at boxes of pills and medicines. They had that thought out right, I'd likely drink myself ill and all, if I lived here. I don't think it's a good idea, Sam, she said quiet. I told her it'd be fine and sent her walking down the drink aisle while I tantled near the entrance, examining letter pads and packs of envelopes. I didn't look up, but I'd glegged the shopkeeper as we'd come in, a bald sod with a band-end wisp of moustache. I could feel his eyes on me. He was thinking – what's he looking at them pads for? Who's Lankenstein going to write a letter to? His mother and father? Katie Carmichael? Dear Katie, remember them times sneaking out behind the school, kissing and giggling? Them were good times, weren't they? But I've got a new girl now, so you don't need to worry about me. All the best, Lankenstein.

I moved down the aisle, among the biscuits. She was far side the shop still, I could see the top her head, shining under the strip light, never mind she hadn't washed her hair and there were umpteen grimings of muck coated on her. She was stock-still. I couldn't tell what she was doing. The bald sod wasn't fussed about her, though, he had his glare my way. I could sneak a watch of him between packets of custard creams, and I saw that, next the counter where he was stood, there was a cold chest stocked with sarnies and scotch eggs. It'd been a calf-headed idea, I thought then, telling her to distract him. We'd got it arse-uppards. It should've been me doing the distracting, for who's more suspicious-seeming – a bonny-faced young lass, or a brazzent-looking farmer in a raggedy jacket, studying letter pads? Arse-uppards or not, though, he was sudden moving off toward her, she must've called him over, codding him she needed help finding a medicine for some ailment. He gave a quick glower my direction as he left his spot behind the counter, I've my eye on you still, he meant, but I didn't give a stuff where he had his eye, he wasn't going to stop me smuggling sarnies now he was other side the shop. I'd bray him if he tried.

I sauntered down the aisle toward the cold chest, scanning the items along the shelves as I passed as if I was thinking what to buy – pasta, rice, gravy granules, no, I'm good for all of that already, I think it'll just be the free sarnies today, that'll be all. When I got to the chest, I gave a check behind, but I couldn't see either of them, he was busy playing the quack, telling her which pills she needed to mend her ailments. I cast a look over the sarnie shelf. All lined up in plastic triangle cases, it started my juices running just seeing them. I was about to take one, but then I thought, it was something queer that I couldn't hear them. If he was informing her on the medicines then certain I'd hear him chuntering, and then it flashed sudden in my head, what if she'd took off? The thought of it took me hold an instant, I hunched for a sight through the lower shelf cracks, and I saw I was being daft, I could see the both of them, they were close by each other and she was saying something to him, too quiet for me to hear. I hurried back to taking the sarnies. It was her fault, all these questions about Katie Carmichael, making me think like that.

I started stuffing them in my pockets – prawn mayonnaise, cheese and pickle, they were the only two labels I saw. I filled two into each the outside pockets, then I crammed the insides as well, my jacket was so swollen around my nethers it looked I had it mighty bad with the haemorrhoids. You have anything for that, do you? Hmm, well, let me see, I might have just the thing.

I tucked a bottle of water in the band of my kecks, and I was about done, ready to make off out the shop, when another thought stole into my brain – most the sarnies I'd took were prawn mayonnaise, but what if she wasn't partial? There wasn't sense in it, course, if I'd used a bit of gumption I'd have said to myself, how do you know she likes cheese and pickle, how do you know what sarnies she likes, except for pork and apple? But my gumption wasn't strong enough to wrestle the thought out, and I started searching for anything different. Behind the counter was empty, they were still other side the shop, so I started fingering through the ones at the back. There were a couple of ham, and I pulled them from the shelf, but as I did it I knocked another packet off and it broke open on the floor, spilling shreds of lettuce on to the spanking clean tiles. Poor bald sod, he kept the place so tidy normaltimes, and I'd gone and made a muck-hole of it, but no matter – here he was coming round the aisle corner, ready to clean it up. He marked the sarnies sticking out my pockets and he clocked right away what was going on, shouting, oi, you thievin' tyke! but he wasn't so sure of himself to do anything on me, he just stood dithering, his bald slap gleaming beneath the light. I kicked the fallen sarnie at him and scarpered.

She was stood outdoors. Her eyes were hid from me by the lettering on the window but her mouth was open in a small circle, saying something, I couldn't hear what. She looked like she was blowing out a candle. All I could hear was the bald sod behind going, oi, you, oi! I didn't know what he thought he'd do if he caught me. I darted out the shop, snatching a tin of beans off a shelf as I ran out the door.

She was stood on the pavement still. Come on, quick, I told her, and I took hold her hand. Come on! I shouted, pulling her along with me – not that there was chance he'd catch us up, but I wanted to run away like we had the day before, laughing like half-brains. Greengrass! I shouted, get back here, you old devil, then I turned round and smashed the tin of beans through the shop window. We slowed a moment and watched as the window caved in like it was being sucked by a whirlpool, and shards of glass shattered on to the floor and into the boxes of onions and potatoes. Poor bald sod, he was holding his hands on his head, he thought he'd get scratches all over it.

We had to make a sprint for it then, folk would be popping their heads out of windows any moment – what's all this racket? I'm drinking myself ill in here, you know, I can't be doing with all this kerfuffle.

Come on! We ran down the street back the way we'd come. We kept on at a fair crack and I had to ease off time to time when I realised she couldn't keep up so well and I was tugging at her arm. Greengrass! I shouted once, but when I looked across at her she wasn't laughing, her face was fixed straight ahead. She needn't have worried, no one was going to catch us now, we'd reached the oilseed fields, and when I glegged behind there wasn't anybody in sight.

The path through the fields was too narrow for us to go side by side, so I had to let go her hand. We slowed to a walk, and I marked that my blood was pounding and my head spun a little when I looked about at the sea of yellow quivering all round. Then I noticed she'd stopped. She was twenty yards back, she must've flagged out after the running. I walked back toward her, tickling my palms along the tops of the oilseed, and I thought, maybe I'll show her now what happens when you split the flowers open and the seeds spill out, but when I got closer I saw it wasn't the time for that. She was bluthering.

You hurt me, she said, her cheeks slippery with tears. You broke my bracelet.

20

We returned to the wood, and rested out the afternoon, owing to it started raining. She hadn't been too keen to stay there, but I told her it was sense to wait while the rain stopped, eat us sarnies, before we moved on. She must've understood finally that was the best way for it, because she didn't fratchen with me, she followed as I led her into the more sheltered part the wood, where we seated up in a thicket of ash trees, using our bags as buffits. She was tetchy, though, I could tell. One point, she said we should go back, and I had to tell her she wasn't being sensible. She kept herself lipped up then and whenever I spoke something to her, like – are you dry enough? Or, did you see him with his hands on his head? – she'd say, I'm fine, or else she wouldn't say anything at all, just look in front at the soggy ground with a yonderly face on her.

We sat munching us sarnies in quiet, the rain pattering on to the leaves overhead. I needn't have fussed about getting the wrong choice, I saw now, because she scranned down the prawn mayonnaise fair sharpish. I wished then that I'd took more, smuggled some in my bag as well, for we only had six between us and that wouldn't last beyond tonight. She didn't mawnge about it, though, just kept up her silence. I didn't know what she was so bothered about. It was only a bracelet. It could probably be fixed and all. After we'd got back to the wood, I'd watched her as she unfastened the clasp and held it in front of her an age, fondling it round with her fingers to study where it was dented, demonstrating what a cruel bastard I was for mangling it. Then she'd opened up her bag and placed the bracelet on top for safe keeping. Once she'd done that she had nothing to show me what a bastard I was, so since then she'd spent the afternoon touching her wrist instead, finger-stroking where it had marked a band of red.

Who ever heard of a bracelet being so special as all that, was what I wanted to know? It looked cheap anyhow. Thin and tinny, faded, it was probably a present from the Cyclist. Then it hit me. It was him gave it to her. That was why she was so heart-sluffened I'd bent it. I watched her rubbing the wrist. She was only making it worse – it hadn't been so red, firstly, it just needed leaving be was all, then the mark would quiet down. I stared at her, but she wouldn't look over. She was lost with her thoughts. What's Marsdyke ever given me, anyway? A prawn sandwich, anything else? No, that's about the lot.

I'll fix it for you, the bracelet, I said. I'll take it in a shop, Whitby or someplace, have it fixed.

She carried on gawping ahead.

I don't care about the bracelet.

Right you are, I thought, so why've you got a slapped arse of a face on you, then?

No, I'll fix it, I told her. In Whitby or somewhere. We're not too far away. I'll show you when the rain stops, you can probably see it from one of the high parts, up on the Moors there.

We shut up a while, listening to the rain sile down. It'd be a time yet, before we got out the wood and I could show her that.

It's only bent a little anyhow, I said.

I don't care about the bracelet, I told you. It was from a Christmas cracker or something.

The set of her face didn't even change when she said it, I marked, though she kept her gaze away from me. Christmas cracker, was it? What breed of nimrod did she think I was?

She fell asleep toward the end the afternoon. All she'd had to eat was a couple of prawn sarnies and a palmful of nettle flowers, so I wasn't much capped she was drained already. She lay on top her bag with her eyes open a while, glazed over staring at the roof of the wood, until she drowsied away. Her head was drooped backward, with nothing to prop up on, her neck stretched taut and white, tendons running lines under the skin. What did it matter I hadn't gave her a bracelet myself? It was a band-end gift, probably cost him less than a pound, and anyhow, she'd not done a great lot to earn it off me, was the way I should've been thinking, it wasn't me spending them afternoons by the fire with her.

I didn't much feel like sleeping, so I went for a walk round the outside the wood, never mind it was teeming still. Maybe clean some of the muck off me. I took the empty water bottle to fill up, and soon as I stepped in the open, I was drenched with warm, claggy rain, and I wondered if maybe we were in for a thunderstorm. We'd be holed up in that wood for a while longer if one came, and I was itching to get on, specially now as she had a munk on. She'd be right, once we were going again, I knew. I strayed a way off from the wood toward a higher point from where I could view down across the plain, not fussing about the wet.

I reached the perch of land and scanned through the hagmist of rain, picking out what was visible below. Not Whitby, certain, or even the sea, the sky was that thick – mostly what I could see was the oilseed fields, not so bright and sparkly as earlier, dulled now, bleary, hugged around Garside, which was no doubting empty, all the folk retreated indoors with their beer bottles. Poor bald sod. He'd be mopping up floodwater until Christmas unless he'd got that window boarded up already.

A tiny drop of water was hanging off my eyelash. I blinked it off, trailing my view along the bank of hillside bordering the plain, and I marked a great sandy block sat halfway up, not far past the village – Garside Manor House. That was somewhere I'd not be taking her. I couldn't even if I'd wanted, mind, for they didn't let people in any more. When I was a sprog it used to be open for the public, they gave guided tours of the grounds and some of the rooms – herds of tourists gawking at tea sets and chandeliers with a hundred lights, and ropes stretched out to keep you from mucking the walls. Which poor bugger was it, had to replace the light bulbs each time they bust, was what I wanted to know? Not the family who owned the place, certain. They were too busy sat fuddled up in the private rooms, a giant coal-cob fire blazing as they blathered about the Glorious Twelfth and how much land they owned. Are you sure we don't own the village? Are you really? Not even a part of it? How awful.

Before they stopped the tours, the family used to bunker up in them rooms while the goggle-eyes shuffled along other side the wall, staring at gold-framed paintings of the ancestors – a row of red-cheeked old bloaches with hair perms and grouse strung over their shoulders. All these stern faces sneering down. Well really, one of them is saying, his eyebrows snarled into crows' nests, I certainly don't approve of this – tourists trampling through the manor house. Quite so, pipes up Lord Lancaster the Second, from a painting further down the row, and have you seen? Chinese, some of them. Chinese, of all things.

Of all things, says Eyebrows.

It's indecent, says Lord Lancaster.

You know, goes another bloach in the middle of the row, we *did* own the village once, back in the day. Eyebrows and Lord Lancaster lean in for a listen. Yes, he carries on, there was a time when you could look out from one of the south-facing windows, and as far as the eye would reach belonged to us.

The good old days, says Eyebrows.

The good old days, says Lord Lancaster.

I turned back toward the wood to go dry off, the whole my body slathered with rainwater. They got their good old days returned, them bloaches. A government subsidy, not long back – Maintenance of Sites with Historic or Special Interest, it'd said in the newspaper, and they closed the place up afterward. The bloaches were fain pleased, that day. Father wasn't. Where the fuck's t' sense in that, giving all that brass to them fuckers? Tha can't eat a manor, eh?

She was sat up, awake, when I got back. Just been off on a wander, I told her, and it seemed she wasn't mardy any more, for she gave a quick laugh when I said that, probably owing as I looked a champion sight, sogged through as a newborn lamb. You'd have to be proper daft to go on a wander while it was siling down like this. She was right, it was funny, I had to laugh and all. I sat down on my bag-buffit and shuftied myself comfortable, spying over when she wasn't looking, tracing an eye over the shape of her. She had her chin rested on her palm, and I could see that the red swell on her wrist had near died away. I knew it wasn't so bad as all that. It'd only seemed so bad because she'd pestered at it.

We ate the rest the sarnies, her looking up into the dusk above the trees. It'd stopped raining, I marked. I hadn't noticed until then because there were still raindrops sputtering down aside us, but that was just water caught in the trees, gathering on the leaf-ends, dripping off.

We settled for the night soon after, ready for an early start. I lay down, churning over my plans for the morning. Food – that was first thing on the list, I had to work out how we'd get enough to eat without too much palaver about it. We were less than a day's walk from Whitby, and there'd be a vast of chances to sneak food there. We could even earn us some brass if we stayed long enough, kippering fish or something, so we'd be able to buy our food. I could get her bracelet fixed then and all

Inside my head was too aflunters to sleep straight away, there was so much to get framed up. My brain cogged away with ideas, most of them daft – we could stay in a bed and breakfast, get fish and chips from that famous cafe, go on the Dracula tour. We'd rent a house, someplace small, the both of us could get jobs, go out to work daytime and have the nights to usselves, alone next the fire. I started to tire soon enough, the ideas that'd come in such a rush at first starting to ease off, the cogs slowing down to a halt. I dropped off, my thoughts lying scattered around my mind, and the smell of wild garlic drufting into my nostrils from some part the wood, woken up by the rain.

21

I got up early, feeling bruff, fit for anything. I could see outdoors the wood it was a gradely day. The rain clouds had buggered off west over the Moors to go piss on the Dales and it was belting bright and warm, perfect suited for us to get moving. Good morning, I told her, but she didn't stir. I knew she was half awake, though, one portion of her brain left switched on same as a duck or a chicken roosting, always alert for Mr Fox or some other bastard might come along and catch her unawares. There wasn't time to let her snoozing, though, I had to rouse her up, tell her the plan.

She jerked awake when I tigged her on the shoulder – don't worry, I told her, it's not Mr Fox, you stay lay down a while if you like. I'm going to fetch us breakfast. She looked at me, wary. Bloody marvellous, she was thinking, he's going to bring back some nettle flowers, is he, or a handful of garlic? I put her straight, though. You wait here while I tread over to the next village, Ugglebarnby. I can't likely go back to Garside – they'll have the shop fixed up with barbed wire all round by now. I'll bring us back some more sarnies, enough for a couple of days this time. She sat up, a patch of pink one side her forehead where she'd been laid. Her arm hurt, she said. I want to go back. Not now, I told her, but I didn't say it sharp – I smiled at her, friendly – it's too late for that, after what we've done. Then I told her my plans. About Whitby, and the Dracula Tour, and renting a place to stay, and I must've got het up explaining it all because she was tensed stiff, froze looking at me like a caught animal. It'll be fine, I said, we just need to keep careful a while first, is all. Okay, she said. If you say so. When she said that, I filled my boots so swell I could've bust the leather.

Just you wait while I fetch breakfast, I said, grabbing up my bag. I was minded to run the whole way there and back, only she'd think I was even more touched than she already did, if she saw me bolting off.

I cracked on over the moorland, keeping high along the hillside brim of the plain, other side from the manor house, until I passed Garside below and I could see further on toward the coast. The landscape that direction was broken up with population as the valley lowered and flattened for Whitby, veined with the dark-green slits of tree-lined ghylls joining into the Esk. Not far off, down the hillside, was Ugglebarnby, and more on I could see other villages dotting a line eastward, sucking off the river as it wound to the sea.

Someplace lower down a cuckoo was calling, the sound lulling through the still. Cuck-coo, cuck-coo, a fair bonny noise it was, but that just got me thinking – how was it such a sweet-sounding creature could be such a miserly tyke, always looking for some other poor sod bird to dump its eggs on? It capped reason, that. And why didn't the other birds have a bit more gumption, getting tricked so easy? You'd think they might mark one of the eggs was twice the size the others. Or, when they hatched, that there was one chick looked mighty different from the rest. Ee, he's a big ugly bugger, that one, must take after your side the family.

It was quiet about when I got into the village, but not so quiet as it was in Garside. There were some locals around. Two old women were resting up on a bench outdoors the pub, and a school-lad stood at the end of a garden path, his satchel by his feet. He was examining a bug crawling along the top the garden gate, nudging at it with his finger. I gave him the wink as I came past, but he was occupied with the bug and he ignored me. There was a shop, I saw now, up on the right, not far past the pub. I didn't look on the old girls as I went by the bench, I kept my sight straight ahead, but they weren't paying any heed to me anyhow, they were too busy nattering.

I hear tell he's hired out t' village hall for it.
Has he now?
He has. And he's getting a mobile bar in.
By! Is he indeed? What's that, then, mobile bar?

I don't know. But clogs'll be sparking that night, tha can be certain.

Their conversation trailed off as I reached the shop. All I'd do, once I was in there, I'd grab up a bagful of food and scarper. Let them chase me. I'd run them knackered, if I had to.

It took a couple of laps round the aisles before I was certain – it was empty. Shopkeeper had popped out, so I took my chance to stock up – sarnies, crisps, pork pie, scotch eggs, sausage rolls, apples, and two big bottles of water. I checked about, but there was no one coming still and I thought maybe I'd pile in some more, keep us going for a week, but then it started fixing in my head that maybe one of the old girls owned the shop, or the both of them did, and part of me didn't feel right taking too much, so I fastened my bag and made off. And I saw her face. I knew it was her, immediate, I wasn't dreaming it up. I bent down for a closer look, and the first thing I thought, before my head got befuddled all these other questions trying to cram inside same time, was how happy she looked. The photograph wasn't took long ago, from the looks of her, but she was wearing a different school uniform, so I knew straight off it was took in London. She had a smile on her I hadn't seen before and it jabbed at me sudden that she'd never looked like that with me. I shelved it, mind, when I glegged the headline.

MISSING GIRL, 15, SIGHTED WITH ABDUCTOR

A Danby schoolgirl, who went missing from her parents' home on Sunday, was seen yesterday in the North York Moors village of Garside with the man police say may have abducted her.

They were seen as the man, Sam Marsdyke, 19, robbed a local grocery store.

My eyes flipped further down the column:

. . . a previous charge of molestation was brought against him.

I snatched up the newspaper and hurried out the shop. The old girls were still nattering, but I didn't hear them. My mind was jenny-wheeling. The man police say may have abducted her. Abductor. That was a new one. Add that on the list. Man that was a new one and all.

The school-lad had gone, picked up by the bus. He'd probably took the bug on with him to show his mates. That was all he had to think about, catching bugs, he didn't have to worry about abducting and robbing grocery stores and previous charges of molestation, he was too young yet. I upped pace, leaving the village and following the path halfway up the hillside until it levelled out into a small clearing. There was a scrap of burnt ground one side of it, beer cans lying about. I gave one a kick down the hill. Any town or village you went, there'd always be idleback nimrods around, getting puddled. I checked I was alone, then I sat down and laid the newspaper on the ground. There was another article down the side – FALCONRY CENTRE IN ASYLUM SCANDAL – but the main story was us, her face part-way down the page, staring up at me, look how happy I was before I met you, Lankenstein.

A Danby schoolgirl, who went missing from her parents' home on Sunday, was seen yesterday in the North York Moors village of Garside with the man police say may have abducted her.

They were seen as the man, Sam Marsdyke, 19, robbed a local grocery store.

Josephine Reeves, 15, was reported missing by her parents on Monday afternoon, and police intensified their search later that evening, when it became apparent that Mr Marsdyke had also disappeared from his parents' farmhouse only half a mile away from the girl's home.

This is not the first recorded incident involving Mr Marsdyke. Three years ago, a previous charge of molestation was brought against him.

Police believe he may have been planning to accost Miss Reeves for some weeks. He had been seen with her a number of times in the month leading up to the disappearance.

Until yesterday's incident at the grocery store, police had been limiting their search to Danby High Moor and > page 2

I turned over. There was a block of writing continued down the right side the page, split in two by another photograph, this one of me. I was sitting in the tractor with a big grin on my chops. It wasn't a recent photograph, not near, it must've been took five years back, because it was the day we got the new tractor, and Jess was still a whelp – she was stood on my lap, poking her head through the steering wheel, she didn't look older than two months. Father looked happy as a sandboy. He was stood next the tractor with his hand on the engine and a catie-cornered smile straggling his face. Janet had come round that day, I remembered, she took the photograph. It must've been her gave it the police.

. . . the surrounding area.

According to a witness, Mr Marsdyke stole groceries from the store before forcing Miss Reeves to leave with him and smashing the windows of the store on his exit. The owner, Michael Stainthorpe, described the girl as 'nervous and tired, but in good health'.

He added: 'He'd forced her into the robbery, because she got my attention while he wasn't looking and she told me he was going to rob my store. Then he threw a tin of Heinz beans through my window.'

Miss Reeves' mother made this plea: 'We knew immediately what must have happened, and then when we heard what he did to that poor girl before – we just don't know what that boy's capable of. Somebody must have seen them.'

Mr Marsdyke's parents declined to comment.

Police are appealing for anyone who might have seen the pair to come forward. Mr Marsdyke is described as tall, thin, and wearing a torn brown jacket.

The search continues today.

I folded up the newspaper and slid it in my bag, behind the food. Then I made back to the wood. So, here was another I'd forced against her will, then. I didn't know why he was glibbing about her saying that. *She told me he was going to rob my store.* That capped it all, that did. It was me had told her to get his attention, daft bald sod, he was just twined because I'd thrown the beans through his window. She'd laugh when I showed her it.

Whitby was out now. We'd be spotted, certain. Only choice now, to my telling, was to hide out on the Moors, and then ship off overseas. Do a Sidney Swinbank and disappear into the ocean. I was walking back, listening to the distant peck, peck, peck of a woodpecker, when I stiffened up, sudden, as a thought snagged in my brain. I couldn't show her the newspaper. She'd see about what happened with Katie Carmichael. There I'd been, gibbering about kissing and giggling and wagging lessons together, I couldn't have her reading I'd a previous charge of molestation brought against me. I started getting something flowtered, thinking what to do, until I realised it was no bother, I wouldn't show her the newspaper, I'd just tell I didn't have time to take it because the shopkeeper had copped on to me. I could tell her what the article said, myself. I felt easier then, and I shaped up the story in my head as I neared the wood.

It was near midday, a humdinger of a sun up, and I was mafted from walking so quick with all that weight of scran and water on my back, so it felt fresh and cool stepping into the shade of the wood. The light slatted through the treetops, scattering shadow patterns all around. It minded me of the disco-ball hung up to the ceiling at the End of Year Party, twisting rods of light round the canteen, over the dancing throng and over me stood next the stack of chairs and dining tables, my new shirt flashing red. I looked a right bobby-dazzler, Mum'd said. I looked a right bugger, more like. I smiled, thinking on it. That was another item I could tell her. She might think I was touched again, mind, saying the wood looked like a disco, and truly speaking it wasn't too similar – there were no lasses chundering in the deep-fat fryer, for one thing, and I didn't have a bloody nose from clogging with David Arckles.

I came into the thicket where we'd camped up, but she wasn't there, she'd gone for a stretch of her legs in the sunshine. I set my bag down and went out the wood. I looked around a moment, then I returned to the thicket, for she was off on a more distant wander and I couldn't see her.

It was probably best not telling her about the newspaper. It was too maggot-eaten with lies. Once I'd left out the part about a previous charge of molestation, and Chickenhead's statement, and that she was nervous and tired and I'd been planning to accost her for weeks, there wasn't a mighty lot else left. Only the bald sod glibbing about what she'd said to him, and the police were searching for us, but I wasn't mooded for telling her any of that, neither.

There was a worn piece of ground she'd been laying on, and a mangled clump of burdock, all bent and broken from where her bag had been. We had to find a new hideout now, I knew. There wasn't choice but to keep moving, covering our tracks, now they were on to us.

We'd need to steal a boat. Unless we stowed away in a liner, or on a mighty great tanker going out to the oil rigs. That was no good, mind, we couldn't live on an oil rig, stranded, middle of the North Sea in a city on stilts, with the wind battering away and a hundred lusty black-hands ogling a bikini calendar. When was the last time you saw a woman, eh? A real one, do you remember? Not me – last thing I rutted was a skate's mouth. No, an oil tanker wasn't suited for us, it'd have to be a liner, from Whitby or Scarborough, one of them big buggers taking folk over to Europe, there'd be plenty enough of them, certain.

I got up and trod over to the edge the wood, glegging out at the landscape. It was a cracking day, still. I let the sun warm my chops a moment, eyes shut, feeling the heat on my lids, then I went back to the clearing and got the newspaper out.

Mr Marsdyke's parents declined to comment. That was one good thing, at least. Sod knows what they'd have said if they had. Bone idle, allus in trouble, nowt t' do wi' us. I wondered if the newspaper had sent someone round to the house, toe-ending their way through the sheep shit to the front door? Mum appearing in her housecoat – we an't nowt to say to you. Father sat glaring at the television behind, listening. They'd have had the police round and all, asking questions. When did you last see him? Where do you think he might be? Has he been behaving strangely of late? Course 'e's been behaving strangely, 'e's allus behaving strangely, the nazzart.

It was gone two o'clock. I took a walk to the viewpoint over the plain. I could see Garside Manor more clear today, the sun slapping against its great sandy walls and the glint of light reflecting off the windows like flies on a sponge cake. I looked out over the oilseed fields, and Garside, where the bald sod was in his shop gabbing at any as'd listen – oh, all the newspapers have been here, that's right, the shop's never been so busy – and I looked out further at the small dark gash of Whitby on the coast. Then I turned round and scanned over the Moors, but there wasn't sight of her.

She'd be fine on her own for the time. She was too smart for them to catch her. And anyhow, I felt calm on my tod, with her off someplace else a while. It bated me yearning her. It was worse, somehow, when I was with her.

22

I bided in the wood as the shadows of trees crept round the clearing. She'd been gone two hours since I'd got back, and a thought was settling, something had happened.

I shouldered my rucksack and set off, bugger knows where to, she might've been anyplace. Lain on the heather, her leg broke from slipping down a buckle in the ground, or lost, her bearings swallowed up by the Moors. I hadn't a sign of her, as I scanned out again from the viewpoint, she could've been sat next the idlebacks' bonfire for all I knew, giggling herself daft as they larked about telling jokes and chucking stones at beer cans.

I walked a wide circle around the wood, one eye busy for clues of what direction she'd gone – a footprint, or something dropped to the ground – but a half-hour later I was back at the viewpoint, thinking what to do. If she was down there on the plain, she'd need be careful. By now all the villages would be crawling with police, and an uprising of shopkeepers. Could've been she was hid waiting behind a wall or a bush for them to clear off, that was why she'd took so long. They'd have her if she wasn't patient, and then it'd all be over, some copper marching her to the door of a police car – there, that's one of them caught! Now, you can't keep quiet forever, lass, where is he? Where's Lankenstein, then? A small smile showing on her lips. You're a mentalist if you think I'm telling you. Right, if that's the way you're going to be, you can get in the car and we'll see what Chickenhead has to say about it when you get back, shall we? He opens the door all stern-faced, waiting for her to climb in the back – and look who's there, sat aside the window. Stone the crows if it isn't old Greengrass, spluttering his innards into his mucky red neckerchief. The door locks behind her and the copper's face appears at the window, giving the nod toward Greengrass. We found him up at the manor house, he says, he was leading the tourists on a trip round the grounds.

I decided I'd search otherways from the plain and the coast, into the Moors. That was the only way she could've gone, else I'd have seen her. I set off across the small moor leading toward Goathland and the great expanse beyond.

The problem was, my brain was in a nazzartly mood, playing tricks, befuddling me with doubt. Are you sure you hadn't made a plan with her before you left, to meet up someplace else? You must've forgot because you were upshelled seeing the newspaper. I closed my eyes, trying to remember what I'd said, and I was fair sure, last thing I'd told her was to wait there while I got breakfast. My brain could riddle with me all it liked, but that was what I'd said, certain, and I felt a spark of anger she'd ignored me. Why'd she gone off bogtrotting, when I'd told her to wait? She was too mooded for doing as she liked, was why. I'd have to put her right. She couldn't go behaving like that any more, we had to be more careful now the police were looking for us. She didn't know that yet, mind, I had to give her that.

I pressed on, a muck-lather of sweat greasing my forehead and itching at my pits. It was a teasing piece of moorland, this, small enough I could see the limit of it all sides, yet it'd still take another hour getting past, even at the crack I was on. And each step, I knew I might've been going the wrong direction, moving away from her. There was a dirty smirk of chimney smoke up ahead, over Goathland. Some cloth-head had a fire going, no matter it was a mafting hot afternoon. I headed toward it, though I wasn't minded for going in the village, I didn't think she'd likely be there – I'd skirt round instead, get on to the Moors proper, where I could scan out over the vast. I quickened onward. This wasn't real moor, this part. The Moors laid themselves bare to boulders of wind that had swelled for miles, gathering and gusting and preventing all but the deepest-rooted, thickest-skinned articles from surviving. This cosy stretch of land here was coddled with woods and villages protecting it. Most of it wasn't even heather, it was lush blankets of long grass swooning in the druft.

I was nearing Goathland, close enough to see the bright-coloured movements of tourists tantling about, but something made me stop a moment – my brain wasn't done niggling at me still. A thought floated into my head, simple and innocent as a bird flying through the kitchen window. What if she'd snuck away on purpose? It certain wasn't a stretch of the legs she'd gone for, it didn't need half a day for that. And I'd know if they'd found her, there would've been plenty enough footmarks around the wood, they'd have been waiting there to catch me anyhow. It started panicking about my head. I should've thought it earlier, I was soft in the brain, waiting all that time for her to come back. It was the bracelet still. I shouldn't have left her, I should've seen she was mardy again – what if they found her before she came to her senses? It was his fault. What did he think, he'd bought her a gradely present, a sneck-lifter, she'd let him do what he liked after he gave it her? The great nimrod. I had a picture of her sat on a hump of ground, bluthering, her face all smeared and the bracelet turning round and round in her fingers, why did he have to do it? Everything would be fine if he hadn't broken it.

I passed through the wood by the side of Goathland, hiding once behind a tree when I thought I heard a tourist near, strayed from the village. I waited, listening for voices, until it turned out to be a squirrel scraffling in the undergrowth and I carried on, careful down a dip, over the railway, then up the other side to the top, where the Moors bulled up in front of me. Well, ramblers, it's a gradely day for it, there's no doubting. The clearest yet – the twitchers will be out in force, an afternoon like this, the hides'll be full. Oh, they will, you're right about that. And what are you spotting for, yourself, Lankenstein? Meadow pipits, is it? Grouse? The heather's thriving with them right now, before the shooting season starts. I looked away over the Moors. No, no, it's a different breed I'm after. Girlspotting is what I'm at. Is that right? Well, good luck to you, you don't see a great many of them round these parts, I must say. Not really the habitat, what with the wind and the cold and blather, blather, blather – I stopped listening then, my senses locked on something else, for I had a sighting.

Two miles off, a prick of blue was creeping northward. Back the direction we'd come. She was off home, then. Found her way smart enough, I had to give her that, I didn't know how she'd managed it. Maybe she'd left herself a trail. Oldest trick in the book, I should've thought of that one – dropping a stone, or a balled-up sweet paper, every few yards when I wasn't looking. What was that? I narrow my eyes at her, suspicious. Nothing. Here, would you like a sweet? Smart as she was, mind, she didn't think things out enough sometimes. She was too stubborn-minded. Flighting off because she had a munk on. What, did she think everything would fettle up normal again, did she? Back to the visits up the field, watching the progress of the lambs, and going down the Betty's Sister for a drink? Oh, she'd like that, would Chickenhead, she'd be filling her boots.

I kept my eyes on the blue mark up ahead, moving quick away. She had a fair steam on. It was strange thinking we'd been running through Goathland the day before yesterday, a pair of convicts, and now she was here, a blue mark escaping home. She'd forgot all that now. She was too busy thinking on the tea she was going to eat, and her comfy bed with its fresh sheets and snug of pillows all plumped up ready for her. She'd half forgot about me – I was shoved away to the dust-cupboard of her brain, with Greengrass, and the bald sod, and all the other leftovers of her memory. A mole's skull; elegant strawberries; a tin of beans flying through the air, glass shattering everywhere. Oi, Greengrass, budge over, will you, you're taking all the space, you fat bugger. The bald sod pushes forward, straining for a view out the cupboard door. Who's that through there? he says, there's someone in the front with her look, he's got all the space he wants in there. That's the Cyclist, I say. I can see him, grinning, talking to her. Said something funny, have you? She thinks he has anyhow, she's laughing her arse off at him as he sidles over and whispers something in her ear. She's still at the giggles when he stretches her arms up and slides her shirt over her head, Greengrass and the bald sod clambering over each other for a gawp, their lollickers hanging out their mouths.

I could see the outline of her now. She'd come to a fork in the path and stopped, hmm, which one was it, someone's moved the sweet papers. I slowed up, ready to duck to the floor, but she didn't look round, she was on the move again, thinking to herself, now, what am I going to tell them? Thought I'd go on a little holiday for a few days, get away from it all, see the countryside – really, you shouldn't have worried. Chickenhead lifts an eyebrow. Did you now? And what were you thinking, bringing him with you? You don't know what that boy's capable of. But I didn't know any of that, I'd not heard about Katie Carmichael. I wouldn't have done it if I'd known that. Well, anyway, it's all over now, there'll be nothing to worry about once you're back in London, thank God.

I stalked half a mile behind, chewing on a sarnie. She'd not ate or drank anything since the day before, far as I knew, I was capped she had the strength for it, the speed she was keeping. Most folk would be done for by now, not an inch of wick left in them, lagged out on the heather with the worms gathering round waiting for the end. Not far now, she was thinking. She'd be home by night at this crack, the banners fluttering above the gate – WELCOME HOME! NOW LET'S GET THAT BASTARD, LANKENSTEIN! – Lionel barking himself daft, Chickenhead crying buckets. We've been so worried about you, darling, we were expecting the worst, she says, the eyes gleaming with tears, watching as the wriggling head of a maggot pokes its way out the mushroom. Ey up, lads, I'm through! Follow me. Chickenhead bluthering away. Butch up, would you, what do you think it's going to do – bite you? It's a mention of protein, is all, you daft trull, you're lucky I didn't do anything worse, injected them with blowfly vaccine, then you'd be crying, right enough. There was a droning noise far off, a fighter jet, taken off from the base at Leeming Bar, out on a practice flight. A grey plume showed its path as it began a circuit of the Moors, waking all the idlebacks still slumbering in bed. She'd stopped to watch it too, and I started into a jog. The jet was tearing across the sky – there's the Dales look, glossy green hillocks rolling to the west, and the farm down there, Sal working the flock glancing up to check if Father's about to belt her. She was running, I had to laugh at that. Did she think she could outleg me? No food since yesterday and she thought she could outleg me. The rucksack was bobbing up, down, she kept looking round every while, glegged me gaining on her, but she kept straight on, like an animal running in front of a vehicle, fixed on its course. It wasn't long until she started flagging, and I clasped an arm round her, pulling her toward me with the rucksack buffering against my front. It's all right now, it's all right, but she was flailing her arms behind her, scratching at my face, the hot scorch of a nail dragging across my cheek. Hush up, I told her, hush up. She wouldn't listen, though, they could hear her in Whitby, she was beldering that loud, hush up, I had to clout her round the jaw to make her stop. She lay on the ground a time, curled in a ball with the lip wibbling. I looked about, making sure no one had seen us, then I rooted in my bag for a decent-looking sarnie. She'd feel better when she'd ate something, I told her.

23

She'd finished struggling, so we sat on us bags nice and peaceable with a prawn sarnie and a pork pie on the ground between us. She looked tired. All the dander had gone out of her – I told her she should have a kip, get her strength up. She wasn't listening, mind. She sat, sluffened, not touching the food I'd gave her. Now, I said, lively as I could, you can't goat around any more, things are serious now. Then I learnt her the sightlier parts of the newspaper article, and she lifted her head up, seemed I'd snared her attention at last. They know about us robbing the shop in Garside, I explained, there's police all over looking for us, so we have to tread careful, you can't go taking off like that any more. Do you understand me? It was like chiding a puppy for being naughty – she looked up at me with big eyes brimful with guilt and nodded. I smiled at her. Don't worry, I'm not angry at you, I'm glad I found you, is all, we can get back on track now. Thinking caps on, eh – we need a plan. She smiled back, and I thought she'd forgave me for hitting her, but it was all a show, I found out then. I turned round to scan the land, and next I knew she was fetching me a sharp kick in the knackers and legging it away. I watched, crumpled on the floor, pain firing through my nethers, as she bolted off.

She only got a couple hundred yards before I caught her up and tackled her to the ground. I held her down, our faces close together, as she hissed and floundered like a bust tyre. What'd I told you? What'd I told you, eh? I had to be firm with her, it was the only way, she had to stop behaving daft. I kept her pinned, waiting to see if she'd say anything, but she had her head turned sideways, she wouldn't look on me.

I knelt up, letting go, and she quieted, lying with her eyes open staring out across the heather. Come on, then, I said, and after a moment she got up and walked over to the bags with me, at heel,

I didn't have to hold on to her. Course, she couldn't be trusted yet, though, not while she was in this mood. I was right, being firm with her. That was why I had to keep her penned secure. I unfastened one of the longer straps from my rucksack and tied her hands together behind her back, careful not to hurt her wrist in case it was still sore. Then we set off walking, and I was glad she'd learnt she was best keeping peaceful, she didn't try bolting or anything stupid, though I could mark her fidgeting at the strap whenever I glegged away, and the waterworks came on a couple times, no matter she pretended otherwise when I turned to look on her.

She wanted to know where we were going. Best hiding place on the Moors, I said – the Hole of Horcum. She asked me what the fuck was that. Likely she thought I was taking her to some giant well, the way the name sounded, we were going to hide out with the frogs, bats flackering about us faces in the dark. The Hole of Horcum, I told her, is a dip in the land – a crater a mile wide full of ditches and crags and patches of forest. She kept quiet. I tried making talk a couple of times afterward – looks like we're in for a champion summer, and the like – but she was on conversation strike, she didn't speak a word the next hour as we traipsed south, over Rosedale and Wheeldale Moors, past Cropton Forest, toward the Hole. The only thing she spoke was that she wasn't hungry, when I asked her if she'd have a bite to eat. Course not, I said, joking with her, you only ate recent, didn't you, what was it, a day ago? She didn't answer. She'd have to eat soon, I knew, else she'd pass out, but I wasn't going to argue with her, because it'd just make her worse.

We'd both have a proper feed soon anyhow, when we got to Whitby. Fish and chips on the seafront, claggy with vinegar, and a mighty dollop of steaming mushy peas. That'd sort the job. And just as I was thinking it, she started talking again. It was the queerest yet, it all came out in a rush so fast I could hardly mark what she was saying, she was like a tree branch snagged on a riverbank, sudden broke free into the current. Yes, the lambs would be all born by now, I answered her, no, they had a while yet before they were ready for selling. She quickened her pace as we nattered on.

I thought, this is what it'll be like, us pair chattering away like budgerigars, not bothering about anybody but usselves. I felt so bruff, thinking about it, I could've leapt a drystone wall.

She was still on about the lambs and I was so flowtered listening she near escaped me, breaking sudden into a run as I noticed there were people up ahead. I caught hold her arm and pulled her toward me, she shouted the start of something so I clamped a hand quick over her mouth and pushed her to the ground, dropping down aside her. They fortunate hadn't marked us, they were too far off, facing otherways, bent down examining the heather. I took my hand off her mouth, but she started to shout again so I quieted her up, I had to be firm. She couldn't free herself with her hands tied behind her, but that wasn't going to stop her struggling, I had to keep my hand pressed hard on her back, she was squirming like a fresh-caught fish. They were studying the heather, they must've seen a rabbit, or a grouse, they were looking where it'd gone. They gave up before long, walking off away from us, and it wasn't until I glegged the four-by-four with its yellow and blue squares that I understood it wasn't ramblers, it was police. I clamped tighter over her mouth, my palm hot and sluthery with spittle as I watched them get in the vehicle and drive off east along a bridleway, the direction of Goathland, and Garside. Gawbys. We'd have no trouble keeping hid, if they thought we were around them places still.

It was late afternoon by the time we reached the Hole. It'd been slow going, as she kept needing to stop and rest and I didn't want to risk getting her twined by hurrying her. We halted up at the lip of the Hole and viewed out over it. Even she must've been impressed, a sight like that. It was shaped in a bowl, like a giant football stadium, the great sloping sides coloured different either end. The Gorse against the Bracken. The south-facing half was a semicircle of bright yellow, still blaring in the afternoon sun; the other half was in shade, grim brown with smears of green. We made our way toward the bracken end, and I undid her hands so she could step easier down the steep bank. I didn't need to worry, for she was too tired to try codding me. She went down before me slipping and stumbling, gripping hold the stiff stalks of the bracken to balance herself. It reached thick up to our chests, blocking sight of the ground so we couldn't tell where we were stepping. I kept us moving toward a crag of rock halfway down, the bracken thinning, growing through the cracks of stones and boulders. We settled usselves in the gap between two mighty stones, where it was wide enough she could lie down to sleep while I sat keeping watch, busying myself cutting another strap off my rucksack with a sharp piece of rock. When I'd done, I stored the bags together in the gap and moved quiet off the stone for a walk down the bottom. There was a pool of water I washed my face in, checking regular uphill there wasn't a ruffle in the bracken and a small, escaping body. She was asleep when I got back, her eyes were shut anyhow, but I could see my bag had been shifted, and when I looked in later I was gradely pleased marking she'd drank some water and ate a sarnie.

The moon was half showing, yellowish, and her skin glowed pale and cold in its weak light. She didn't look uncomfortable, mind, her lips and her eyelids closed soft. She always slept peaceable like that. I sat silent, watching, while the Moors whispered and rustled and sighed above us, and I thought, what the bugger was it so noisy for, it was the middle of the bleeding night?

It was black when I woke her, the moon clouded over. She didn't look much pleased about it, her eyes two reluctant slits and the skin underneath all crozzled with drowsiness. Time to go, I said, getting the straps ready.

We made steady progress over the open moor, no matter I was carrying both bags and I only had a dim-shaped idea of the route. I looked behind at her. She had her eyes down toward her hands, tied in front her body now. I'd made a leash and attached it on to her, and I thought she might've took badly to it, but she wasn't playing up, she was keeping a decent pace, it was only a few times the strap pulled taut, and then I just had to give a couple of tugs and she sped up. She had her strength back, certain, after eating something. I felt easier now – we'd be in Whitby by morning if we kept like this. Everything was fettling up like I'd hoped, and I thought, right, what can we talk about, I'm mooded for a good old natter. I couldn't find the proper-fitting subject, mind, so we trod on, silent.

We were on the right path, because I could see the great walls of the military installation at Fylingdales off one side, two red dots marking the radar discs. What did they think – there was going to be a war? The Battle of the Farmers and the Off-comed-ones. Colonel, come quickly, I've picked up something on the radar, it appears to be advancing this way. I think it's the onslaught of the giant tomatoes. A short way on from there, a dull shape came into view ahead, upright, still, man-sized. We paused up and waited to see what it would do. She was sudden all nerves, I could hear the slight shaking in her breath. I tried to take hold her hand but she moved away. Whatever it was, it was alone, I was sure, I'd looked all round but there was nothing else except for this bleary shape in front. We couldn't wait there all night, so we moved forward, slow and watchful. And did we laugh when we saw what it was? We near fell over usselves, we'd been that daft, worrying it was a policeman or the like. It was a tumulus stone. I should've known when it didn't shift for five minutes – we'd reached Lila's Cross. A fair old time we'd have been, waiting for that to move, it'd been there a thousand years already, seven foot tall and rooted in the ground straight-backed as a Barwick maypole.

Then it came to me, here was a subject we could talk about, and I explained her the whole history of the cross – how the minister Lila took an arrow in the eye for his master, King Edwin, and Edwin had been so heart-sluffened at his death he buried him under the very spot, his flesh by now passed into the turf, the worms sheltering in his bones.

I was fain pleased at myself, remembering the story, and I told her about a couple of others – Ralph's Cross; the Bride Stones – near enough reading them off my memory from years before when Mrs Pocklington had gave us the lesson of the history of the Moors and the Angles and the Vikings, and I'd been glued to my seat hearing it. I dropped back level with her, smiling, and looked at her face. She seemed she was crying again – she was all puffy-eyed, and I tried to touch her cheek to wipe off the dampness, but she wouldn't let me. She was near undone with tiredness.

And here's the best story of all, I said, but she wasn't going to look at me. The Fat Betty – do you know what that is? Not a pub, not rightly. It's a mighty great stone on the Moors. I fancy them lot in town don't know that, eh? The story goes, there was a farmer round these parts whose wife was named Fat Betty, owing to her size. The two of them had been to market one day, and the farmer was riding their horse and cart back home that night, through a thick fog, Betty sat in the cart with all the goods they'd bought, and the ones they couldn't sell, when Betty fell out. Problem was, the farmer didn't mark she'd gone until he got home and looked in the cart. He went straight back looking for her, searching all along the track they'd come, but she wasn't anyplace to be sighted. She was lost to the Moors – no one ever saw her again. But the queer thing was, along the track, halfway across, a lumping great white stone had appeared. No person knew what it was, or where it came from, except that it'd never been there before that night.

She'd lost interest, though, digging her heels refusing to move, but the walk had sapped her and I hauled her onward. Nothing like a story to pass the time on a journey. The Tumulus Tales. Forty-odd burial stones stood on the Moors, and each its story. I told her all the ones I knew, guiding her through the dark a couple of steps behind, pulling her along like a dog on a lead. We were like Herriot and his faithful companion, come by, there's a good lass, now, I've a warm fire and a plate of liver for you when we get home, how does that sound?

A change in the light was the first sign of Whitby. It was black still when we got near, so the dull fug of orange sat over the town showed us the way. We didn't head straight there, though – we angled toward the coast just south of it. It was too parlous yet, staying in the town. We had to hide out a while longer, fettle up our plans, figure out how we'd manage stowing on a ship, bide a time until our faces weren't so fresh in folks' minds – until they were half-forgot, crumpled up at the bottom of the dustbin, sogged with gravy leavings and budgerigar shite.

There were fields now, cut into the moor, and paths, walls, a road. There was one wall I couldn't find a gate for, and she wouldn't go over the stile, so I had a job hoisting her up by the armpits, my fingers pressing into the fleshy tops of her breasts. She wasn't mighty chuffed about it, but I ignored her, it was her fault anyhow, not going over by herself. We were on a path, moving downhill, hedgerows either side and sand dusted over the floor, the sound of cold, foamy waves crashing against the cliff, and the path opening out on to a great rocky beach. And then the sea, the lull of the sea, a salty mist stinging up our nostrils as we ran on to the beach. Dark, brooding cliff stretched both directions unbroken, except for one small pip of light nicked into the coastline – Whitby. We moved otherways from it, toward the dark. I was as good as dragging her along now, she was that tired. She was weak as a bandy-legged lamb, she'd have laid down right there, on the high jagged rocks climbing out the swirl, if I hadn't towed her on. I'm looking for the right spot, I told her loud over the spray. I wasn't worried about finding one. This stretch of coast was riddled with caves and tunnels and boggle-holes worn into the cliff, I knew – I'd spent hours and hours here before, playing at smugglers with Jess. We'd hide out in the boggle-holes, riling Mum and Janet right up for disappearing the whole afternoon, searching for forgotten smuggler hoards, ancient stashes of tobacco or jewellery untouched for a hundred years. Bracelets? I'll show you bracelets – gold, silver, studded with diamonds and rubies stolen from the Orient, you don't get those in a Christmas cracker, do you?

We tried a couple of likely-seeming gaps that turned out to be flood-caves, before we found the champion spot. It wasn't mighty large, but it was snugly hid. In the crook between the cliff and a jetty of rock was a boggle-hole with a low, pooled entrance you had to slide in lengthways so your backside was sopping, but then it opened into a small cavern high enough you could kneel inside. I'd need to get a light, or some matches, as I couldn't see hardly anything, but it was perfect. It had a dry, sandy floor and enough space the both of us could lie down. No smuggled booty, mind. She rested down, her body juddering sobs and a quiet whimper coming from her. The journey had took a toll, she wasn't in the best shape. She'd be fine, though, after a rest. I was thinking to untie her, but I knew she might sneak off when I was asleep, so I felt round the walls at all the stalactite formings hanging down over us heads, and I found one that curled from the ceiling in a ring on to the wall. It was the best luck yet. I knotted the wrist leash to it and then I set about making another, ripping the last strap off my rucksack by rubbing it up, down over a rock, and leashing that one to her ankle. Afterward, I lay down next her, rolled on my side, the sound of spray outdoors and the damp heat of her body and flutterbugs of excitement skittering in my belly, thinking what I'd do in the morning.

24

A slant of light was glimmering on the entrance pool. Another belting day, with any luck. I craned forward for a look outdoors, and I thought I'd never seen the world looking so gradely, it was that postcard. Past the rocks I could see a vast of bare beach and beyond that the surf, eddies of water gathering, swelling unstoppable forward – crash – gliding racing bubbling then, retreating, drawn under the pull of the next. Mum, Father, the weather's champion and we're both doing fine. And the best of all is there's no other bugger around, we've the place to usselves. Wish you were here, love, Nimrod.

She was lain on the sand still, and I whispered her my plans. I'm off to get us some food, I told her. I explained she had to stay put, for the time. I made sure the straps were tied fast, and I left off.

After I'd climbed the path to the cliff top, I stepped toward the edge and stopped a moment to look out over the sea. I was stood above where our house must've been, fifty yards beneath. Inching forward until I could see down the face of the cliff, I tried to gleg the entrance pool, but there were too many rocks in the way, overhanging, so I moved off, taking the cliff path toward Whitby.

There were plenty of folk about, most of them groups of tourists tantling through the cobbled streets from shopfront to shopfront, cooing at the windows. I followed behind when they herded off, and looked what they'd been staring at. It was always some feckless trunklement no one would ever buy – a silver plate knife and fork set, or a plastic fish with a clock lodged in its gut. I got bored before long, so I trundled down to the centre of town where the harbour was, huddled round the sides the river as it widened and slurped into the sea. There was a stink of fish, and stacks of empty lobster pots everywhere. A few fishermen were fettling up their boats, but they paid no heed of me. I had a look round to see if there were any cargo or passenger ships, but they must've set off from a different port, here was all fishing fleets, save for one small, open-decked affair with a sign aside it. BOAT TRIPS – SEALS – BIRD ISLAND. This is it, love, I've found us the perfect place to live. An island, miles away from anybody, fleece-white, plastered in puffin shite. Then I saw what I was looking for. A length of rope, damp and heavy, coiled up by some crates. I checked none of the fishermen were watching before I hung it over my shoulder and went off on a food search.

There were plenty fish and chip shops one side the harbour, doing business already, folk stood scattered along the quayside poking tidgy wooden forks into cartons. I slunk past them to the empty, wind-bassocked pier, studying the situation over. Trouble was, if I ran off without paying, people would look, they'd mark my face, my clothes, someone might snout I was one of the Moors convicts. I had to think a way of doing it quiet, unnoticed. The days of smashing windows were over now, that was sure. Further down the pier, a seagull was perched on the rim of a dustbin, jabbing at the rubbish. After a couple of tries, he stabbed something and yanked it out, flapping down to attack it on the ground. As I came closer, I saw it was a bent-up fish box. He had his head inside, scraffling along the tarmac with his wings half-spread, warning, bugger off, this is my dinner, you get your own. Don't worry, feller, I told him, that's just what I'm thinking about. He clocked me when I reached the dustbin, one eye examining me over a piece of cod mushed to his cheek. He watched me a moment before returning to his scran, and I marked, as he chased at a stray chip, that he had a crammocky, hobble-hopping walk. His left leg was gammy, swollen up at the knee, he couldn't put his full, fat weight on it. You've got some gumption, I'll give you that, I told him, that's smart thinking, getting your scran out of there. He looked up. Sod off – I'm eating. Right you are, right you are. But when he turned his tail on me, I had a gleg in the dustbin to see what he'd left. It was near full with fish boxes. I looked round, but there was only an old couple staring to sea, so I reached in and pulled one out.

Bloody hell, they've not much of an appetite, the tourists, there's plenty left in these, some of them are hardly touched. But Hobble-Hop wasn't listening, he was busy slotching down a chip. I found a couple of boxes that weren't too bent, and I collected up the remains from six or seven others, shaking them into the good boxes, peeling off the batter where it'd clagged on the sides.

She was awake when I got home. She looked knackered still. Her eyes were bloodshot, and the sand had rubbed a pink patch on her cheek. I untied her from the leashes and put the fish boxes on the sand in front of her. I was something surprised when, after staring at them a moment, she started eating. Not a mighty amount, only a couple of mouthfuls, but enough it'd help get her fettle back up. When we'd done eating, I put the leftovers in a corner, and tied her up again, hands behind her back, and just one leash this time, round her ankle, now I had the rope. It was a gradely job – tighter, firmer, but a longer tether, so she had more room to move about. We sat quiet the rest the day, listening to the waves lash the beach, except for I went out once to fill up the water bottles from a stream, and had a small explore, investigating in rock pools and stalking the limpets.

We lay more snug together that night. I pressed in close against her back and, when I thought she was asleep, I put the arm over, resting my hand on her belly. We stayed like that most the night, warmth breeding between us, the tickle of her hair on my face.

In the morning, before she woke, I took her rucksack outside and opened it up. There wasn't much in it, just a couple of shirts and no underwear and another pair of jeans. I rooted around a minute until I found the bracelet, then I went back indoors and put the rucksack where it'd been. Her eyes were open. She must've seen I'd took it out, but it didn't seem her brain was switched on yet, she didn't shift her stare on the wall. I gave her a kiss on the cheek and told her I was off out again.

It was darker today, a mizzle coming in off the sea, filming my skin with wet. There was a greasing of mud on the cliff path, and I had to mind as I walked along I didn't slip. For a moment I imagined a crowd of people on the beach, ogling for a sight of my broken body, lying dead on the rocks. A helicopter, blasting a circle of sand as it lowered down, the crowd parting as men in bright-orange jackets jogged out, none of them knowing there was another body not far off, hid in the dark, slowly rotting, the bone beginning to jut through and seagulls squabbling outside the entrance, attracted by the smell. That was enough of them thoughts, though. Today was going to be champion, the best yet.

Whitby wasn't so busy as the day before, owing to the weather. These tourists here today, walking unsteady along the cobbles, were likely here for the week. They looked bored enough, trudging round in their anoraks. There wasn't a week's worth of shops to goggle at, a single afternoon and you were done in, wondering why Dracula ever bothered coming here. Not me, though, not today, I was all attention, marching up and down on the lookout for something better than a fish clock. A jewellery shop, that was what I was after, and it didn't take much searching until I found one. *Abbey Jeweller's – purveyors of fine Whitby jet*. They weren't glibbing and all. The glishy black stones were set into most the items in the window – rings, earrings, necklaces, they looked proper sightly on the female with no body, her white neck smooth and firm as a birch trunk. How do you fancy a bite of that, Mr Dracula? Oh she's attractive, there's no argument, but I prefer something a little fleshier, myself.

I went inside and a bell rung above my head. There was no one in the shop, and I felt sudden I should leave but before I had chance there was a female at the counter. She had a great smile on her, which sagged and wilted as she took me in, looking me up and down.

Can I help you?

I set the bracelet on the counter. She studied it a moment, then she rolled her eyes slow back up to my face, as if I'd just placed a turd before her.

It's bent, I said. It needs fixing. She was looking at me, the raggy jacket with muck smeared down it, my face black as a miner, clots of cack stuck to my boots that I was likely treading into her carpet.

But when she'd done inspecting me she smiled, proper friendly, and picked up the bracelet.

Who's it for?

My girlfriend.

Well then, she felt the kink in the metal, I suppose I'd best see what I can do. She put it on a shelf behind her. I stiffened up then, because I knew she was going to tell me a price, and I didn't want to tell her I'd no money and I'd have to pay her later, she'd been so friendly. She must've seen what I was thinking, though, because she smiled again and said, there's no charge for that, dear. Come back in an hour and I'll have it ready for you.

I was smiling like a half-brain when I came out that shop. There was a young couple outside, holding hands, looking at the jewellery. See – not all folk are bastards, eh, there's some of them are proper friendly, if you look hard enough. But they must've thought I was one of the bastards, for they sidled away fair sharpish. Not that I gave a stuff. I had an hour, so I went down to the pier – and who was there? My old mate, Hobble-Hop. He had a fat chip sticking out his beak.

Mornin'.

Mornin'.

I told him what'd happened at the jeweller's, while I pulled boxes out the dustbin, collecting handfuls of wasted food into an unbent one. Do you think that bald sod would've said something similar, do you? Don't worry, Lankenstein, there's no charge for them beans – they're on me, they are. I might not've thrown it through his window if he'd said that, the glibbing bastard. I tossed a decent piece of fish to Hobble-Hop and he stumbled after, necking it in one. Looks painful, that leg does, feller. He angled a look at me, the gammy leg dangling useless above the ground. It gives me some jip sometimes, you're right. Any more fish? I fingered through the waste to find him a tasty bite. Someone had thrown away a toy plastic Dracula. He was trying to climb out of a crisp packet. I tell you, the things people will chuck, eh, and I wiped the slutherment off with my sleeve, pocketing him as I threw a bit of battered sausage on to the ground. Anyhow, Hobble-Hop, much as I enjoy our natters, I've got to be picking the bracelet up soon, so I'll see you later. He watched me turn to leave, the head cocked, wondering if I had another piece of fish for him. I laughed. He was certain bone idle, old Hobble-Hop.

She'd done a grand job, the woman in the shop, she hadn't just straightened out the dent, she'd buffed up the whole thing so it looked better than ever, better than it looked when he got it her. I thanked her, three or four times, and I was about to leave when she said, can I get you something to eat, dear? I've some sandwiches left over in the back here. But I told her, no, thank you. She didn't know I had the box of fish and chips hid under my jacket.

It was a gradely view from the cliff top. All the fishing boats out at sea, small dark clouds following behind them, gull flocks, scavenging after the nets. There were no liners, mind, or cargo ships. Seemed Whitby was all fishing. I wasn't flowtered, though, because I had a new plan – we'd steal a boat. That way we could go wherever we fancied, we'd sail about and land someplace and move on when we got bored. We could go on day trips, anyplace she wanted, all she had to do was say where. I was coming down the snickleway path from the cliff, shaping my plan, when I heard voices on the beach. I turned round and made back for the cliff top to belly down and peer over the edge at who it was. Ramblers. Four of them, sat lined up with their backs against the cliff, a heap of anoraks piled on the sand aside them as they basked their chops toward the sun. They were close to the house, other side the rock jetty, almost in earshot of her.

I took Dracula out the pocket and propped him up aside me so we could spy down together at them. He looked proper dapper, in his pointed shoes and glishy black coat-tails, a sly grin on him, his mind up to some kind of devilry. One of the females stood up and paraded up down the line of them, something that was clear very funny because I heard the dag-ends of their laughter float up to me. Fucking ramblers, they got everywhere, they'd be pestering at the fishermen next – tell me, is it true, do some fish have feelings, can they fall in love? I marked Dracula had his eye elsewhere – on a scattering of rocks nearby us. I gave him a smile, understanding him, and went over to gather a few of them up, rolling them back to my spot in a collection, huddled together like a group of heads.

The female was still on her feet talking, I bided until she sat back down before I pushed the first rock off the edge. It bounced twice against the cliff face, small explosions of stone and soil busting showers into the air, and it came down with a great clobber on the sand a few yards off. They were rooted to their seats shuffling about in dafflement, what was that, what was that? I aimed another, and this one was better directed, it was dropping right on to them. There was a clump of yellow flowers halfway down growing out the cliff face, I had to smile at that – you could've picked a cosier place to live than there, couldn't you? Well, we could've, yes, but, what with house prices round here these days, and anyhow, it's a princely view. I was lost thinking what sound would it make, but near the bottom the rock hit a jut on the cliff face and bounced forward, over their heads, landing in front of them. They were up sharp enough now, it was an avalanche, run, run for your lives! I rolled another, but I rushed it and it ended in a rock pool. By then it was too late, they were long gone, fleeing down the beach with their anoraks fluttering behind them.

When I got back in the cavern, she was snoozing, laid up against the far wall. I watched her a while, but I didn't want to disturb her, so I just left the bracelet on the sand by the fish box, so she'd see it when she woke.

She was mighty lagged out. She slept into the afternoon, and I started getting stalled waiting so I took off on a walk. Further down the beach, after I'd been going a while, there were two sprogs playing in the surf, splashing each other and running away from the waterline as it chased toward them. It was hard to believe there were so many bastards in the world, looking at them sprogs. Their father looked like one, mind. He chided them as they scuttled back to him, sod knows why, they were only larking about. I watched the three of them as they walked away toward Whitby, the sprogs staying obedient at heel a long time, until finally one of them made a bolt for it and the other ran after, ignoring the father waving his arms calling them back.

She was awake, sat up, the bracelet still on the floor where I'd left it. She hardly marked me crouch up to her, she hadn't touched her food, neither, far as I could tell. I held the bracelet up in front of her. Just for a second, her eyes fixed on it, then she went blank again. It's buffed up and all, look, she put a shine on it for you. Good as new. Better. She was away with the clouds, though, I didn't know what was the problem with her. Someone come in and stole your brain while I was gone, have they? I know who it was. It was bloody Greengrass, wasn't it? Up to his old tricks. Greengrass! Greengrass! But she didn't think old Greengrass was so funny these days, she didn't even tweak a smile. I tilted her forward, unsnecking the cord off her wrists. Now, let's have a see if it looks bonny on you, shall we? I twisted the bracelet on to her good wrist, pressing her fingers together so I could squeeze it past the bunched flesh of her hand. She sparked up then, wriggling in my grasp, oh, so you've still a bit of buck about you, then, good, I was starting to worry you'd turned into a gawby while I was out. I had to tie her hands behind her again, mind, and she quieted straight away when I'd done, the eyes blank again, you wouldn't guess anything had happened except for she was breathing heavy after the effort. I knew I had to try getting her talking quick before her mind drifted away. Do you like it, then? It's better than new now. She looked straight at me, no expression on her. Thank you *so much*. And that moment, never mind it was half-dark, never mind her sobbing, never mind she was mucky and scratched all over, I'd never seen anything so beautiful as her face looking at me. It was no bother, I said, it was no bother at all. I felt like I was going to gip, she was that beautiful. I bent forward and we kissed. My body clocked off then, all parts of me stopped aflunters like the blood had forgot which way to flow. It didn't matter we'd waited so long, it was all worth it now, her soft hair flooding through my fingers as I pressed her toward me. I'd never leave her, she wouldn't always need the rope, that was just for the time, we'd move out of the boggle-hole soon, we'd go to bleeding Europe.

I didn't know how she did it, she bust out of the wrist cord somehow. I must've put it on aslew when I retied it, she was sudden a hubbleshoo of thrashing arms and shrieks echoing round the cavern near deafening us both. I held her down and fastened her tight. She wouldn't stop crying. Her face was covered in sand glued on with tears, and I didn't feel angry at her, I felt my gizzern tighten looking at her like that. I'd never leave her, she knew I'd never do that. We pressed us mouths together, hot and slubbery, the four eyes streaming tears, and it was queer but the first thing I thought was, she must've ate something, for I could taste vinegar on her mouth. The thin slice of pale flesh widened as her jeans pulled down, baring her thighs and her knees and the muscles on her calves straining taut. She wouldn't do it again, she promised me, as I untied her hands again so she could take off her shirt, stretching her arms above her head, a tang of sweat coming off her body as I held into her, careful I didn't press against the bracelet – I couldn't likely go back to the shop tomorrow as well, you should tell that girlfriend of yours to be more careful, Lankenstein, I can't keep doing this for free, you know. She had to keep still, I told her, but she wouldn't listen, she never listened. You're stubborn as a sheep to dip, you are, and I laughed, come here, give me your hands again. It was getting daft, all this tying, untying, tying, untying. She lay writhing on her back with her arms under her, rigwelted, struggling to get up. I had to smile then, for there was a picture of Popeye's wife on her underwear. She had these giant eyelashes and a ringlet of hair curled on her forehead, and she was giving the wink with one big eye – I know what's under here, she was saying. I had a fair idea, myself, but I wasn't going to find that out yet, it wasn't time, so we just laid down listening to the waves and I held her tight, I told her I'd find out tomorrow where we'd steal the boat, we wouldn't have to stay there much longer, I'd have everything fettled up soon enough.

25

In the morning there was a small splattering of sick in the sand by her head. Not a mighty amount, a dribbling. I scooped it up and threw it outdoors, then I dressed her back up, which was no easy job as she wasn't mooded for helping, she was someplace limp between asleep and awake and her body was heavy as stone.

I sped along the cliff top. Wait until I told Hobble-Hop about all this that'd happened. He'd pop his clogs. The sea was calm today, all the grim weather had disappeared over the Moors and I could see small black dots in the distant ocean, trawlers out netting cod for me and Hobble-Hop's dinner. He wasn't there, though, when I got to the pier. I collected up some food and sat on the railing dangling my legs waiting for him. I was there almost an hour and I near gave up and left, until finally he appeared, he must've slept in. I wasn't riled, mind. It was good to see him. At first, he didn't look much familiar, he flew in so smooth and graceful, it was only when he dumped down on the rim and near fell into the dustbin I knew certain who it was.

Mornin' feller, owt fresh?

He gave me the eye a moment. Thought I'd stole all the food already. But he didn't need bother worrying, there was plenty in there, he could see so himself now, as he picked out a whole box and dropped it on the floor. He didn't have much of a hunger today, though, he left all the scrag-end pieces and just picked at the choice bits. Go on, then, he looked up at me, I can see you've something to tell. I smiled. He was no calf-head, old Hobble-Hop. I told him the whole story, and he was mighty interested, watching me all the time. Looks like you're going to breed her sometime soon, he said. Then I told him I was going to get her some jet, something gradlier than a tin bracelet, a necklace or similar, but I needed some money first because I didn't want to steal anything off the woman in the shop. He mulled it over a moment, then he went back to his box. No, sorry, can't help you there, lad, it's beyond me. He tossed away a chip. Folk certain put a lot of vinegar on their food, don't they?

I marked sudden there were two lads watching us from the railing other side the pier. Fucking freak, one of them said, and he turned to walk off, laughing, but the other sudden darted at Hobble-Hop, hissing and wheeling his arms. It boggled him, and he lost balance, flapping his wing against the tarmac and the gammy leg trailing useless until he righted up and flew off, skriking loudly.

I watched them traipse off toward the end the pier. They had their shirts untucked, their school ties made into short stubs like the nimrods in my class used to have them. They didn't notice me follow behind, they were all concentration kicking a pebble between each other. They got to the end and slouched over the railing. One of them gobbed into the surf. Oi, nimrods. They swung round, confused. You think you're funny, eh, chasing him like that? They were betwaddled something champion, they'd not have been more capped if Dracula himself was stood there chiding them. Now, dear fellows, of course I don't want to do this, but you can't go behaving in that manner, I'm afraid. I'm going to have to drain the blood from you. I stepped up to the bigger one, him who'd run at Hobble-Hop, and I could see he didn't know what to do, he glegged at his charver but he didn't know what to do neither, it's not every day you meet a convict on the pier. What the fuck's your problem, freak? I made a grab for his tie but the ground was slippery from the sea-spray and I skidded, he pushed me in the chest, knocking me over. Fucking freak. I looked up, not a cloud in the sky, there was a seagull gliding about, I couldn't tell if it was Hobble-Hop or not because the legs were tucked in. I got a kick in my side and I doubled over, closing my eyes a moment. Sod off Cyclist. Another kick, on the leg, and I felt a cold splat on my cheek. Let you out the mental hospital for the day, have they? I tried to get up but my stomach cramped. Bracelet? What sort of present's that? But they were running away laughing, they couldn't hear me.

I touched my cheek and a syrupy drool of gob clung to my finger. I wiped it on my jacket and got to my knees, picking up the pieces of food that'd fallen out my box. Hometime. She'd be wondering where I'd got to, by now.

I walked careful slow down the path from the cliff, limping like my old charver on the pier. My leg was getting an ache up from where I'd been kicked, jipping each time I stepped on it. A proper resting was what it needed. We'd stay indoors now, the afternoon and the night, and I'd spy about for a boat early next morning, while she had a lie-in. I walked past one of the rock-bombs from the day before, half buried in the sand. I had a go digging it out with my foot but there was no shifting it, it was there forever now so I left it be and scrambled round the rock jetty. I don't know what you're idling at. She's been waiting an age already, she likely thinks they've caught you, and here you are digging at rocks. I've never known the like – you wouldn't find my husband, Mr Popeye, doing anything like that, believe me. She was right, course, so I hurried on, my brain filling with the night before, and the smell of her, the flesh of her thighs – it didn't matter she'd let the Cyclist spend them times with her, he was forgot now. There was only me. I'd forgive her everything. Popeye's wife gave me the wink. Don't worry you've been too long, she's waiting for you, and who's the one with the key, anyhow? She gave me the wink again – it's me, of course. I slid in through the creep-hole and I thought, I'd need to put something on the sand underneath, make her comfortable, a shirt, something out the bags, but as my eyes tuned to the dark and I viewed round I realised the cave was empty, she'd gone. All there was left was the rope coiled on the sand like a giant dead worm, and the bracelet, lying there next the two rucksacks.

I thought sudden I heard her and I scrabbled out the door, but when I looked about there was no one there, only a pair of seagulls fighting in the sky. I'd wait for her to come back. Middle of the night, that was when I'd get looking for the boat. She could come with me, if she wanted, or stay at home, as she pleased. I'd not tie her up again. We'd sail without stopping, we wouldn't know where we were until morning and the sun rose up, a vast of orange over the water edge. So, that's where we are – the middle of the ocean, no land for a hundred miles all round.

My leg throbbed each time I got up, like there was a lead ball trapped inside that dropped whenever I moved, but I'd been wrong thinking it needed a resting, that was just making it worse, so I went outdoors for a walk on the beach to get the blood moving. It was cold out, evening setting in. Someplace distant an engine was buzzing over the water. When we were on the boat, I'd know where she was the whole time. Drifting out to sea, nobody to bother us, only the tug of the engine and the seagulls mawnging that the fish net's still on the deck, and all the things that'd happened floating further and further away. Daft bleeding gulls, following an empty boat – Hobble-Hop was pissing his kecks laughing at them. This here's a passenger boat, you cloth-heads, passenger boat for two. We'll land up wherever we want. There's the place, see, a viewsome-looking spot of land, that – full steam ahead, no folk there, no puffin shite, nothing. But wait on, spoke too soon, look. Should've known it was all a bit too postcard, Father, what're you doing here? Come to give you a braying, Nimrod. Right you are, and no better man for the job. Do you hear that – Father's come to give me a braying, come all this way, he has. But she wasn't listening, she was stood with her back to me, nattering away, it wasn't until I craned my neck to look round her I saw she was talking to Norman, sat in a new vehicle he was showing her. Nought to sixty in seven seconds, I could hear him saying, a gash of a smile on him. Nought to sixty in seven seconds, what the fuck do you know about that, Norman? She gave me the wink. Daft sod.

There was a noise then, and we all looked round. Eh up, what's this, another boat? Father was chuntering something. Quiet up, Father, there's plenty time for the braying afterward, let's have a see who this is first. It was the police – the southern copper and his herd of gawby sergeants. They were in an orange lifeboat, buzzing toward us bouncing on the waves, their hands on top their heads keeping their helmets on. They reached the shoreline and skidded on to the beach. I stood rooted as they jumped out the boat and the waterline drew back splashing over their boots. Afternoon, fellers, I said, then I turned and ran for it along the beach. Greengrass! The wind was rushing against my chops and down my nostrils. Nothing like the sea air. Best treatment there is. Greengrass! Get back here you old nazzart! Greengrass! Sorry fellers, but you'll not catch me. And I was right – a gap was opening up behind me, but what I hadn't clocked was another group, in front, coming straight toward me. I near ran right into them, one of them was shining bald and these two red ears sticking out, he belted me in the stomach, taking the wind out of me. No need for that, fellers, you've got me now, but they were teeming round, pressing me down, a swarm all over me like maggots at a dead sheep. He's secure, someone was shouting. Course I was bleeding secure – I had about eighteen handcuffs on me. Father and Norman and the girl had gone now, I was being marched to the lifeboat. One of the police was poncing in the surf, trying not to get his kecks splashed. You're fucking insane – tied there like a dog, another was spittling in my ear, and he must've belted me again, because I blanked out after.

26

There's a small smear on the ceiling I've never marked before. I gawp at it a time, studying what it is. Damp-rot, shite, blood – sod knows how it got there, or if it's mine. What's queer is, I feel something frammled, thinking about it. Spent all this time never noticing it and now I'm off out and there's sudden a new piece of muck on the ceiling, and I don't feel ready, somehow, I need everything settled familiar before I leave it.

He's got the television on next door. I'm not much capped at that, mind, he's always got the bleeding television on, he watches it right through the night sometimes – if that is what he's doing, watching it – so I can go forty, fifty hours straight with that noise piercing through the wall. Sometimes I wonder how it is the whole wing can't hear it, but he's a big bugger and I don't say anything any more.

I keep my stare on the smear. He's not going to bother me now. I've spent four years waiting for today and I've gradlier things to think on now I'm about free. He can have his television as loud as he sodding likes – he's as cloth-headed as the rest of them if he thinks I'm twined about that any more.

*

I didn't rightly know where I was at first, it took a time for my brain to stop jenny-wheeling – the last I remembered before the police cell I was fetching fish and chips back to the cavern. All I had aside from that was snags of memory. Norman showing off his new vehicle; bruises on my wrist like the one I'd gave her; dinner on a plastic tray under the door and it was the best thing I'd ever ate; the driver taking me to the prison. They love beasts where you're going, lad.

If they'd put me straight in a maximum security, it wouldn't have been worse. Even a Category A would've been snug compared with where I went first off, down the valley. They all knew there, course, what I'd done. They read about it in the recreation room in *The Blatherskites' News*, them that knew how to read, and for them that didn't, there were plenty fain glad to tell the story. Brutal abduction ordeal over. Girl recovering at home with parents. Abductor on remand in local prison. Motivation may have been sexual.

They knew about Katie Carmichael and all. There was a nimrod I'd been at school with, Ricky Morlock, was in for selling drugs in the toilets of the After Dark in Thorpe Head. He'd a gob on him like a muck-spreader, scuttering my history about the wings until the whole place was teeming hate for me. No matter they weren't better than a pitful of robbers and muggers and drug dealers themselves, I was the foulest of the lot, was their opinion. The first week, a mob of them came in my cell and dragged my kecks and my pants down and pushed me against the wall, then this grinning fucker called Swiss punched me in the knackers, enough times I pissed blood the next two weeks.

I learnt quick enough after that where to hide myself after breakfast was finished. Recreation room until midday, while the officers were in watching the television, and then the library, where no one else ever went save for an old boy who was always there falling asleep over *Maps of the British Empire*. Every day, he was in his spot reading that same book, he must've known it arse-uppards. The choice wasn't too gradely, mind. The months I was there, I read *The Scorpion Man*, *Angels and Demons*, *Strange Fishing Tales*, and plenty others besides – they were better than pissing blood, for all they were bad. One day I was reading a book about haunted castles in Scotland, and on one of the pages somebody had wrote along the side: *Barnes is a dickhead bully and a coward and if he touches me again I'll stab the bastards eye out with this pencil.* I didn't know who Barnes was, and the writing was faded from age, but it seemed I wasn't the first who'd hid out in the library.

*

I get up off the bed, marking the position of the smear, and go over to the window. It's an open prison, so there are no bars blocking the view, but that just makes me laugh – I've never seen what's so open about it, myself. It's not like I've been able to come and go as I please, pop to the shops, go on a wander, unless it's been approved and planned out by the warden, and even then I've always had to heel to my soppy sod of a parole officer. Well, it is a prison, after all, isn't it, we do have to respect that – you can't swing a cat in an alleyway, can you? No, you can't, very true.

It's a bastard of a day, shuttering rain, but I can still shape up the hills off in the distance. First thing I'll do, tomorrow, is go to them hills. The time I've spent, staring at them, thinking that must be why they put the prison here in the first place, so they're just in eyeframe, teasing. Come for a walk over here, the hills are saying, but the moment you walk toward them you realise all the land's level for miles around like a mighty tablecloth pulled flat, pulling you away, so the further you walk, the further away they seem. All you're allowed to walk in is three acres of landscaped grounds full of ponds and fountains, you'd think it was a prison for second-home owners. I took a walk around the grounds this morning, said goodbye to the ducks and Fat Lip the gnome, then I came indoors and that's when I noticed the smear.

I turn away from the window and go to the shelf, where my few books are propped up and, lodged between, the booklet they've given me – *Adapting to Freedom*. I pull it out and take it over to the bed. Some gradely advice in here. *You may find these first few months a frustrating time. There will be moments when you might feel lonely, and bored, before you regain employment and a social network. Don't let yourself become inactive during this time. Develop a hobby: a sport, a volunteer group, a cookery class – not only will you learn new skills, but you will also meet new people . . . a perfect opportunity to start new friendships.*

Cookery class, they'd love that one, wouldn't they? I flick through until I get to the picture, tucked in the middle the booklet, and I take her out, waiting a moment listening that no one's in the corridor. Then I unfold it, laying it on the bedsheet and spreading it smooth so it's perfect straight and neat, except for the fuzzed edge one side where it'd been careful torn out a magazine by one of the perverts.

*

Once I'd learnt I was safe in the recreation room and the library, I mostly avoided many more clobberings. I rare saw any other prisoners the whole day through, except for Maps of the British Empire – it was like twenty-four-hour bang-up, apart from at meals. Even then, though, they mainly ignored me. They were concentrating too hard slotching up their dollops of food, and anyhow, they couldn't do much on me with all them wardens about. There was piss in my mug a couple of times, when Morlock was serving the line, but I learnt fair sharpish to check for the slummery layer on the surface before I took a sup. He'd always gleg over at me from his bench, Morlock, nudging the rough-arsed skinhead next him, their faces creasing with halfways smiles. It was like being at school again. The food was shite there and all.

Any bother like that didn't last long, though. Morlock, Swiss and the rest moved on before I did, to higher security prisons across the country, or back out, to mind to their drug rings.

And I had the court case to go to and all. A great wood-lined hall full of folk I'd never seen before, all of them ready with their tuppence-worth. Mr Marsdyke, you understand the seriousness of the charge brought against you? Oh, no doubting it, Your Honour, but the problem is you've got the wrong person – that's him, Mr Marsdyke, up on the balcony there in his funeral best, he understands the seriousness of it, certain enough, for who's looking after the farm while he's stuck here, eh? Sal? Not likely, Your Honour, you see she's nothing but a withered sack of an animal now he's worked her half to death. It's true, it's true. True? What the fuck do you know about it, bald sod? She was just the distraction, we planned it together, you never worked that one out, did you? But there's no stopping him once he gets going, she was clearly under duress, I could see that from the moment they came in. Then he's off with the story of the beans again, we've heard that one before, but the lawyer wants to examine it some more, he even asks him what kind of beans it was, like that's the key to it all, and the bald sod goes all serious-faced a moment – they were Heinz beans, Your Honour. I didn't see her. They'd set the room so as we couldn't look on each other, or, more rightly, so she didn't have to look on me, it was too distressful for her, was what the lawyer said – I didn't even know where she was, they'd hid her someplace. The times she had to go up on the stand I was took out by a pair of lugger-buggers and we sat in a small room with a list of Right Honourables carved into a board on the wall. The lugger-buggers were itching to give me a clobbering, I could tell, waiting for me to try something, but I didn't give them chance. One of them had a piece of snot rattling in his nose the whole time, but he didn't even realise, the great plank.

You've to promise me, Sam, it'll never happen again. You've to promise me, you hear? But it was too late for all that now. I'd broke the promise and she'd never be able to leave the house again, Delton and the town and *The Blatherskites' News*, there was no escaping from them now, she couldn't even look at me, sat stone-still next to Father, she had her eyes in the roof-beams the whole time.

You ran away together, but it was your premeditated aim to abduct her, and when she tried to escape from you, you took your opportunity. It was your intention to rape her, wasn't it? Objection! Objection? I didn't see what he had to object about. What he really objected about was he had to defend me in the first place, that he was the unlucky sod got pulled out the hat by the court. We were like them twins that get born fastened together, so there's no choice but going round with the other, no matter he hated me and wished the whole time I wasn't joined on to him. Hello, ladies, you're looking elegant tonight, I must say, can I buy you a drink? You can, yes, but what's that thing stuck on your back? Oh, that's Lankenstein, just pretend he's not there. Did you know there were caves in the cliff? How did you know where to find a rope? Was it the first time you'd visited the caves, or had you been there before? Yes, I admit it – sheepdogs *are* more intelligent than other dogs.

There, I said it. Lock me up, Your Honour. Lock me up and throw away the key. And by the way, tell me, why've you got a Wensleydale on your head? That's what they're kept for, is it? I should've known, such a meadow-munching breed as that. Coats? Hats? Not good enough for us, I'm afraid, we're going to be turned into judges' wigs. It all fit in place now, you had to laugh. Unless you were Chickenhead, course. She's not laughing. She never is, Your Honour, she's the grummest creature you'll ever meet. She's sitting there, quiet, with the dad holding on her arm, but she's ignoring him – she's only interested looking this way, her eyes boring holes through me until I have to gleg away. The dad's proper befuddled, stood in the crowd outside as the lugger-buggers barge me through, all these cameras clicking away, you have acted in a cruel and pitiless manner and your sentence must reflect the particularly frightening nature of your crime. I catch the dad's eye a second through the crowd, he doesn't know where to look, his face all sorrowful. Thank you ever so for the mushrooms – it wasn't your fault they were mawky, I knew that all along, but then Chickenhead's pulling him away and I lose them in the throng and I try to sight the girl but they've smuggled her off already.

*

Old people are the most difficult, it says. Least likely to accept it's a *Fresh Start* and change their mind about you. She's not interested in that, though. She just looks out at me, same as ever, them big eyes piercing right into me. It's all right, there isn't anyone to bother us, it's just us here. I meet her eyes, touching round the outline of her, mighty finger-worn now. It's all right, she is smiling, there isn't anyone to bother us here.

*

After the court I got shifted down south, further from home than I'd ever been before. Carted five hours in a cage like a two-shear off to market, stopping to pick up other mawngy sods on the way, all this orchestra music drufting about the van the whole journey, the drivers whistling away in the front. I was fain pleased, mind, they took me so far away. For one thing, I knew Mum and Father wouldn't visit me. I hadn't liked it when they'd come to see me in the first prison. We'd never had a mighty amount to talk about before, so we certain didn't now. Hello, Mum, Father, anyhow you'll never guess what I've been up to. Getting belted in the knackers, that's what, oh, and I'm a pitiless abductor. The couple times they'd come, Mum just twittered away, filling up the time slot, and I knew she felt it was her fault at root, no matter what Janet told her, if she'd brought me up different I wouldn't have turned out half-baked. I couldn't say anything to her, not with him sat there. She was thinking it was the same as budgerigars and she could've cared for me better, changed how I was kept, given me a mirror and a bell I could balance on my head, then I would've been different. I didn't want to see her. Both times she just sat there blathering about the weather and Janet's new hair but all the while I knew that was what she was thinking; and I didn't want to see Father because he was a grum bastard wouldn't once look at me, I didn't know why he even came anyhow.

The other reason I was glad to move so far away was I didn't think I'd be known. It wouldn't be like down the valley, where they'd read about me in the newspaper and I had to stay in the library the whole time, I'd be able to go about unnoticed now. I was green as cabbage-looking, though, if I thought that. Prisons are worse than any town or school you can think of – all any prisoner is fussed about is fags and gossip. They knew who I was before I even stepped on the wing. Fashioned up a name for me and all. Ripper. Sometimes it was Pete, or Yorkshire, but most times it was Ripper. I should've been chuffed, rightly, for most the perverts were just Beast, or Nonce, but I was pissing blood again soon enough. There were others got it worse, as this was a Category B and some of them were in for fouler than I'd done. Near all the perverts ended up on the Rule, sided off out of harm's way in the Vulnerable Prisoner Unit, and I could've asked to join them, said I was in danger out on the wing, but I didn't fancy getting cosy with them lot. I just wanted to be left on my tod. I could frame myself for the clobberings – it was the noise of the place that undid me.

The shouting, clanking echoes that never stopped. They rang in my ears, addling my brain, everyplace I went I felt penned in by them until I could hardly move. I riddled the answer soon enough, mind – if I wanted to be left peaceable, I'd have to stir up some bother first. That was when I started my attacks. They were small at first, throwing pens or cups, and always at band-end weaklings I knew wouldn't do me over. That would get me a couple of days of quiet in segregation. Then I upped it. I clouted an officer on the shoulder. Belted another weakling until he was senseless with the battery out the video projector, wrapped in a sock. They were never interested why I'd done it – they couldn't shut me away quick enough, twenty-eight days a stretch. And that was gradely by me. Peace. Nothing but the white wall glaring back at me, and my thoughts to turn over, and every now and then, hello, a dollop of feed on a tray sliding under the door. There was a cost for it, course. Another year inside, at least.

*

He's on his way, not long now. He'll sit on the bed next me, blathering on, now, let's have another practice shall we? Can you tell me a time when you've succeeded in a challenging situation? They're bound to ask you that, any job you go for. Well, let's think, there's the time the ewe was stuck in the cattle-grid and Chickenhead was stood over me with her pipes steaming until I got it out. That count, does it? Does it! It's perfect, Sam, you'll knock their socks off. She just smiles. There you go, then, it's as easy as that. Obviously that's the first thing your father will ask if you go back to the farm – when have you succeeded in a challenging situation? – but she's smiling still, because she knows I'm not ever going back there again.

I flatten out the picture, and feel down the length of her back, over the smooth white skin and the fragile curve of her spine, and I remember for a moment the mole's skull, perfect delicate and unharmed. She just smiles, her head turned round to look at me, them big eyes and the little tweak of the mouth. Here's one for you, a challenging situation – Wetherill coming back into the

206

classroom, picking up the blackboard eraser, What's this? Marsdyke! You forced me against my will, you can't really deny it now, can you? Can you? There were bruises all up my arm, after all, what more proof do I need?

*

I wasn't mighty popular after I started the attacks. The times between segregation I got beaten regular, and all over the shop now – in my cell, in the showers, in association. The officers let them at it mostly. They were just biding for their next chance to send me to segregation, and course I gave them plenty. They started treading careful around me, like I was a bullock might charge them any moment. It couldn't go on like that for always, though. The warden got wind before long. He said I was a danger to myself and to others and I had to go on the Rule, which meant I was off to the Vulnerable Prisoner Unit with the perverts.

Life was fair different in there. I was still Ripper and Pete, but when these lot said my name they didn't spit or snarl it, they spoke it high and mighty, like a title. They liked me in there, because I was one of them. It was mostly perverts, together with crammocky old fellers who'd been inside half their lives, and a few barmpots who'd missed the bus to the mental hospital and ended up left in the VPU, the prison sump-pit. These were the ones most likely for a battering, or a breeding, by the other prisoners out on the wing.

No matter they liked me, I was never thick with any of them. Most were either quiet and skulking, or they were flibbery-gibbets yammering in your ear about what they'd done, what the others had done, what they were going to do – they never gave you any peace. They were better than the other lot, mind. And I got to understand there wasn't nothing too different about me, most of these had done worse – raped a female, or a sprog. One had bred his own sister. What I'd done wasn't much compared to that, owing as my luck had run out at the last moment.

I didn't tell them that at my treatment, though. I just sat, pretending to listen while they put ticks on my parole card. I should've been grateful, the perverts told me, getting the treatment, for you didn't always get it if you were in less than six or seven years, and once you'd bided out the treatment your parole card would be blistering red ticks. It was proper calf-headed. There were classes on Victim Empathy and umpteen short films of lads and lasses copping together in supermarkets and pubs and going on dates in fancy restaurants, feeding each other prawns out their fingers. Bugger knows what they wanted us to learn. Did they want all us perverts lining up in supermarket aisles waiting to meet a female? Then there were classes with Richard and Luke, all these diagrams of Relapse Prevention Strategies and Offence Cycles, and how high-risk situations can be avoided. The teachers had to be men, course, else we'd have paid no attention – if it'd been females we'd have been too busy dripping gozzle on us desks and thinking what we'd do to her to listen what she was saying. Not that there was a champion amount of listening going on anyhow. Most the lesson, the perverts at the back the class were studying each other's picture stores, doing swaps.

That was when I got the picture. Stole it when one of them was looking otherways and hid it under my writing pad. It was a fair piece of luck, because most the time the perverts hoarded their pictures sharp-eyed as a Scotsman burying brass. She was likely the prize of his collection and all, the little smile on her like she'd just been sent out the classroom, all she did was she drew a cat in her textbook, that's hardly a crime is it? Bugger knows where he got hold of a picture like that, but it was his own fault, not being careful enough.

I stayed in the VPU the rest my sentence in the Category B, until I got enough red ticks and the transfer order came to move me to the open prison. That was when they fixed me with my parole officer. Mawkish sod, he was like the dad some ways, wouldn't say boo to a goose. I could imagine it, the pair of them trying to shoo the goose in the coop, fussing, the goose parked up, not moving. Round your side a little, that's it, that's it, not too fast, don't want to frighten her. Now m'lady, bedtime I think, come on now, let's not have a scene. This way, this way – well, can you believe it? It would seem the lady's not for moving.

He's got me a place in a hostel, some town nearby, he'll keep calling in on me, he says. He's been coming to the prison most days now that I'm near the end my stretch, I've hardly had any peace from him, though there's been other things to make up for it. I've been on two outside visits a week since I got here. Never mind I've had to spend them with him, sat in tea shops listening to him talk on about bank accounts, I've still been able to view out the window behind him at all the females walking past outside.

*

She's staring at me, looking right into me. I suppose you won't be needing me any more, will you? A whole world of other girls out there. I smile – she's just teasing with me, I know, and I tell her she's wrong, she's got it arse-uppards. She's a mentalist if she thinks I'm letting go of her now. I'm sat on the bed smiling, when there's a knock on the door. My parole officer. He's the only one knocks like that.

Yes, I say, folding her back inside *Adapting to Freedom*.

He steps in and stands in the doorway, a great daft smile on his chops and his hands on his hips.

Fit and ready?

I just fucking know he's a rambler.

Near as. I haven't packed yet. Won't take long, mind.

Good, good. He's looking round the room, taking it in, as if he's leaving it himself and wants a good last sight and he doesn't have to be here next week, coddling some other pervert. He picks up a bag by the doorway and comes to sit on the bed next me, without asking. Then he goes quiet a moment, and I know we're going to have one of our chats.

How do you feel, Sam? Ready?

Course.

It won't be easy, you know. Adjusting. Getting back in the swing of things.

I know. We've talked about it.

I'm not glibbing – we've certain talked about it enough. How it won't be easy meeting people. How some people might be unwilling at first to accept I've changed, they might give me the cold shoulder. I had to laugh when he told me that. Adjust? What does he think it was like before I was locked up? Who does he think I was – Postman Pat?

So, he says, have you thought about your plan of action for tomorrow?

Some.

Well, go on then, tell me your thoughts.

I want to have a walk. I want to see them hills, I say, nodding toward the window.

He lips up a moment, looking out. He's likely thinking, hmm, a walk, let's make a checklist – packed lunch, Thermos, Ordnance Survey map, woollies. But all he says is, okay, that's fine. Should probably wait a few days first, though, get settled in, feet on the ground.

Right.

Now, Sam, I've got some things for you here, your own posse-sions, that you gave in at first reception. He sets the bag by my feet. Okay, he taps the bed, I'll be back in half an hour, drive you to the hostel. He stands up and smiles down at me. See you in a bit.

When he's gone I walk over to the window for a last look of the hills, and I picture him up going home after work, greeting his wife, and I wonder if he's as chirrupy as this the whole time. Can he shut away thinking on the scutter portion of his day when he kisses her hello on the cheek, or is there a griming he can't ever wash off, like a miner, or a fisherman always reeking cod?

The bag's got my boots in it, and my jacket, soap-smelling and faded now, all the layerings of muck washed away. I put the boots on first, then the jacket, still comfortable after all this time, and I start to pack up my trunklements. There's not much – toothbrush, a few books, and the picture. I take her out for a moment, then I fold her back inside the booklet and put her in my jacket pocket. And who's there? Old Dracula, that's who, dapper as ever, seems he's escaped the washer. Who'd have thought it? The old team back together. The keyhole blinks as people walk past outside, and

I slip him back in the pocket to guard over her. It's a fair important job, I tell him, she's all I've got, for the moment. Then I sit down on the bed and I wait, Dracula's head poking out the top the pocket, the sly grin on him, watching, on the lookout.

Acknowledgments

I would like to thank Zoe Waldie, Jenny Hewson and everybody at RCW and at Penguin, with special thanks to Peter Straus, for committing so early and wholeheartedly to the book, and to Mary Mount, for her discerning, and considerate, editing.

Also, thank you to Maura Dooley and Pamela Johnson at Goldsmiths; Jennifer Barth; David, Dom and Aodhnait; my family; the Tiptons; and Arnold Kellett, whose *Yorkshire Dictionary of Dialect, Tradition and Folklore* proved a useful and interesting aid.

And above all, for everything, to Tips.

About the author

About the book

Read on

Insights,
Interviews
& More...

A Conversation with Ross Raisin

Luke Christie

Does your affiliation with Yorkshire trace back to childhood?

Yes—I am from Yorkshire. Not the North Yorkshire that the book is set in, but West Yorkshire, where the wool mills used to be.

Describe your childhood.

As a child, you would most likely find me walking on a hill in oversized grey clothing, which may sound idyllic to some, but when you're thirteen you'd probably disagree. I think because I was always quite skinny, my parents tried to dress me in large shirts as a disguise, and they thought I didn't like bright colors, so these clothes were usually grey, I am today wearing a medium-size purple jumper.

Your name, tell us about your name.

My full name is Ross Radford Raisin, which never fails to amuse people. I hope I'm not giving a bad impression of my mum and dad here. I should just say that they are wonderful, supportive people with a sense of humor, hence the name, which I have always liked. I'm not sure where Raisin comes from, though, as I don't know much about my dad's side of the family. I know more about my mum's: they come partly from Argentina, and my great-grandmother was forced to marry her uncle, so she escaped to Turkey and had an affair with a fighter pilot.

When did you first take to writing?

I'm not sure that I have yet. I find writing difficult and slow.

What were you reading in your teens?

Horror—James Herbert, Dean R. Koontz, Stephen King, Ben Elton, Graham Greene.

What kind of extra-literary jobs have you held—anything dangerous or notably mundane?

I have always worked in restaurants and hotels, as a barman, waiter, dishwasher, manager or porter. I still do, as a waiter. I enjoy it, I think I'd go mad without it: writing involves sitting in the library on your own trying not to fall asleep; ▶

> " I have always worked in restaurants and hotels, as a barman, waiter, dishwasher, manager or porter. I still do, as a waiter. I enjoy it, I think I'd go mad without it. . . . "

working in a restaurant means you get to talk to people.

Which football team do you root for?

Root. Well, I root for Bradford City. I begin every day by looking at the club Web site for news (our reserves just lost to Huddersfield, our local rivals, who, even though a division above us, average much smaller crowds). You might not know much about Bradford City—they are in the bottom division of the English League—so here is a potted recent history:

1995: Mid-table in the third division, a not-so-local, fat, rasping businessman takes over the club. His name is Geoffrey. He promises us a future beyond our wildest dreams. We are a snowball rolling down the hill, he tells us. He invests money into the club, lots of money. He argues with the Huddersfield chairman in a live radio discussion. We love him.

1996: We are promoted to the second division.

1997–1999: More and more money invested in the club. We start to dream of the Premiership. We don't think much about where the money is coming from. We are a snowball rolling down the hill.

1999: We are promoted to the Premiership, captained by our star player, our hero, Stuart McCall.

2000–2001: We enjoy a magical time in the top division; we go to Manchester United (and lose 4–0); we buy expensive, celebrated, glorious players, who come from places like Italy, not because we are paying them £20,000 a week, but because they love the cold, windy, ex-industrial feel of the city.

2001: We are relegated. Our manager leaves. There are allegations that Geoffrey has been trying to pick the team. We begin to realize that the money has been borrowed, at high interest rates. Our snowball is at the bottom of the hill, thawing, unpleasant things it picked up on the way sticking out from it.

2002–2007: Geoffrey leaves, a rich man (allegedly, allegedly). We are relegated (twice), close to bankruptcy, crowds down 300 percent, the banks want their money back, we have no money or, at some points, it seems, players.

2007: In the bottom division, it is the end. But then Stuart McCall (the hero) comes back as our manager. A local businessman takes over as chairman and clears the club's debts with his own money (allegedly). There is a surge in ticket sales, we begin the season well, previously disgruntled supporters feel fresh hope and start looking at the club Web site every morning. We are a snowball rolling down the hill . . .

I look forward with interest to seeing how much of this gets edited, and how much of it is libelous.

Describe the objects on your desk right now.

Let's see. To answer this I will need to go over to the desk, which I don't work at because it is an impenetrable jungle. It is too small, really, with the computer ▶

behind it balanced on a fold-out camp bed covered with a piece of cloth. There is: a Bradford City mug containing pens; three manuscripts of *God's Own Country* (the novel's title in England); tissue paper, looks used, not mine; two horse chestnuts; a booklet of new menu descriptions; a Bradford City paperweight; a cutout "win a holiday" competition page from a magazine; books; files; and, I suspect, somewhere, the pile of CVs that my girlfriend has been this morning stamping about trying to find.

Does music play any part in your writing process?

None. I struggle unless everything around me is completely silent.

What is your favorite word in the English language?

At the moment: crop-dusting. It is a word Australian waiters use to describe when they fart at one end of the restaurant and walk the smell through to the other side.

Name your pastimes.

Pubs; theatre; playing squash; camping (I've only done it once, but I really liked it); Bradford City.

What has been your fondest experience on a train?

A lady in Anne's dad's village, who has a season ticket to London, very kindly gave us a booklet of the complimentary tickets she receives. So now, whenever we go to Yorkshire (Anne is from Yorkshire too) we go in the first-class carriage, which is brilliant, because you get as much free tea as you like, they keep filling your cup up. My least fond experience on a train was when I was coming back from holiday and a Frenchman stole all of my underpants.

What are you reading these days?

Illywhacker, by Peter Carey; *Herzog*, by Saul Bellow; *So He Takes the Dog*, by Jonathan Buckley.

Can fiction save the world?

Only if you are posh. This is Anne's answer, but I kind of agree with her.

What must you do before you die?

Write past page two of my new novel.

> 66 My least fond experience on a train was when I was coming back from holiday and a Frenchman stole all of my underpants. 99

You Look Like a Farmer in Those Clothes
A Note on Farming in Britain

WHEN FOOT-AND-MOUTH DISEASE first struck the UK in 2001, and our TV screens were filled with images of spasm-legged cows and giant pits of smouldering cattle, one of the most striking things about it was the picture behind the pyres—of farmers, crying, desperate, beaten. But it wasn't just these farmers struggling to contain their emotions that made it such compelling viewing, it was also the very fact of them being on the television at all.

Yes, we have Emmerdale, and the Archers, but until that spring I really don't believe that most people in this country had ever given much of a thought to what actually goes on inside a farm. Food is eroticised these days like never before—if I flick through the TV schedule on

A sheep

my sofa now, I can see that there are eight food shows on terrestrial I could watch today if I wanted, all of them emphasising the same message: that only a complete loser nowadays doesn't know how to spatchcock a quail. The TV chefs will no doubt stroke their scallops and slap their beef as they dribble about the quality of the produce, but as for the producers, I dare say you won't learn a great deal.

This was one of the reasons I decided to set the book where I did, on a small hill farm in North Yorkshire. Not simply, I must admit, because I care about increasing people's awareness of real country issues (although I do), but because I saw a fairly unexplored subject that I could make a story out of.

And if you want isolation, disenfranchisement, gossip and muckraking, a farm is the perfect setting for a novel. The common image of the British farmer is of a tight-lipped, dirty simpleton, grumbling. He is male. He wears funny clothes. People will joke that he

Farndale

is an inbred. Of course, my novel isn't exactly a ringing endorsement of the clean-cut, bushy-tailed optimism of the British farmer, but what I will say is that farmers in this country are marginalised to the point of myth and, not uncommonly, fear. Unlike in France, where farmers have considerable cultural and political significance, agricultural workers in the UK—even though farming accounts for almost 15 percent of the GDP—are rarely seen or heard outside of an epidemic crisis. ▶

> 66 Of course, my novel isn't exactly a ringing endorsement of the clean-cut, bushy-tailed optimism of the British farmer. 99

You Look Like a Farmer in Those Clothes
(continued)

The disconnection between shoppers and the source of the food they buy is greater than ever before—a problem exacerbated by the stranglehold of the supermarkets and, paradoxically, the glossy TV shows that supposedly increase the viewer's food awareness. The only farms you tend to see on these programs are small, organic producers, with bustling farm shops, run by, say, the posh woman who came down from London to set up her free-range goose flock. There is, of course, nothing wrong with these places, and long may they continue to thrive, but the impression such shows give of the countryside is often misleading. It is part of the same glamorisation of the rural that encourages us to escape to the country and do up a barn. Or lionises the butcher's shop as a place for special occasions and the well-to-do. I suppose it was inevitable that many butchers would develop this image—as sellers of premium, expensive meat—because in lots of instances it has been the only way to survive the supermarkets, which can provide a large choice of very cheap meat. In London these days you can walk for miles before you find a butcher and, more often than not, their existence is possible only because they are situated in one of the rare neighbourhoods to not yet have a supermarket.

A new Tesco opened at the bottom of my road in London a couple of months ago. A Tesco Metro, more precisely, the smaller version of the giant supermarket that brands itself as a kind of local "corner

The Hole of Horcum

shop." The real corner shops in the area were understandably displeased at the new arrival, and began a petition to encourage shoppers to veto the store. I don't know what has come of this, but I can see clearly enough that Tesco Metro is already by a distance the busiest shop in the area, and the business coming into local stores has declined as a result. This is bad news for suppliers as well as retailers. Supermarkets are not interested in getting their supply from small farms (unless it is for their organic range, with a picture of a smiling farmer on the pack, patting his cow). Supermarkets want large amounts of consistent produce at low price. The only sources able to supply this within the UK are the big specialist farms able to operate with reliable, factory-like efficiency. Each time a new supermarket opens, their orders increase, and they become more powerful, gobbling up the smaller farms which simply cannot compete.

The big four—Tesco, Sainsbury's, Asda/Wal-Mart and Morrisons—control over three-quarters of grocery sales in the UK. Competition between these companies ▶

> ❝ Supermarkets are not interested in getting their supply from small farms (unless it is for their organic range, with a picture of a smiling farmer on the pack, patting his cow). ❞

You Look Like a Farmer in Those Clothes
(continued)

ensures that prices stay low. Julian Hunt, editor of the *Grocer*, ran an article in *Farmers Weekly* magazine a couple of years ago about a survey that had recently been conducted: in 1998, an average basket of thirty-three popular food and drink items cost £37.50. In 2005, the same bag of groceries cost £37.30. Great for the shopper, this deflation, but not so good for the farmer, whose share of the sale price keeps on dwindling—generally, farmers now receive less than eight pence of every pound spent on their produce. At the same time, prices for fertiliser and grain are increasing (wheat prices have spiralled this summer); subsidy payments are more difficult to obtain and generally encourage the bigger, more efficient producers; and it is ever easier and cheaper for supermarkets to buy cheap supply from abroad (production costs of Brazilian beef, for example, are one-third of UK levels).

It is no wonder, then, that farming jobs are being lost. You rarely read about this in the mainstream media. The only mention is usually to be found in industry journals, like *Farmers Weekly* (a great magazine, by the way, full of interesting facts and surveys—for instance, one poll found that 73 percent of farmers believe big cats are at large in the UK countryside). In September 2005 the magazine ran a survey of young farmers and found that 36 percent of them had no intentions of ever taking over the running of the family farm. When asked what might persuade them to stay, the resounding answers were: better pay (65 percent), less red tape dealing with subsidies and supermarket paperwork (52 percent), and greater optimism within the farming industry (48 percent). The general feeling was that there are better prospects elsewhere.

Sam Marsdyke, the main character of the book, certainly has no hopes of taking over his father's farm (though, clearly, for a few reasons other than the bleak state of the farming industry). Mind you, even if he did want to, this summer's latest onset of foot-and-mouth, and the subsequent collapse of lamb prices, would probably have left him no choice in the matter anyway, because for a small, remote farm like theirs, it would likely have spelt the end. ❧

> **❝ Sam Marsdyke, the main character of the book, certainly has no hopes of taking over his father's farm (though, clearly, for a few reasons other than the bleak state of the farming industry). ❞**

All photos courtesy of the author

A Brief Glossary of Yorkshire Food

This is of course by no means definitive, and no doubt there are other counties that probably lay claim to some of these dishes, but no matter, I'm putting them down here as Yorkshire.

Yorkshire pudding

No arguments about origin here. Cheap, simple, stodgy food. A batter, similar to a pancake mix, with milk, flour and egg, whisked together and cooked in a shallow tray so that the sides rise to form a sort of cavern. This is the beauty of the Yorkshire pudding, because inside this cavern you can put whatever you like. Beef and gravy is traditional, but it also makes a good dessert, with treacle inside, or, as a starter, a wet salad of lettuce, spring onion, vinegar and sugar. Supposedly, it came about as a starter in order to fill the guests' bellies up before they came to the main course, so they didn't eat as much of the expensive stuff, like meat, but I'm not sure if I believe this.

Suet pudding

Again, this isn't really a pudding, it's a kind of upside-down pie, usually filled with steak and kidney. Suet is the dense fat around beef kidneys, mixed with flour to make the dough that encases the pudding.

Faggots (or savoury ducks)

Pork leftovers, stewed and minced, then moulded and clad in caul (a membrane), with jelly on top.

Lots of this food might not sound nice, but it is, believe me.

❝ This is the beauty of the Yorkshire pudding, because inside this cavern you can put whatever you like. ❞

Fish and chips

Yes, I know, you get them all over England, but Yorkshire has the biggest fish and chip shop, so I'm having it. Harry Ramsden's in Guiseley holds the world record for the single biggest order of fish and chips: 490 servings in an hour, when an army regiment passed through in 1949. Traditionally cod or haddock is fried in beef dripping, and served with mushy peas.

Parkin

A heavy, dark gingerbread made with oatmeal and black treacle, eaten on Guy Fawkes Night (November 5th). This is the night that we celebrate the foiling of the Gunpowder Plot of 1605, when a group of Catholic conspirators schemed to blow up the Houses of Parliament. To mark it, children make a cloth dummy of the chief conspirator, Guy Fawkes, who gets impaled on the top of a large bonfire and incinerated.

Liquorice

A black root, which grows in the ground and is turned into sweets. Pontefract, in West Yorkshire, has been making liquorice since medieval times.

Wensleydale

A beautiful, mild, creamy white cheese, made at the factory in Hawes in the Dales. Traditionally eaten with apple pie. "An apple pie without the cheese is like a kiss without the squeeze," apparently.

Fat rascal

A currant tea cake, kind of like a rock bun. ▶

> " Pontefract, in West Yorkshire, has been making liquorice since medieval times. "

Rhubarb crumble

Not so long ago, 90 percent of the world's forced rhubarb came from the Yorkshire Triangle around Wakefield. I just looked that up on the Internet. If it is true, then I can only assume that most of you in America don't know what forced rhubarb is: it's a sweet, stringy, red stalk used for puddings, grown in artificially dark surroundings, thereby "forcing" it to grow bigger as it strives toward the light. This technique was discovered by a Chinese builder who lost his hat, accidentally dropping it on a rhubarb crop—when he eventually found his hat again, the rhubarb underneath had grown markedly bigger than its neighbours. This fact does not come from the Internet, but from a dim part of my memory, another admittedly dubious source of information.

Yorkshire Tea

Not food, but deserves a mention, I think, because it is very good tea. Strong and rich, with pictures of Yorkshire on the box. Also, like most people in Yorkshire, the Yorkshire Tea people are good people. When my girlfriend's sister, Vicki, was travelling round Australia, she couldn't find any Yorkshire Tea. So, exasperated, she wrote to the company asking if they knew where it is stocked. They wrote back, telling her the two stores where you can find it (one is in Darwin, the other somewhere else) and, together with the letter, they sent her a small package of Yorkshire Tea bags to keep her going. Other tea companies take note. ❧